FAITH AND THE FORMULA

FAITH AND THE FORMULA

Clint Smith

DEEDS PUBLISHING | ATLANTA

Copyright © 2013 - Clint Smith

ALL RIGHTS RESERVED - No part of this book may be reproduced in any form or by any electronic or mechanical means, including information storage and retrieval systems, without permission in writing from the authors, except by a reviewer who may quote brief passages in a review.

Bible verses on pages 158, 244, and 302 from New International Version
Bible verse on page 259 from King James Version

Cover photograph by Bill Cobb of SkylineScenes.com

Published by Deeds Publishing
Marietta, GA
www.deedspublishing.com

Printed in The United States of America

Library of Congress Cataloging-in-Publications Data is available upon request.

ISBN 978-1-937565-83-1

Books are available in quantity for promotional or premium use. For information, write Deeds Publishing, PO Box 682212, Marietta, GA 30068 or info@deedspublishing.com.

First Edition, 2013

10 9 8 7 6 5 4 3 2 1

Acknowledgments

Most importantly, I give thanks to God for blessing me with the opportunity to pursue the project and for sending His only begotten Son, Jesus Christ, to give us all the gift of eternal salvation.

Any book project that becomes a reality is a group effort. I want to thank my mother, Evelyn Smith, for her love, support, and prayers. I could not have completed the book without the love, patience, and input of Cammie Connell.

The technical support of my friend, David Sexton, was a tremendous asset. The great team at Deeds Publishing made the effort rewarding and fun. Bob, Jan, and Mark Babcock are hard-working, dedicated professionals who truly understand the current landscape of the publishing industry and the great opportunities that abound.

Finally, my friends at First Redeemer Church in Cumming have been stalwarts of support in prayers and motivation to me. We trust the Lord will make *Faith And The Formula* a great witnessing tool.

To my parents, Charles and Evelyn Smith, for their love, faith, and spiritual leadership

Contents

Chapter One—A Friend Lost	13
Chapter Two—An Amazing Discovery	25
Chapter Three—The Wild Odyssey Begins	33
Chapter Four—In a Fog	43
Chapter Five—Lovely Tiffany	49
Chapter Six—"The Load"	57
Chapter Seven—Looking for a Little Help	65
Chapter Eight—The Race	69
Chapter Nine—Nelson Porter	75
Chapter Ten—European Adventure	83
Chapter Eleven—Alone in Denmark	91
Chapter Twelve—The Old Factory	97
Chapter Thirteen—Rusty Shaw	103
Chapter Fourteen—The Mysterious Jon Actund	111
Chapter Fifteen—The Face Off	119
Chapter Sixteen—Meeting the Inner Circle	129
Chapter Seventeen—Confiding in Each Other	135
Chapter Eighteen—Courage to Worship	145
Chapter Nineteen—A Flicker of Hope	153
Chapter Twenty—An Uncomfortable Place to Live	159
Chapter Twenty-One—In Need of Comfort	161
Chapter Twenty-Two—Inside the Empowerment Brigade	163
Chapter Twenty-Three—The Fountain of Youth	167
Chapter Twenty-Four—A Debate	173
Chapter Twenty-Five—Background	179
Chapter Twenty-Six—One-on-One	185
Chapter Twenty-Seven—The Clones	189
Chapter Twenty-Eight—The Headache	197
Chapter Twenty-Nine—On the Road	201
Chapter Thirty—Trapped	205
Chapter Thirty-One—Incarceration	209
Chapter Thirty-Two—St. Augustine	221
Chapter Thirty-Three—Nancy!?	225
Chapter Thirty-Four—A Surprising Encounter	231
Chapter Thirty-Five—The Aging Conference	237
Chapter Thirty-Six—Refuge in the House of the Lord	245
Chapter Thirty-Seven—Renewing Acquaintances	251
Chapter Thirty-Eight—Woman in the Spotlight	259
Chapter Thirty-Nine—Porter's Patience	271
Chapter Forty—Back in the Game	275
Chapter Forty-One—Tiffany's Plea	289
Chapter Forty-Two—The Truth	293
Chapter Forty-Three—A Dilemma	299
Chapter Forty-Four—The Most Important Decision of Tim's Life	303
Chapter Forty-Five—Resolution	307

Chapter One—A Friend Lost

Friday, June 7, 9:43 a.m.

Tim Jennings was a man of conflicting, even colliding emotions. The loss of the only person he ever loved tormented him. However, he had found someone new who was attempting to fill the emotional void in his life but he was not sure that he wanted the void, the emotional gap plugged. As an escape, Tim retreated to his successful professional career because it was an area of his life that brought a sense of satisfaction.

"You know what my goals are in the business. This industrial film stuff is only a stepping stone because I want to shoot documentaries all over the world and hook up with a company or somebody that will bankroll my ideas," Tim explained. "But I don't see me in your settled down world." The business afforded him opportunities to travel. When he was in college, he had plans to become an archaeologist and travel to remote locations but that dream never happened.

"You have to be realistic because you still have to live somewhere," Tiffany Baker said. "Why not here in Atlanta with me?"

"It won't work."

"You're impossible!" Tiffany said. "If there's something else, you need to tell me what it is."

There was nothing wrong with Tiffany Baker. "You're perfect," Tim said. "But I don't like it when women pressure me."

"Don't worry. I won't pressure you anymore. Good bye!"

Tim cringed. "What do you mean?"

"I mean I don't think we should see each other for a very long time," Tiffany muttered. "At least not until tomorrow night."

Saturday, June 8, 5:36 p.m.

Tim's mind raced back to the night one year ago. Nancy was a magnificently attractive woman with green hypnotic eyes. Her long brown hair, nestling softly on her shoulders, never seemed to get tangled.

Tim cried as the memories came back. It was Memorial Day weekend; they had a fun day planned at Lake Lanier. Nancy had packed a basket full of picnic food. Lance McMichael, Tim's best friend since the third grade, had loaned his boat to them—a fishing boat with an outboard motor.

The couple spent most of the day boating, swimming and skiing, then relaxed on the beach until dusk. Tim remembered turning to admire Nancy's natural golden beauty.

As darkness fell, Nancy argued that a quick spin under a shining moon would be fun, and she wanted to go alone to prove that she was capable, even though she had done it twice before. Her flair for adventure and the dramatic was alluring to Tim, but sometimes scared him. He watched her cast off from a grassy hilltop overlooking the lake as the last light from the sun disappeared.

Tim became frantic after an hour passed and she was not back. A cool breeze stirred as he sprinted down to the shore. He remembered seeing a man and woman docking a boat a few hundred feet up the shoreline. After stumbling along the muddy bank, he reached the dock.

Tim convinced the old man to take him to search for Nancy. After about ten minutes on the lake, they came upon the boat, floating on the surface of the water. Tim's gut ached and his palms sweated as their craft eased up alongside the boat. Nancy was not on board.

Shouting her name, he jumped into the water and swam a wide perimeter several times around the empty boat but saw nothing. A sheriff's dive team was called in but they could not locate a body or any evidence of Nancy Proctor. The authorities ruled the incident a drowning.

Tim's big Irish setter brought him back from his memories by a wet slobbering lick. Soon Tiffany would be knocking on the door so Tim grabbed an empty box of Ritz Crackers with one hand and an empty plastic RC Cola bottle in the other hand in a frantic last minute attempt at housecleaning.

They had decided to spend the evening at home, which pleased Tim greatly because Tiffany was a gourmet cook and he welcomed an occasional opportunity to stray from his usual diet of frozen pizzas and TV dinners.

Tim thought he loved Tiffany but he wasn't sure.

"You need an interior decorator to give this place an overhaul," Tiffany said later in the evening as she prepared their dinner. "Actually, you need a woman's touch." She was a beautiful, statuesque blonde who had a radiant complexion that stemmed from her pure countenance and her Christian faith.

"Do you think we'll have any leftovers?" Tim asked.

"Possibly."

"If we do, we can give them to Lou. That dog loves table scraps. By the way, you need to keep Lou for about a week because I've been invited by an independent film company to go to the Himalayas with them as an assistant to the producer. This will be great experience for me and a chance to make some contacts!"

"The Himalayas? Why?"

"They're going to search for Noah's Ark, the Bible myth," Tim said cautiously.

"It's not a myth. It's an historical incident from Scripture," Tiffany protested.

"Whatever! All I know is that people have been looking for that ark for ages and have never found it. Some astronaut even devoted about ten years of his life searching for it."

"Well, that doesn't mean it doesn't exist."

"I don't care whether it exists or not because I'm just glad to be able to go on this trip."

"Did it ever occur to you to ask me what I thought about the trip?"

"Yep."

"Then why didn't you say anything?"

"Because you would have told me not to go but I can't pass up this opportunity. And you know something? If we got hitched, we would be having this same type of argument about twice a month."

"We're not arguing."

"Yes, we are so let's change the subject. How's the spaghetti coming along?"

Monday, June 10, 9:11 a.m.

Tim, camera operator Bud Pope, and Lance McMichael arrived together at the construction site on a sweltering summer morning. The heat hung over the city like a thick, itchy wool sweater. Tim was afraid that by afternoon the heat would be unbearable so he wanted to get the job finished as fast as possible.

Occasionally, Lance came along on jobs. Tim and Lance had been inseparable through the years. Lance was a tall, fun loving fellow with a great sense of humor. The two young men played sports together in high school.

Tim's assignment was to film the president of Premium Construction and Associates in various poses in front of equipment and the building that was under construction at the site as he discussed the attributes of his company.

Lance often assisted in the projects by holding a clipboard and taking notes for Tim as he shouted out his thoughts about the shoot as it unfolded.

As Tim looked up at the sun, he saw a massive steel girder dangling above, suspended by the company's biggest crane. The girder was about thirty feet in length, ten feet in width and five tons in weight. It had a big banner with the company logo draped across it. The company president thought it would be a neat idea to have the girder come down above him and hang suspended in air as he made his closing remarks for the film.

George Petrie, the president of the company, received a telephone call several minutes before the commercial was to be shot. "I understand that you have some knowledge of the Florida Everglades. You did archeological digging down there. I read your bio on your website," Petrie said to Tim as he walked away. "I have uncovered some interesting information that could make your experience in that section of the country very useful. Frankly, that's one of the reasons I hired you." He hurried off to take his phone call.

"How about if I help out and stand in for the guy until he gets back?" Lance offered. "You can go ahead and set up the shot."

"O.K. Bud, get over here," Tim said.

Bud had found a shady spot next to the Port-a-John and it took several minutes for him to get the camera set. "I'll make sure you get the entire banner in the frame," he said.

Tim looked up at the girder and the chains attached to it. "Lance, do you know how much life insurance you have?" he shouted.

"Enough to start my own goat farm to go along with my fifty acres and a mule."

"It's forty acres."

"What?" Lance laughed. "You want ten of my acres. Well, you can have it, but not the mule."

Tim forced a grinned as he made his way to the refreshment stand for a swig of soda. Suddenly, Tim heard a tremendous crashing thud and a scream of terror and pain. He whirled around and saw a horrendous sight. The huge girder had come loose from its supports and collapsed to the ground. Dust and debris floated through the air as people ran frantically in all directions.

Tim sprinted up to the location and witnessed a sickening, sad, and horrifying situation. Protruding from underneath the steel girder was a leg and a barely visible hand. A stream of blood flowed in front of Tim's feet.

"Lance!" Tim shouted.

Tuesday, June 11, 8:19 a.m.

The ring of the telephone broke the morning's silence. Tim arose from the couch in his den. In his state of half slumber, Tim believed for a moment that Lance McMichael's death had been a dream. It was only a fleeting, yet uplifting, moment until the pain and gut-wrenching truth of reality hit him upside the head.

Tim was a handsome thirty-eight year old man with wavy brown hair and an athletic appearance combined with a normally confident presence that had carried him far in his professional life. But the confident exterior had melted away as he reeled from the second death of someone very close to him. He was like a frightened child.

The phone rang again.

"It's Bud. There's something strange going on with Lance's death."

"What do you mean?"

"They can't find the guy who was operating the crane that dropped the girder. He's disappeared."

"Are you serious?" Tim shouted.

"When the police and the dude's boss tried to find him at the site to ask him questions about what went wrong, he had disappeared. The cops discovered that the support chains didn't break loose with the girder. The chains had been loosened intentionally!"

"What are you saying? Lance was murdered? You're telling me a perfect stranger murdered by best friend," Tim scoffed. He grabbed the pillow from the couch and squeezed it.

"All I know is that they need to talk to the crane operator and he must have taken the next boat to China because he be gone!" Bud said.

"What was the guy's name? They shouldn't have much trouble finding him."

"I don't know his name but the cops are probably gonna be calling you. They called me last night."

Lance McMichael was one of the most likeable dudes anyone could ever meet. "Nobody would murder him!" Tim said. "They must have been targeting the company president."

Late in the morning, Tiffany visited Tim. She gave him a big hug. "I'm sorry about Lance."

"I want you to stay with me today. Please!"

Tiffany simply smiled and kissed Tim on the cheek. "Will you go to church with me on Sunday?" Tiffany asked when she returned from the kitchen with two cups of coffee. "You need to visit more often… especially with the experiences you have suffered through. It will be good for you."

"I can worship anywhere I want like my van, at the donut shop, at the park, you name it," Tim said.

"You need to fellowship with other believers in church!" Tiffany stared blankly at her boyfriend. "Are you sure you have been saved?"

"Yes. I ought to know, shouldn't I?" Tim laughed nervously.

"I'm worried about you," Tiffany said.

"The only thing I'm worried about is solving Lance's murder," Tim said. "I'm meeting with the detectives tomorrow."

Wednesday, June 12, 8:53 a.m.

Tim arrived at Atlanta Police Headquarters for his appointment with the detectives assigned to Lance McMichael's case. In the lobby, he walked through a sea of blue clad officers. Five minutes later, Tim was sitting in a tiny office. It had a bookcase, a worn out coffee maker, an oversized wall calendar that featured photographs of motorcycles, and not much else. Tim squirmed in his chair and looked across a battered wooden desk at his two inquisitors.

"I'm Detective Grover." He was a young black man of average build. He wore a gray suit with gold cuff links. He pointed to his associate. "This is Detective Howard Welch."

The other detective was a white man, bald, fat and middle age. He wore a blue blazer that was two and a half sizes too small, polyester gray slacks and a clip-on blue tie.

"How well did you know Lance McMichael?" Grover asked.

"He was my best friend."

"I asked you how well you knew him."

"Since the third grade. Real well," Tim said.

"Do you know of any reason why someone would murder him or have him murdered?" Grover asked.

"Not at all. Lance was a great guy. Everybody loved him."

Grover adjusted his tie. "Sam Reed didn't love him."

"Who's Sam Reed?"

"He's the crane operator who dropped the slab of concrete on your friend. He's got an interesting past. What do you know about Reed?" Grover asked.

Tim glanced quickly at Welch and then at Detective Grover. "I never heard of the guy."

"He's a small time crook," Grover said. "This construction company doesn't do a good job of screening their job applicants. Reed did time for petty larceny, stealing a car, and trespassing."

"I don't think Lance would ever get mixed up with someone like that. He was too straight," Tim said.

Grover flipped a paper clip in the air. "What about drugs? Did he get high? Was he hooked? He might have owed some dealer a big debt."

Tim laughed. "Not Lance." He looked at Welch. "When are you going to say something?"

The fat man grimaced and looked down at the dirty carpet.

Grover continued. "He could have been in debt. You see, this Reed. He was only working for someone else. He did the grunt work."

"I don't understand," Tim sighed. "What's going on here?"

Grover pointed at Tim. "A simple 'yes or no.' Level with me. Was Lance McMichael involved in anything illicit?"

"A simple no!"

"How well did you know the owner of the company, Mr. Petrie?" Grover asked.

"Not well at all. It was the first time my company had ever worked with him," Tim said. "It's more likely that they wanted him dead."

"It is probable that Mr. Petrie was actually the intended target," Grover said. "Do you know someone named Saul Marino? They call him 'The Load.' Do you know him?"

"No," Tim said. "I'm glad that we are off the wild goose chase about Lance."

"We believe that these two men had some business dealings together in the past. Illegal activity," Grover said. "Marino has been known to eliminate rivals."

"This is all new to me," Tim said.

"You're free to go," Grover said. "Make sure you don't cross paths with Marino because he's dangerous!"

Back at his office, Tim could not concentrate on his work. A walk in the nearby park after his grilling by the police had done nothing to clear his mind.

Bud Pope walked into the room. He was an overweight slob who was described by some people as a slacker. He was balding on top, never tucked his shirttail in and had a plump belly. "The cops called before you got here."

"I got grilled for an hour. What more do they want?" Tim grimaced.

"They want the video."

"What video? You mean the video of the accident?"

"I didn't tell you before because I thought it was too morbid or gruesome or something but the camera was running when the accident happened."

"You're telling me we can watch Lance get killed?"

"I've seen the footage and it's not a pretty sight."

Tim stood up and walked to the other side of the room. "How did the police know about the video? By the way, they are following the premise that Mr. Petrie was the intended target, a scenario that makes more sense."

"I agree, and so in an effort to be helpful, I told them about the video. And they think it could help in the investigation."

"Well, I want to look at it before we turn it over," Tim said.

"Are you sure about that? It might shake you up too much," Bud protested.

"He was my best friend and I want to look at it."

They walked into an adjacent room that was used for editing video footage. The room was equipped with the most modern equipment available. Bud put a disc into a video machine and fast-forwarded for approximately thirty seconds, at which point he pushed the play button. "Get ready."

Tim squirmed and fidgeted in his chair as he watched the seconds leading up to the accident. "I had my back turned when it happened." He watched as the steel girder fell on his friend. "Stop it!"

"I told you not to watch it!" Bud stammered.

Tim was red-faced and seething. "Rewind it because I want to watch it again. Did you see what happened? That worthless piece of trash carefully positioned that girder over Lance."

They watched the sequence again as the girder crashed to the ground, sending dirt, dust, and gravel flying.

"Do you want to watch it again?" Bud asked.

"No. You can see that Reed in the corner of the screen sitting in the cab of the crane. I want you to center that part of the frame then zoom in on the picture until I can get a good look at his face."

"Why do you want to do that?"

"I want to know exactly what he looks like because when I find him, I'm going to kill him!" Tim shouted.

Bud approached a mini-cooler in the corner of the room and pulled a can of Cherry Seven-Up from the top shelf. "You know, man, you need to chill out and let the cops do the dirty work."

"Do what I tell you to do!"

Bud mumbled under his breath and took a quick swallow of soda as he approached the equipment. He centered the image of the cab of the crane on the screen and made Sam Reed's face clearly visible through the window.

Bud blew the shot up several times its original size until Tim was satisfied. Tim leaned forward in his chair as the man's face appeared on the screen, staring quietly for a long time. The man had a thin, angular face with a bushy mustache.

"He's an ugly bird," Tim said. "You might as well let the video run its course and we'll watch the end of it."

"Anything you say, boss, as long as we can get this ugly guy's face off the screen. I've already seen the end. Somebody runs by the camera after the accident and brushes up against it and the lens faces out toward the street now. See. Look at all those morbid people running over each other to get a good look."

Tim found it strangely interesting to observe the expressions of the onlookers as they watched the confusion after the accident. An old woman, a bag lady of sorts, peered at the scene with a solemn expression. She wore an old gray dress with oversized shoes and a Sears department store bag was draped over one of her arms. A wiry little man wearing a cheap dark suit with a polka dot green and white tie came into view. He stood silently with a slight smirk on his face as he munched on peanuts that he pulled from a brown paper bag.

"How much longer does this video… ." Tim stopped in mid-sentence as he glared at the video screen. He blinked several times and strained his weary eyes to get a better look at the unbelievable sight, his dead fiancée, Nancy Proctor.

Chapter Two—An Amazing Discovery

"Can it really be her?"

"What are you talking about?" Bud asked.

"It's Nancy. Look! Or her exact twin or double or something!" Tim screamed.

Bud hit the pause button as they stared silently at the image. "It sure looks like her." Bud had known her in passing. "She's wearing old-fashioned looking clothes, but she never dressed that way."

"It can't be her. It's somebody who looks like her," Tim laughed nervously. "Zoom the shot in for a close up."

As the face grew larger, Tim's stare grew more intent.

"Did she have any moles, bumps, or scars on her face?" Bud asked.

"Nancy had a great complexion and a great face."

"This lady does, too. Wasn't Nancy's hair different?"

"She wore it pulled back on her forehead a little more than this woman, but still this is amazing," Tim said. "She could have changed her hair." He continued to stare at the image on the screen.

"Well, let's finish watching the rest of the video." Bud refocused the screen back to normal depth as the woman turned and disappeared into the crowd.

"I'm convinced that's Nancy," Tim said. His face had turned an ashen shade as he felt sick to the stomach. When he rose to get a cup of coffee, his knees wobbled and quivered. "You know we never found her body at the lake."

"If she survived the waters, don't you think she would have come back to your loving arms?" Bud asked.

"I can't answer that but I'm gonna find out!"

Thursday, June 13, 9:27 a.m.

Tim decided to drive to Chattanooga, Tennessee to visit Nancy Proctor's closest living relative. Her Aunt Linda was a peculiar woman but Tim thought that she might be able to help him determine if the woman could actually be Nancy.

As he traveled north on I-75, Tim felt strangely disconnected from reality. The previous day he had witnessed the death of his best friend and the 'rebirth' of his fiancée all on a single section of video. A strangely, bizarre set of circumstances, Tim wondered if the events happening together could have been more than a coincidence.

Tim had ordered Bud to speak to no one about his theory of Nancy's return. He was troubled and disturbed but had the presence of mind to let Tiffany know that he would be gone a couple of days on 'business.'

Before he departed, Tim phoned the Hall County Sheriff's Department to inquire as to the possibility of dredging the lake once again to retrieve the body, but he was rebuffed.

"Aunt Linda!"

A wiry woman in her seventies had opened the front door of her house. She wore a pilot's leather jacket with khaki pants and cowboy boots. A purple beret rested on her head.

Aunt Linda was a unique woman who owned sixteen acres on Lookout Mountain on the Georgia side of the state line. Her companions were two black stallions, a pig named Harriet, and a one-legged rooster. Her husband, a fighter pilot in World War II, had died six years ago.

Quite a military historian, she had a wealth of information about the Civil War in her home. In fact, an old Confederate cannon stood guard on her front lawn.

Tim reminded her that he once worked as an assistant to an archeologist. "We could team up and scour the countryside up here looking for all kinds of Civil War artifacts."

Aunt Linda had been very close to her niece. "She was so precious to me. Come inside because I've got some old photos of her that I found in the attic. I think you'll like to take a look-see."

She led Tim into her two-story brick colonial-style home that featured a screened back porch. They went into her den, a homey, quaint room with numerous paintings and artifacts that would make a museum curator drool with envy. It had a ceiling fan and blue shag carpeting.

Aunt Linda brought Tim a big glass of lemonade and a photo album from a nearby bookcase. Tim leaned back in a big, comfortable easy chair in the corner of the den and started flipping through the album. About eight photo-filled pages into it, Tim stumbled upon something that alarmed him.

An old and faded photograph caught Tim's eye. For a brief moment, Tim thought he was looking at Nancy. As he read a hand-written caption in the bottom border that spelled out '1945', Tim called Linda over to look at the photo.

"That's my mother. Nancy's grandmother," Linda told him.

Nancy's parents were killed in a car accident when she was six years old but Tim knew nothing of her grandmother. Nancy and her grandmother were mirror images of each other in appearance.

"Isn't that amazing to you? I've never seen that much of a resemblance with a skipped generation," Tim said.

"The strange thing is my mother's disappearance I'll tell you."

"What happened?"

"My father was an intelligence officer in the Army. In the heat of W W Two, he was apparently assigned to…. What ja call it? Covert, yep, covert work in Austria. They think he was captured as a prisoner of war but my sister, went lookin' for him in the middle of a bloomin' war, even though everybody told her not to!"

"How could she travel to Europe? Weren't there restrictions?"

"Yep. But she was a very stubborn lady and usually found seventeen ways around problems like that. She was a bulldog."

"So what happened?"

"They never heard from either one of 'em again."

Linda left the room as Tim flipped through the album once more. He was afraid to alert her to his theory that Nancy was still alive but he knew it was the right thing to do so he called her back into the room.

Aunt Linda drew a long sigh after Tim recounted the story. "What in blazes is going on here?"

"I wish I knew. I wish I knew." Tim leaned back in his chair. "My head is spinning because I truly believe that Nancy is alive."

Linda laughed nervously then looked squarely at Tim. She saw that his expression could not have been more serious. Her eyes became watery as she sat up on the edge of her seat, "How could it be?"

Tim described the discovery on the video footage. "Have you had any hint that she might still be alive in the last year?"

Linda scratched her head and bit her lip. "No. Never."

Friday, June 14, 7:32 a.m.

A streak of sunlight shot through the window, hitting directly on Tim's face. He awoke and forgot for a moment where he was located until all the strange, troubling events came rushing back into his mind at once. He fell back onto the bed in Aunt Linda's guest room.

Tim walked to the window and saw a wondrous view of the city of Chattanooga with the Smoky Mountains standing watch in the background. A hovering mist hanging over the mountains accented the panoramic scene. Out of the corner of the window, Tim could see the crest of Lookout Mountain and a Civil War cannon at Point Park.

Late in the morning, Tim and Linda sat in lounge chairs on her back patio. Linda picked up a glass of ice tea, sipped it twice and said, "Let's look at your situation. Your best friend was killed but you think somebody was trying to murder the man you were working for. Then you saw Nancy on your film. We need to tie all the pieces together." Slowly, she took two more sips from her ice tea. "I think you should talk to that man. Mr. Petrel."

"Petrie," Tim corrected her.

"See if he has some answers."

"I'll do that when I get back to Atlanta. But what about Nancy? Do you have anything I could look through, like family documents or something more than those photos?"

"All her belongings are in Savannah. You know I have a second home down there. But it's empty, no furniture or anything. It has plenty of space, so I shipped all her personal belongings down there for storage."

Tim leaped from his chair. "Then that's where I'm going. She may be there. At least, I might be able to find out more information."

Within thirty minutes, he was back on the road, planning to return to Atlanta and then leave for Savannah on Monday. He wondered how he could tell Tiffany, the girl he had planned to marry, that his long dead fiancée was actually alive.

Tim called Tiffany on his cell phone and told her that they needed to talk. He asked her to pick up a pizza and they would talk over dinner at his place.

Tiffany arrived wearing a lovely yellow and white summer dress. As they ate pizza, Tim explained the entire situation to her. When he was finished, Tiffany was silent.

"Say something," Tim demanded.

"I don't know what to say!"

"We have an honest relationship," Tim said. "I decided to be upfront about it. I need to settle all this in my mind about Nancy."

"I don't believe she's alive. It's absurd."

"In my heart, I know she's alive," Tim said.

"What are you saying? You're leaving me?" Tiffany asked as her face turned red.

"No! That's not what I'm saying!"

"You'll drop me like a hot potato!'

"No! I love you. You know that."

"You two were actually engaged," Tiffany said. "We're not. That speaks for itself." Tiffany stood up and ran to the front door. "Don't call me." She slammed the door behind her.

Tim buried his head in his hands. He could not blame Tiffany for her reaction because it was natural.

Although, he wanted to avoid the issue, Tim knew that if a miracle did happen then he would be faced with a choice. Nancy or Tiffany?

Monday, June 17, 9:43 a.m.

The phone rang.

"This is Detective Grover with the Atlanta Police Department."

"Good to hear from you," Tim said.

"Sam Reed is dead."

"You mean the crane operator? What happened?"

"He was found in an alley in midtown with his throat cut."

Tim decided not to mention his suspicions about the woman in the video until he had time to look into the situation further. With everything else happening, Tim did not want the police to question his sanity.

"We have concluded that Mr. George Petrie was the intended victim in the murder," he said.

"That's what I thought!" Tim said. "Who's behind all this stuff?"

"We're working on it," Grover said. "Our theory is that the crane operator was knocked off simply to eliminate any trail back to whoever ordered the hit. Petrie, among other things, is an importer and exporter of government and business secrets. A salesman, a mercenary to the highest bidder."

"What kind of secrets?" Tim asked.

"How well did you know him?" Grover asked.

"Not well at all. Only long enough to finalize our contract."

"And you say you've haven't had any further contact with Petrie?"

"Nobody could accuse me of being mixed up with his shady deals if that's what you're implying!"

"I'm not implying anything," Grover said. "But I think we should talk to Mr. Petrie."

"Where will you see him? At his office?" Tim asked.

Detective Grover smiled. "No. The Atlanta city jail."

Tuesday, June 18, 9:56 a.m.

"What did you charge Petrie with so that you could lock him up?" Tim asked Detective Grover as they approached the jail on foot.

"We came up with something."

"Are you saying that you manufactured charges against him?"

"He's where he needs to be. Let me handle most of the discussion because these white collar criminals are pretty slick," Grover said. "They're smooth talkers."

Grover and Tim waited in a stark, dingy holding room as Petrie entered. Tim saw him as a distinguished-looking man, despite his orange prison jump suit. He was sixty years old with salt and pepper hair and a somewhat muscular physique.

"I believe you know Tim Jennings," Detective Grover said.

"Yes. I do and I'm sorry about your friend."

"We want to know what kind of secrets you are running," Grover said.

"I don't have the vaguest notion of what you're talking about."

"We know all about your past. You were an up and coming military officer. Then you were dishonorably discharged because of what the military called…. Let's see." Grover looked through a notebook. "Negligent inaction in regards to classified material. In other words, that sounds to me like you looked the other way. What exactly happened, Mr. Petrie?"

"That's classified information," Petrie said with a slight smile on his face.

"That hasn't stopped you before," Grover said.

"What's your next question?"

"When the fed boys get involved, we'll have all the answers we need." Grover loosened his tie.

"I'm honored that you would consider me worthy of attention by federal agents. But I believe you'll be disappointed because I'm no super spy." Petrie almost giggled. "I'm no mastermind and the trumped up charges you pinned on me will never stick because I'm no extortionist."

"Spare us the dribble," Grover said.

"I'm a businessman."

"A very wealthy businessman," Tim chimed in.

"Why do you think somebody would want to kill you?" Grover asked. "We think that slab of concrete was intended for you and I'm sure you reached the same conclusion. So who did it?"

"The police are the protectors of the public safety so that's your job."

"Are you going to tell us anything or not?" Grover shouted.

"I know nothing to tell you."

"We'll get it out of you one way or another!" Grover pointed his finger at Petrie.

"Are you threatening me with physical harm?"

"Let's go." Grover led Tim out of the room. "We're waiting on a detailed dossier on Petrie from the military and the FBI so we'll know more about his background soon."

Chapter Three—
The Wild Odyssey Begins

Tim returned to his office to catch up on paperwork. He entered Bud's office to retrieve a file and grimaced. Bud was not very organized. Stacks of manila folders lay strewn across his desk with barely enough room in the corner of the desk for the Mason jar filled with a mismatched assortment of writing pens.

By attending flea markets and yard sales, Tim had assembled a rag-tag collection of furniture for Bud's office. The sixty year-old desk was made of solid oak. The three chairs in the room were cheap, straight back models that were originally used in a high school cafeteria. Bud was asleep on a sagging, disheveled, and torn brown leather sofa that was positioned against the far wall.

Tim kicked the sofa. "Wake up!"

"What? Who?" Bud stammered as he awoke and fell off the sofa.

"Where's that file with the resumes?" Recently, Tim had concluded that it was time to hire an administrative assistant. "Bud, we're gonna hire somebody soon so I need you to start lining up interviews for the middle of next week."

"You aren't happy with me?"

"Not your position! An administrative assistant."

Later in the evening as he sat down in front of the TV to eat a chicken pot pie, Tim remembered that he had promised Tiffany a week ago that they would attend Wednesday night prayer meeting the next day. He was reasonably sure that after the previous night's developments she would not want to follow up on the plans.

After he finished his meal, Tim called Tiffany to tell her about Savannah. He played the 'optimist card' and acted like he assumed the church meeting with her was still on.

"I'm calling about the prayer meeting tomorrow. Unfortunately, I've got to go out of town so I'll have to miss it. I'm sorry," Tim said.

There was a short period of silence on the other end of the line. "I do not want to talk to you. I'm not going anywhere with you. Why don't you bring Nancy? Good bye."

Wednesday, June 19, 1:03 p.m.

Bud arrived at the office with his suitcase, a bag of corn chips, and a dour expression on his face.

"Where's the Smith and Wesson?" Tim asked.

"Ole S&W is right at home." Bud pulled his jacket open to reveal a holster with a pistol secured in it. An avid hunter, Bud was very comfortable with firearms.

In recent years, Tim had kept a pistol next to his bed for protection. He brought it along for the trip.

The drive to Savannah in Bud's 1989 Ford Escort would take about four hours.

"I hope you got the air conditioning fixed in this thing," Tim said as Bud pulled out of the driveway.

"No problem." Bud pushed the air condition button and the cool air quickly flowed into the car.

As they traveled through downtown Atlanta, the vehicle passed Turner Field, home of the Atlanta Braves.

"What do you think about Turner Field?" Tim asked.

"It's great. Every seat's a good one for baseball. It's better than the old Atlanta-Fulton County Stadium, but fans have a lot of memories from the old place," Bud said. "Aaron's home run. Stopping Pete Rose's streak. My mom even got religion there in 1973."

"What do you mean?"

"She accepted Jesus Christ as her Savior at a Billy Graham Crusade at Atlanta Stadium in 1973."

"Bud, you're not very religious are you?"

"Nope because I am too busy having fun."

A long silence followed as Tim stared out the window.

"Do you really think that woman was Nancy?" Bud asked.

"Yes I do."

"Then why didn't she call you or better yet, knock on your front door?"

"I don't know. None of it makes any sense. Maybe she's in hiding or running for her life, but we're beyond the point of arguing about her being alive because we saw her on the video."

"It could have been somebody that looked like her 'cause everybody's got a double. My girlfriend looks like Britney Spears."

"No she doesn't. She looks more like… ."

"Who does she look like?" Bud asked.

"Let's not get off the subject."

"What is the subject?"

"Nancy, of course," Tim said as he impatiently shook his head.

"Let's be objective about all of this stuff," Bud said. "That video is not irrefutable evidence that Nancy is alive."

"If there's any chance that it might be legit, I can't wait around because Nancy needs me," Tim grimaced. "You did make a duplicate video disc, didn't you? The cops might lose the original, for all we know."

"Yes, of course."

By late in the afternoon, the two travelers were motoring down I-16, southeast of Macon.

"I love Savannah," Tim said. "But here in the middle of June, heat's gonna be rough."

"Well I don't plan on doing much sightseeing while I'm here or lying out on Tybee Island," Bud laughed. Suddenly, he turned somber and serious. "Tim, is there a southern Mafia?"

"I don't know that I'd call it that. There's certainly organized crime."

"It's a strange situation, if she is alive. You're not going to like this," Bud said. "But have you thought about the possibility that Nancy intentionally disappeared?"

"I've thought of everything but that wouldn't make any sense. What would she be running from?"

Bud chewed on his lower lip. "You possibly."

"Don't be crazy. We were in love."

"Do you maybe think she got cold feet about the commitment?"

"Sure and dropped off the face of the earth?" Tim jeered as he fumbled with his shirt collar.

"What other explanation could there be?" Bud passed a pickup truck that was barely traveling above the minimum speed limit.

"Amnesia. She could have bumped her head on the side of the boat, then swam to shore, wandered around aimlessly until she was picked up by somebody in a car. That person could have driven halfway across the country and then finally realized there was something wrong with Nancy," Tim conjectured.

"I don't buy that. Amnesia? That's something out of the movies and besides, she would have I.D. on her."

"Nancy kept all that type of stuff in her purse and she left the purse at our campsite," Tim said. "If she were planning to run off, Nancy would never leave her purse. Women don't do that kind of thing."

Bud grimaced. "I'm afraid she may have been kidnapped. She could have been held captive as a 'you know what.'"

"As a what?" Tim demanded.

Bud frowned and tightly gripped the steering wheel. "As a sex slave."

"I don't want to think about something that absurd."

"It's not that absurd because we gotta face reality, man! All sorts of strange things are going on in this day and age."

"That kind of thing doesn't happen in the U.S.," Tim said.

"Sure it does. There may not be a big market for it but individual people keep slaves. Look at Jeffrey Dahmer. The only difference is he ate his slaves."

"Shut up! Shut up!" Tim screamed.

"Maybe she joined a cult devoted to the weird and the wild."

"I said shut up!"

Late in the afternoon, they reached the outskirts of Savannah.

Tim read the next road sign—Garden City. "Let's spend the night at a motel here."

"Why?" Bud asked.

"Because I'd feel safer and nobody would find us out here."

"Well, there's not much here in Garden City. There's a National Guard training site." He pointed at a sign on the side of the road informing travelers of its location two miles ahead. As soon as they found a cheap motel, they pulled over and reserved a room for the evening.

"We're going out to Linda's house tomorrow morning," Tim said as they entered the motel room. "Maybe we can find out something there."

The small room had two single beds that ate up most of the space. One of the walls had wood paneling and the other three walls were covered with pale green wallpaper. A huge water stain on the ceiling and the mismatched bath towels removed any doubt that they were not staying in a first class motel.

Tim sat down on one of the beds. "Maybe Nancy is living at the house. We'll find out tomorrow, but even if she isn't there, we'll still have a chance to go through the old family stuff."

"I'm really lookin' forward to going through the stuff," Bud said sarcastically.

"Let's watch the news," Tim said.

"No. I wanna watch my TV Land sitcoms."

"You're the shallowest guy I know," Tim said. "I'll go get a newspaper instead." Tim walked out the door and through the gravel, dusty parking lot under a dark, moonless night.

Thursday, June 20, 10:06 a.m.

As Tim and Bud drove to Aunt Linda's house, they passed a famous restaurant, the Pirates' House. The old wooden structure had stood on the spot for centuries, casting an eerie pale on passersby.

"We gotta eat there," Bud said. "It's got everything going for it, including good food and atmosphere."

"One day I would like to do that," Tim said. "It's a pretty popular place."

"Hey! It's the oldest house in Georgia and it's supposed to be haunted."

"By who?"

"I don't know but how 'bout we have lunch there and find out?" Bud rubbed his stomach enthusiastically.

"You know, we're not tourists. We've got work to do."

"True but a guy's got to have fun now and then."

Within twenty minutes, they pulled into a middle-income neighborhood on Tybee Island. Most of the houses were modest, sixties and seventies era two story buildings.

"It's the fourth house on the right," Tim said. They pulled into a driveway and stopped the car.

The lawn was three feet high in tall grass. The house was a two-story red brick colonial model that featured white shutters and trim that were badly peeling. One of the shutters at an upstairs window was dangling precariously, barely clinging to the brick.

"This place needs a mother's touch or a handyman's expertise," Bud laughed.

They walked to the front door and stopped as Tim groped his way through several layers of annoying spider webs. Bud found himself engulfed in a massive, circular web.

"I hate spider webs," Tim groaned.

Two of the front windows had cracked panes.

"How long ago did Aunt Linda live here?" Bud asked derisively.

"It's billed as a summer home but she hasn't lived here in a long, long time."

Tim reached behind the cracked, weatherworn window shutter nearest to the door and pulled out a key.

"Top drawer security," Bud chuckled.

Tim unlocked the big wooden front door and walked in. The dampness and dustiness almost smothered both of them. There was no furniture in the house, not even a folding chair. The walls were bleak and barren.

"We're going into the basement," Tim said as he rounded a corner and opened a door. "I think it's this way." A ramshackle, wooden staircase led down into the deep darkness.

Tim pulled out a flashlight from his jacket and turned it on.

The staircase squeaked as they walked down. At the bottom, Tim stepped into a shallow pool of water and immediately skipped out of it and flashed the light around the basement. The room was small with several old chairs lining the brick walls. A baby's crib rested in the far corner.

Bud screamed.

"What's wrong?"

"Something crawled across the back of my neck."

Tim froze in the cold, damp darkness. "What was it?"

"My trained monkey! How do I know? It was probably a spider."

"Well quit acting like a baby. Ahh. Here's what we're looking for." Tim flashed the light at a wooden filing cabinet with three big drawers, covered with nicks and scratches.

"What exactly did you want to find?" Bud asked.

"Linda said that many of the family records and important documents are here. I'm looking for anything that can help me find Nancy, basically anything from her background that might explain why she's been missing."

Tim opened the top drawer of the filing cabinet and leafed through yellowed, faded papers, most contained in manila folders. The drawer included mostly old warranties, certificates of appreciation, and a batch of old bank statements. Tim slammed the drawer shut, creating a thudding sound that clamored across the dark room.

"Let's try the next one," Tim said. The drawer consisted mostly of old school documents. "Nancy was a good student from way back," Tim said as he looked at a report card from the spring quarter of her third grade. He found many photographs as well. Some of them looked like photos from vacations and there were a few photos of Nancy by herself in what appeared to be a European setting.

Underneath the photos were two folders marked 'Family Medical Records.' Tim looked through the folders and found only doctors' receipts, insurance papers, records of childhood vaccinations, and other miscellaneous documents.

"There's nothing here that's gonna help me," Tim said. But he decided to take the photos and medical records as a precaution.

Tim and Bud returned to their motel room as a steady rainfall descended upon the Savannah area.

Tim awoke abruptly and looked at his watch. He had been asleep for about forty-five minutes. He noticed an envelope on the carpet next to the door. Tim looked across the room at Bud who was snoring most annoyingly.

Tim picked up the envelope and saw that someone had hand-written 'Tim Jennings' on it. He opened it and pulled out a sheet of paper. A handwritten note read: "Meet me at the Waving Girl statue at 10:00 p.m. tonight."

"Who could this be?" Tim whispered aloud. "It must be about Nancy or maybe it's the people that killed Lance."

As he sat down on the bed, Tim considered the possibility that it could be a trap. Nervously, he paced in stocking feet, with his big toe stuck out of one of his worn socks.

Tim decided that he would go to the appointed place. As he aggressively stuffed the note and envelope into his shirt pocket, he decided that he would go alone because he did not want to endanger Bud or be distracted by him.

A sudden strange feeling came over Tim. It was a feeling of trepidation that made him want to escape to a deserted island somewhere, lie in the sun, and sip lemonade all day. He sat down on the side of the bed and reminded himself that only a few days ago, he was leading a mundane but happy life and now he was living a surreal nightmare that was proving more and more unpredictable all the time.

Chapter Four—In a Fog

Tim left a note for Bud to read when he awoke. He drove early to the Historic District of Savannah because he wanted time to think before he approached the statue. Fortunately, the rain had stopped falling. Tim had a keen interest in history and he found Savannah to be fascinating, as he had visited on many occasions.

An organized historic preservation effort began in the 1950s by leaders in Savannah. The Historic District was comprised of over 3,000 structures and 2,300 of them were of historic significance. Approximately 1,700 of them had been restored. The Historic District was neatly arranged, having been laid out in squares many years ago by General James Oglethorpe, who founded the state of Georgia. The squares were basically small, grass-covered parks and most of them included monuments or statues.

As Tim drove down State Route 16, he thought about Tiffany. What would he do if Nancy were actually alive and well? Tiffany had been as good to him as a man could expect, and now he was on the verge of telling her to hit the road. But Tim realized that he had changed since the loss of Nancy. He did not have inner peace or happiness since that tragic day at Lake Lanier.

Tim watched a young couple cross the street in front of him, hand in hand. They were jovial, hugging, teasing, and kissing.

Tim blamed himself for Nancy's death and tortured himself with lonely evenings and desolate thoughts in the months that followed the tragedy.

But Tiffany had helped Tim pull himself out of his malaise and quagmire of despair through her love and companionship. He hated himself for what he was doing to her.

Tim drove through the Victorian District in Savannah which was located south of the Historic District. He looked longingly at the nineteenth century frame homes, many of which were attractive because of their ornate gingerbread woodwork. He almost wished he were alive in that era when he could have lived in one of the homes and claimed a much simpler lifestyle.

When Tim reached the Historic District, he parked his vehicle in Calhoun Square and set out on foot. On the other side of the square, Tim saw an old school building. As he approached the main entrance of the building, he noticed a sign above it that read 'Massie School', the oldest public school building in Georgia.

Tim headed west and entered Monterey Square. He stood in front of the Mercer-Williams House, former home of Jim Williams who became famous in the book and movie *Midnight in the Garden of Good and Evil*.

As the sun began to set, a shroud of fog settled on the city. The rain earlier in the day had made the situation ripe for the fog. But it did not deter Tim as he walked north and entered Chippewa Square. He remembered that Tom Hanks' bench scene in the movie *Forrest Gump* was shot there.

It became difficult for Tim to maintain his bearings with the heavy fog floating in off the river. He walked through a slow, thick billowing patch of fog and rounded a corner and faced the Telfair Academy of Arts and Sciences. Designed by William Jay, it housed impressive American paintings and art of the eighteenth and nineteenth centuries. On a previous visit to Savannah, Tim had toured the facility and been mesmerized by several of the paintings that depicted tremendous battle scenes from wars gone by.

As he walked, Tim devised a plan. He would lurk in the shadows, far enough away from the statue to be hidden but close enough to see the person that appeared. Tim wanted to know what he was dealing with before he showed his hand.

A few minutes before the scheduled hour, Tim stood at the far eastern end of River Street as the fog continued to engulf the area, causing a heavy mist that decreased visibility dramatically. A handful of people scurried about in various directions. A middle-age couple walked toward him, hand-in-hand. After they passed, a teen-age boy, dressed in a leather jacket and gray corduroy pants, glided by on roller skates. Tim was tempted to reach his leg out and trip the kid for endangering other people by flying along on the skates.

Tim walked past the Nouveau Gallery, an establishment that sold local art and stopped in front of Gift Time, a souvenir shop. It was the very last business establishment on River Street.

As he stood in front of the shop, Tim could see the Waving Girl statue through the fog because it was illuminated by nearby streetlights. The statue was erected in honor of Florence Martus who died in 1943. Several miles downriver from Savannah, there was a little island called Elba where a lighthouse stood. The keepers of the lighthouse were a Mr. and Mrs. Martus. When they died, their son and daughter Florence became keepers.

Florence enjoyed waving at the seagoing vessels that passed the island, evidenced by the fifty year period that she continued the tradition. She waved at every ship that entered the port of Savannah, using a white kerchief by day and a lantern after dark. Her legend grew through the years.

Something caught Tim's eye about one hundred yards up River Street, beyond the statue but before the Ambassador Hotel. Two lights approached. As the lights grew closer, Tim squinted into the misty, foggy night, trying fervently to determine what exactly was coming his way.

Tim realized that it was two police officers, each holding flashlights. He considered striking up a conversation with them because their presence would increase the likelihood of his safety, although, conversely, the officers might spook the person. Tim let them pass.

As a slight breeze rolled in off the river, Tim looked at his watch. It was 10:00 p.m. Anxiously, he looked in the direction of the Waving Girl statue, barely visible in the fog. Tim decided to get closer.

Directly across River Street from the statue was a grassy area with a narrow sidewalk, a few trees, and two wooden benches. Tim walked to that spot and crouched down behind one of the benches. As the minutes passed, he spotted a distant ship in the still waters of the Savannah River.

Tim noticed a figure emerge from the fog. The person approached from the west, wearing an oversized gray raincoat with a big parka-style hood atop the head.

Tim peered intently at the mysterious figure but was unable to get a good look at the person. He could not even determine if the person was a man or a woman. Tim looked all around the area but saw no one else in the foggy landscape.

With hope in his heart, Tim Jennings emerged from his hiding place.

"Here I am," Tim said.

The person stood momentarily, then ran into the fog with Tim wasting no time following in pursuit. The person ran up a cobblestone ramp on the right. Tim followed close behind, stumbling over a protruding cobblestone but gathering himself quickly.

At the top of the ramp, Tim faced East Bay Street then looked to the left. In the distance, the Pirates' House restaurant was bathed in light. Looking to the right, he saw the figure running up the street.

After a two block pursuit, he saw the person run into the old warehouse section where cotton had been stored in the buildings in the early part of the 1900s. Tim stopped at a bright street light long enough to see the figure slither into a side door of a warehouse. The door was battered and nearly off its hinges.

Tim stopped in his tracks because he wasn't quite sure he wanted to go inside the warehouse. The smothering fog and the eerie silence of the old dead end street added to Tim's apprehension. He wondered if it might be a trap.

With a hidden pistol at his side, Tim found the courage to enter the abandoned building, plunging into the darkened, cavernous warehouse. Tim's flashlight beamed brightly through the cobwebs and against the old grimy concrete walls. He was standing in a big room with no side exits. Out of the corner of his eye, he saw the elusive figure standing in front of an old cracked window at the far wall. The person was trying desperately to squeeze out of the window.

"Stop running!" Tim shouted.

The person turned around and cowered against the wall as Tim approached then pulled away the hood.

"Who are you?" Tim aimed his gun at a young black male in his early twenties. Underneath his big coat, he wore a faded pair of blue jeans and a sweat-stained white T-shirt.

"Don't shoot! Don't shoot! I'm straight man. I'm straight," the man said.

"Were you waiting for me? My name's Tim Jennings."

"No! I thought you were my probation officer."

"So you didn't put a note under the door of my motel room?"

"Huh?"

"I chased you for nothing," Tim shouted. "I gotta get back to the statue."

Tim returned to the statue and waited forty-five minutes. Nobody arrived.

When he returned to the motel, Tim immediately knew that something was wrong. The door to his room was wide open.

Cautiously, Tim approached. "Bud! Bud!"

A deep, prolonged moan came out of the room.

Tim drew his weapon and rushed in.

Bud was lying on the floor with his hand clasped to his forehead.

The room had been torn asunder. Drawers were open. Suitcases had been opened and plundered and furniture was turned on end.

"What happened?"

"I was watching TV and I guess that I dozed off," Bud said. "Somebody rushes into the room. It woke me up and a guy clubbed me on the head. I was knocked out cold!"

"Did you get a good look at the guy?"

"No. It happened too fast and I was half asleep."

"He tore the place apart looking for something."

Tim explained that he had gone downtown after receiving the note.

"It was obviously a sham to get you out of the way," Bud said. "Only he didn't know that I would be here."

"Good theory. They followed us to Savannah."

Chapter Five—Lovely Tiffany

Friday, June 21, 7:31 p.m.

"I don't think she's alive, but if she is, who would you choose?" Tiffany demanded.

Tim was back in Atlanta, sitting on the couch in Tiffany's living room. Her question made Tim fidget because he was determined to block the choice out of his mind.

"I'd choose you, obviously!" Tim tried to convince himself that his words were true.

"I strongly suggest that you drop this search or whatever you call it," Tiffany said. "If you know what's good for you."

"You don't need to worry about it."

"You're right because I've other things to be concerned about. My Aunt Bess passed away," Tiffany said. "She was very special to me. I'm sure that you remember me mentioning her, don't you?"

"Yes. I'm really sorry," Tim said. He slid to the other end of the couch and hugged her.

"She lived in Dawsonville but she was all by herself with no immediate family." Tears formed in Tiffany's eyes.

"Are the arrangements complete?"

"Everything but the reading of her will by her attorney."

Tim wondered if any other guy on the face of the planet had ever been in a similar situation. He loved two of the most beautiful and caring young women a man could meet and one of them had come back from the grave.

"My parents haven't seen you in ages," Tiffany said as she softly patted his knee. "Why don't we go see them this weekend? Then we'll all go to church together on Sunday."

Tim smiled meekly. "I think I can manage that." He knew that Tiffany's mother was counting on a wedding because she had practically developed a book length game plan for the perfect one and was ready to put the plan into motion.

Tim looked appreciatively at Tiffany. She had a soft demeanor and easy way about her that he found very appealing. He was tempted to drop his mad chase for a ghost and allow himself to bask in Tiffany's love and never look back.

"We'll go up to the mountains next weekend, probably swing by Helen and visit the shops," Tiffany planned aloud.

Tim bit his lower lip, admiring Tiffany's determination to make everything seem normal, but he knew deep down that he could never be at peace until his questions were answered. Was the woman he saw Nancy? Could he love her again?

"Do you know what would be nice?" Tiffany asked.

"What?"

"We should go to an evening concert at Chastain Park."

"That would be lovely," Tim said in a less than enthusiastic tone.

Monday, June 24, 8:21 a.m.

Tim waited outside Detective Grover's office as a woman approached.

"I'm Mr. Grover's administrative assistant. He called to tell me that he will be running a few minutes late. He had a meeting out of the office. Mr. Welch is coming from his office on the third floor to keep you company until Mr. Grover arrives."

"Detective Grover will be here soon," Welch said upon arrival. "Thanks for coming."

The minutes passed slowly, but eventually Detective Grover arrived. After routine greetings, he got down to business.

"Do you know or are you familiar with Saul Marino?"

"Never heard of him," Tim said.

"Saul 'The Load' Marino?"

"Nope but I'm intrigued. Tell me more."

Grover arose from his chair and adjusted the blinds at his window. Streaks of sunlight burst into the dank room. "He's an organized crime leader and businessman."

"He's bad news," Howard Welch said.

"Well, I don't plan to get acquainted with him anytime soon," Tim said. He told them about the incident in Savannah.

"So they turned the room upside down?" Grover quipped. "It could have been Marino's people tailing you for info because of your work with Petrie. Marino and Petrie know each other."

Tim sat up in his chair. "What's their connection?"

"The connection is that we believe Marino was behind the attempt on Petrie's life," Grover said.

"Why?"

"We've got several theories but the most logical one being that they were both after the same prize or goal, or maybe Marino thought Petrie was squeezing in on his territory. Marino's not into stash, loot, drugs, contraband. He's more interested in the intangible stuff," Grover said.

"What do you mean?" Tim asked.

"Government secrets, sensitive documents, private and personal information on people," Grover said.

"What about your job assignments with Petrie?" Welch grunted.

"You mean my assignment—singular. The Petrie job. I never heard of the guy before that job, but there is something I need to discuss with you."

Tim reported in great detail is theory about Nancy still being alive.

"What ya tryin' to pull?" Welch blurted out.

Tim was shocked. "I don't know what you mean?"

"You are claiming that she's lurkin' around in the shadows and then she shows up at a crime scene. There's gotta be something going on," Welch said. "Is she into drugs? Hooker?"

"He's way out of line," Tim shouted. "In fact, I was going to ask you to help me find her."

"It sounds farfetched," Grover said. "Probably a woman with a physical resemblance, that's all. Get us more evidence before we go down that road."

"I will," Tim said. "I will."

"O.K. You can leave," Grover said. "We've established that you don't know Marino, which was our main objective."

Tim turned to walk out, looking angrily at Welch.

"Let us know if you leave town," Welch said.

"For real?"

"That's only procedure," Grover said.

"If I'm a suspect, maybe, but you don't have any right to order me to do anything," Tim countered.

"Let's be safe and stay in touch," Grover said calmly.

Tim stormed out of the office.

In the evening, Tim sat on his back patio and watched his dog as it ran and played. As he attempted to relax under the warm, starry sky, Tim envied the simplicity of a dog's life because his own life was getting much too complicated.

Tim always thought he lived a good life and was a good person, but everything was crashing down around him. The notion that Nancy could be involved in illegal or illicit activities was simply intolerable to Tim and it weighed heavily on his mind.

Later, Tim stretched out on the couch and read some old love letters from Nancy that he had saved in a dusty old scrapbook. With pleasant thoughts in mind, Tim fell asleep.

Wednesday, June 26, 10:11 a.m.

A knock at the front door.

Tim opened the door to find Tiffany standing in front of him in an old Georgia Tech football jersey and a pair of cut off blue jeans. She wore no makeup and her hair was tied up in a ponytail.

"Hi!" She greeted him with the widest and biggest of smiles. "Let's go on a picnic."

"What?"

"You heard me. Let's go on a picnic."

Tim laughed. "I just woke up, I'm not dressed and I don't have any food in the house."

Tiffany closed the door. "It's all taken care of because I took care of everything. I've got a big basket of sandwiches, chips, and drinks in my car."

Tim scratched his head. "You're too much."

Minutes later, they were on the road in Tiffany's car. The young couple's destination was Helen, a quaint, little tourist town with a Bavarian theme. Shops and restaurants of various kinds dotted the landscape of the town.

As they drove north on Georgia Highway 400, Tim thought of Nancy and the day she was lost. The highway ran past Lake Lanier, the spot where she disappeared. As they drove by the Lake Lanier exit, Tim was tempted to ask Tiffany, who was driving, to pull off the highway and go to the lake, but he resisted.

When they reached Helen, the couple walked all over town, visiting the shops. Although Tim was not much of a shopper, he appreciated the fact that Tiffany was having a good time. She bought a stuffed animal, a couple of T-shirts, and some jewelry.

As the lunch hour approached, Tim found a picnic table under a shady elm tree. Tiffany spread a bright red and white tablecloth across it.

"We have it all," Tiffany said.

Tim was quietly deep in thought. He had almost convinced himself that he could have both of them, Tiffany and Nancy.

"When we get married, we'll have picnics every day," Tiffany said with an enthusiastic laugh. "And I'll prepare you a home cooked meal every evening."

"I'll get fat before you know it," Tim laughed. He looked intently at Tiffany. "Why do you put up with me?"

"Because I love you," she said.

"I'm really not worthy of your love."

"Oh yes you are."

"Why are you so radiant all the time?"

Tiffany pulled a bag of potato chips from the picnic basket and placed them on the table. "It's the love of Christ in me. The Holy Spirit." She paused momentarily. "I want you to start going to church with me more often."

"I go with you."

"Not very often!"

"Well you learn enough about the Bible for both of us," Tim said.

Tiffany hung her head. "I'm worried about you."

"What do you mean?"

"You're not saved! You need to accept Christ as your personal Lord and Savior!" she said.

"We've been through all of this before," Tim argued. "I went to church all the way 'til I was sixteen because my parents made sure I was there."

"That doesn't have anything to do with you being saved."

"Well, it sure helps," Tim laughed.

"No it doesn't! You didn't even have a good attitude about it because your parents had to drag you to church."

"Pass those potato chips down here." Tim tried to deflect the subject.

"What are you afraid of anyway?" Tiffany asked.

"I'm not afraid of anything."

"I want you to go to church with me tonight for Bible study."

"We'll talk about it later."

Tears filled Tiffany's eyes.

Tim lost his appetite.

On the way home, Tim agreed to go to church with her. He was a sucker for the tears of a woman.

Later that evening, they entered the front doors of First Baptist Church Atlanta. The sanctuary was almost full so they sat in the third row from the back.

"Give me a quick jab in the ribs if I fall asleep," Tim urged sarcastically.

"You won't fall asleep," Tiffany said.

"I've never been much for Holy Roller music," Tim said.

Tiffany opened her Bible. "The emphasis on Wednesdays is studying Scripture. I want you to learn one Bible verse a week because I know that you can do it. I just know you can."

"I don't think so."

As the service began, Tim fell asleep.

Chapter Six—"The Load"

Thursday, June 27, 11:09 a.m.

Tim sat in a metal chair and looked through a two-way mirror as Saul Marino was interviewed by the police. He was a huge man with a balding head, an upturned nose, and a small scar that ran across his left cheek. He wore a beige summer jacket with an open collar, button down blue shirt, and red scarf around his neck.

"Let's review the life and times of Saul Marino," Grover said.

Marino pulled a pack of cigarettes from his pants pocket, calmly selected one, lit it, and puffed away.

As cigarette smoke encircled his head, Grover took a manila folder from his briefcase and opened it on the desk. "We know all about your activities in Cuba. Funneling information to Castro."

"Don't make me laugh," Marino said. "That's hearsay. Gossip." The man spoke with a high-pitched, nasal tone.

"You'd be six feet under the jail right now if a couple of key witnesses had not mysteriously died," Grover said.

"Hey! Life's got a lot of twists and turns. What can I say?"

"We also know that you've been very adept at corporate espionage," Grover said.

"I bet you've made a killing in that field, haven't you?" Welch shouted.

"I'm a business consultant, a management adviser," Marino said with a forced smile.

"How much did you get paid for tipping off that snack food company about their competition's ad campaign?" Grover asked.

"My only involvement with that company was when I won a complimentary month's supply of cheese chips. I could use a bag right now."

"You have a neat knack for covering your tracks but we know that we have a bunch of dead people that have some type of connection back to you," Grover countered.

"I find you to be very abusive," Marino said. "My attorney's making arrangements to free me. You don't have any grounds to hold me."

"What can you tell us about Petrie?" Grover pressed.

"I can tell nothing except that my attorney will be here shortly and I'll be on my way."

"We're going to prove that you were responsible for an attempt on Petrie's life that killed someone else," Grover said.

"All I know is that Mr. Petrie is incarcerated and I have no desire to be associated with him," Marino said.

"Listen, we've already traced both of you to the common objective of stealing classified and confidential information," Grover said.

"Ole Petrie snatched some info right out from under your nose, didn't he? No honor among worthless thieves," Welch growled.

"You're beginning to bore me." Marino chewed on a fingernail.

"We know that you and Petrie were mixed up with something in Europe. Germany, England, or maybe Denmark," Grover said. "It's something pretty big, isn't it?"

"Let your imagination run wild!" Marino laughed.

Tim waited patiently in Detective Grover's office before George Petrie was brought to the interrogation room. He noticed a collection of ceramic hippos on the bookshelf behind

Grover's chair, a twice bitten strawberry doughnut and a half a cup of cold coffee on his desk. Tim got comfortable in his chair and watched through the two-way mirror as Grover and Welch led Petrie into the room.

"We realize the past few days have been difficult for you," Grover said.

"Yes," George Petrie said.

Howard Welch spoke up. "You're an educated man. What made you go bad?"

"I'm not such a bad guy. My mother, my great aunt, and my dog all love me."

"Let's get straight to it," Grover said. "How long have you known Saul Marino?"

"I've known The Load for about a year."

"I understand that one of your contracting firms did a project or two for his industrial development company. Is that right?"

"That's true."

"What happened? Give us some details."

"I reviewed Saul's portfolio and became very impressed with his foreign ventures. I traveled to Italy to tour a factory owned by Saul. It was legit but then I found out about an underground enterprise that Mr. Marino has been engaged in. The primary purpose was to gather, extract, or heist information of a valuable nature from corporations, governments of North America and Europe, including military sources, and medical and science organizations. Then he would sell it to the highest bidder."

"How did you find out?" Grover asked.

"The Load told me," Petrie said. "He bragged about it like a rooster."

"So he wanted you to become a business associate?" Grover asked.

"More accurately.... He wanted me to become an agent."

"An agent? What do you mean?" Welch asked.

"Marino wanted me to gather information. He wanted me to basically become a spy. As a result of my business ventures through the years, I have made many impressive contacts."

"Why did you do it?" Welch asked. "You've had a clean record and a good reputation."

"Why do you think I did it? The greenbacks, dinero, money!" Petrie said.

"So you admit you're a crook?" Welch asked.

"Not at all. I was in a financial bind at the time and I had creditors coming down on me. My youngest daughter was about to enter college so I needed the money."

"Don't be trying to get our sympathy," Welch growled.

"I'm not!"

"Give us more details about what you did and did not do," Grover instructed.

"I decided to funnel information that would not hurt anybody. I really meant no harm."

"Give us some examples," Grover said.

"Industry trade secrets, government research, medical research. Stuff that would become public knowledge eventually anyway." Petrie glanced at Welch.

"Tell it to the judge!" Welch said.

"A very intriguing situation developed," Petrie continued. "There have been rumors through the years that the Nazis had experimented with anti-aging drugs. Apparently they thought it would be possible to create the perfect race of humans by breeding and training. They wanted ethnic purity but also wanted to defy the aging process. They had the best and the brightest of scientists, chemists, medical researchers, and practitioners gathered. Eventually, they developed a formula to stop the aging process. They tested it on prisoners of war. The first few human guinea pigs died, but then they came up with a less volatile mix. People didn't expire, but the aging still continued."

"Where did you hear all this?" Welch asked.

"I heard it from Saul. He picked up on it from his many European contacts. The rumor was that they finally came up with a viable formula and had successful experiments done on POWs."

Tim listened intently.

Petrie reached for a glass of water on the table in front of him as he continued. "However the war was coming to an end. The Nazis surrendered and apparently these POWs who had been successfully tampered with simply circulated back into society. There was a factory near Bremerhaven, Germany that was the experimentation site but got bombed and battered during the war. The scientists fled, some of them to Copenhagen, Denmark. No one knows what happened to the drug or the formula, but I've heard rumors that there is some kind of activity going on there now… I mean at the factory. It's very mysterious."

Detective Grover wrote a few notes on his pad and motioned for Petrie to continue.

"But here's the most important part of the story. Marino told me that he had stumbled onto something big on this issue and I figured out that he had discovered the anti-aging formula. I think he feared that I would steal it from him, so he tried to eliminate me."

"Fascinating story," Detective Grover said. "So the Germans were serious about all this, huh?"

Petrie chuckled. "True and the scuttlebutt is that Hitler himself actually ordered the original experiments. A German, Dr. Herman Bron Wagonheimer, is believed to be the one who developed the theory and came up with the drug. All his notes and lab documentation disappeared and were believed burned during American bombing raids."

Grover loosened his neck tie. "Continue."

"If Marino ever had the formula in his possession, I planned to make a copy of it for myself," Petrie said. "He eventually found out about my plan and tried to get rid of me. That bit of motivation accounts for the 'accident' at the construction site."

Grover leaned back in his chair and stared at Petrie for thirty seconds.

"What's wrong?" Petrie asked.

"I'm trying to determine how much of that story is true and how much of it is horse manure," Grover said.

"Every last word of it is true."

"Did you ever get a copy of the formula?" Welch asked.

"Maybe I did. Maybe I didn't."

"We'd like to have a look at it," Welch said. "Where is it?"

"We might be able to make arrangements but of course, you would have to ensure something for me. My freedom!"

Detective Grover laughed under his breath. "I'm not here to make any deals with you."

"You'll never get your hands on the formula!" Petrie declared.

"I could care less about that crazy formula, if it does actually exists," Grover said.

"Personally, I'd like to hang both you and Marino from the same tree," Welch said.

"You don't like me, do you?" Petrie countered.

"I think that's enough for now," Detective Grover said.

Tim looked out the detective's fourth story window below into the city of Atlanta. He watched the people in their cars drive by and pedestrians walk up and down the streets. Most of the foot traffic was provided by college students who attended Georgia State University. The main campus was located around the corner block.

Tim thought about Petrie's claims and wondered what life would be like if the story about the anti-aging formula were true. Tim envisioned a world populated entirely by an endless supply of college students, dope heads, and nerds. The practical effect of a formula would have such a profound impact on culture. There would be no elderly for families to care for and nursing homes and assisting living care centers would go out of business.

Tim wondered if Nancy could be somehow involved with Marino and Petrie and the anti-aging formula. Why else would she have shown up at the construction site that day?

That evening, Tim stayed at home in front of the TV with a frozen pepperoni pizza and a can of diet cola. As he watched the Braves baseball game, his mind continually drifted back to the aging story. He wondered if Nancy could be doing some research on the issue and perhaps the government had secretly recruited her. He remembered that she had done considerable volunteer work at a local senior citizen center and worked as a college-credit intern for the Association of the Aged and Retired (AAR).

Tim decided that the AAR connection was worth pursuing.

Chapter Seven–
Looking for a Little Help

Monday, July 1, 10:11 a.m.

Tim called ahead and spoke with Mrs. Edith Woosterhouse, the Regional Director for AAR . When he walked through the front door of the modest two-story office building, he saw a white-haired woman in a blue pants suit sitting behind a reception desk, munching on a bag of pork rinds. She wrinkled her nose upon every bite.

"Good morning. I so enjoy seeing young people take an interest in retired folk," the woman said. She offered a pork rind to Tim.

"No thanks. I have an appointment with Mrs. Woosterhouse."

A wiry, short, middle-aged woman emerged from behind a partition.

"I'm Mrs. Woosterhouse. My word, you're a handsome young man! Isn't he, Barbara?"

The receptionist smiled.

Mrs. Woosterhouse led Tim to her office. It was a small musty room with several oil paintings hanging from the wall and a potted plant in each corner. Tim sat down in a wicker chair while the woman sat behind her desk.

"Do you recall a college student from a few years ago named Nancy Proctor? I believe she worked for you."

"Ah yes, Nancy Proctor. Such a lovely young woman, the poor dear. I understand that she drowned up at the lake."

"She was my fiancée."

"OOOOOOh, I'm so sorry."

"She worked directly under you, didn't she?"

"Oh, yes and she was a diligent young lady with plenty of initiative. In fact, she also worked part time for the Gerontology Alliance at the same time."

"What type of responsibilities did she have with you?"

"In the beginning, she answered phones and did clerical duties. But I recall that she had some specific interests and I gave her a research assignment that she wanted."

"And what was that?"

"I don't recall," the woman said.

"Try to remember."

"You know that I'm not as young as you and you can't expect me to remember every detail of this office from several years ago," Mrs. Woosterhouse said. "But let me go back to our filing room and see what I can come up with. I may have a copy of her work."

Several minutes later, the woman came back to the room. "She completed three research papers for school credit." Mrs. Woosterhouse fumbled through three notebooks that she had retrieved. The first report was entitled 'The Best Retirement Meccas: Albuquerque to Zebulon.'

"I may have to read that one," she mused.

The second report was called 'Pets and the Elderly.' The final report was entitled 'Theories: Halting the Aging Process.'

"May I look at that last report?"

From its contents Tim read, "As soon as we enter this world, our bodies begin dying. A bouncing baby represents the joy and expectancy of life and the unpredictable and fascinating journey that everyone experiences. As teenagers, we can't wait to grow older. We long for independence. We want time to progress so we will not have to suffer the indiscretions and humiliation of youth. We have no thought or concern that every day that passes plunges us closer and closer to our inevitable demise".

"Would you like a beverage?"

"What? Huh?" Tim looked up to see Mrs. Woosterhouse standing over him.

"A beverage, a pop?" she asked.

"A Coke would be great."

Tim flipped to the next section of the report, entitled, 'Telomeres and the Molecular Clock.' He read that "Telomeres are the genetic material at the ends of chromosomes. In fact, telomeres are the strands of DNA in each cell. As time proceeds, cells will divide and then replicate. The telomeres that are on each chromosome will get shorter and shorter. Ultimately, cells can no longer reproduce. We must somehow eliminate telomere loss. Atherosclerosis, arthritis, dementia, and other ailments are all related to changes that are cellular in nature as the old clock on the wall continues to tick. There have been many scientific discoveries recently that have chronicled the important details of the cells' timing process to the extent that there exists the distinct possibility of simply stopping the molecular clock... ."

Chapter Eight—The Race

Tuesday, July 4, 5:00 a.m.

The Peachtree Road Race was a big tradition in Atlanta that attracted 60,000 runners. They convened early in the morning on the Fourth of July at Lenox Square Mall to run 6.2 miles down Peachtree Street. The race attracted serious and casual runners from all over the world.

Tiffany was a fitness buff who had participated in aerobics classes for several years. Eventually, she decided to take up running. Tim, on the other hand, ran on a rather consistent basis. But he never enjoyed it as he much preferred playing tennis.

The Peachtree Road Race was a big festive event of fitness, community spirit, and freedom as the country and Atlanta celebrated its independence on the Fourth of July. It was one of Atlanta's premier events.

Tiffany arrived cheerfully at Tim's home before the sun rose. They planned to run the race together. Along the drive to the rail station where they would board a public transit train and commute to the starting line, Tiffany talked about many subjects, including matrimony.

"Reba and Doug have set a date. It will be in October and they're going to have a lovely ceremony in Helen. Have you noticed that everybody we know is getting married?"

"Noticed what?"

"I've got another friend, Sophie. Her boyfriend.... Listen to this. He parachuted into her backyard from a helicopter with a dozen long stem roses, a box of chocolates, and a self-portrait."

Tim looked glumly at Tiffany. "I'm not jumping out of an airplane."

"Silly, I don't want you to jump out of an airplane."

"Then what's the moral of the story?"

"The moral of the story is that some people know how to treat a woman right."

"How about the fact that I'm spending a holiday with you preparing to push myself, sweatin' and churnin' with 60,000 other runners when I feel like crashing on the sofa all day watching Wimbledon?"

"I want to get married," Tiffany blurted out.

"Tiffany, we're not ready. Be realistic and don't start that business about your biological clock either because that clock's gonna be tickin' for a good long while."

Tiffany turned pale and sat silently for the duration of the ride.

When they reached Peachtree Street, Tim and Tiffany found the section of runners that they had been assigned to run in, the middle of the pack. Most of the runners were standing around and talking but some were stretching.

"Let's join the fun," Tim said as he plopped down on the sidewalk and stretched his hamstrings. Tiffany followed his lead.

At 7:30 a.m., the elite runners started the race. The remaining runners were organized into eight sections and released to run in ten minute intervals.

Both sides of the race route were filled with family, friends, and general well-wishers for the runners.

One hour later, Tim crossed the finish line, generally pleased with his performance.

Somewhere after the midway point of the race, Tim had lost track of Tiffany. He waited for her at the finish line in anticipation of her finish. Five minutes later, Tim felt a tap on his shoulder.

"I finished fifteen minutes ago," Tiffany said. "I've been looking for you. How did you do?"

"Not too bad." Tim's ego was flattened.

Wednesday, July 5, 8:33 a.m.

Tim waited at the Donut Den on Roswell Road as a short, skinny, pale man in his late forties walked in. He was dressed in a knit golf shirt and sweat pants. Tim motioned him over to his booth.

"Hi, Otwell. Sit down."

The man had a distinct nervousness about him. He pulled out a cigarette from his pants pocket and lit it.

"Still smoking after all these years?"

"Til the day I die," Otwell said.

"Are your contacts with the Feds still down at the Richard Russell Building?"

"Sure. I know who I need to know."

"We're talkin' CIA here." Tim briefed Otwell on what he had learned about the anti-aging formula, Marino, and Petrie. "Find out if any federal agencies might be on the case. What they might know about the story."

"Afraid it is going to cost you a little more," Otwell said. "This sounds like a bear of a story."

"I don't care because I think Nancy is involved. Get the job done."

"Anytime I put my neck on the line, I think about my kids."

"You don't have any kids," Tim said. "Don't be such a drama queen!"

"It keeps me in the right frame of mind!"

Tim met Otwell through a friend who worked for the FBI. The friend introduced him because Tim needed some odd jobs done at the office and Otwell appeared to be eager to do labor work.

Otwell was a mysterious character who might best be described as a latter day hippie. He had a brilliant mind but poor grooming habits. Tim quickly recognized that he had stumbled upon an interesting, intriguing, yet somewhat perplexing person.

After the third time he cut Tim's grass, Otwell became more sociable. Initially, Tim thought Otwell was bluffing when he claimed to know many government operatives, insiders, and "shakers that move things", as Otwell put it.

Later, Otwell claimed he could ensure that a long-awaited IRS refund check would be in Tim's mailbox within three days. "Give me time to do my thing," he said. Tim scoffed but on the third day, he opened his mailbox and was pleased to find the check waiting for him.

About a month later, Tim discovered that federal law enforcement authorities had mistaken him for another Tim Jennings because he received a letter stating that his house and automobile were about to be seized and he must appear at the Russell Federal Building within a week. As Tim ranted and raved about the obvious mistake, Otwell laughed and said, "Leave it to me. I'll take care of the problem."

Tim declined the offer.

Otwell laughed smugly.

Later in the day, Tim received an e-mail from the federal government. The text read: "Our sincerest apologies. The Timothy Jennings in question is a different person. We regret any inconvenience this mistake may have caused you."

Chalking it up as a coincidence, Tim decided to refrain from discussing the issue with Otwell. He simply refused to believe that such an odd character could have that much influence.

The morning after he received the e-mail, Tim arose early and walked groggily to the front door to pick up the morning newspaper. He opened the door to find an unshaven Otwell leaning against the threshold. He held the newspaper in his hands and cheerfully tossed it to Tim.

"Piece a cake baby. Piece a cake," Otwell said.

"You cleared up the mistaken identity?"

"Piece a cake!"

Tim smiled as he thought about his past encounters with Otwell. He finished off his cocoa crème donut. "Get back to me as soon as you can with some information."

"Aye, aye, sir," Otwell said.

Thursday, July 6, 4:47 p.m.

Otwell stood with hands on hips in front of Tim's door.

"Who is that?" Tiffany asked.

"Why, if it isn't Otwell," Tim said. He decided not to share anything about Otwell with her. "He's a bum who's probably looking for some money for a drink. Go on in and I'll get rid of him."

With Tiffany out of the way, Tim motioned for Otwell to follow him. They got in the front seat of Tim's car. "What did you find out?"

"Nice car you got here. CD player and everything."

"Let's have it."

"Chill man and you'll be fine. There's a Nelson Porter with the CIA who specializes in contraband and suspicious activities of individuals and organizations that threaten United States' security. He's a key player in the agency. He's working on the anti-aging stuff here in the States and I think he's deployed field agents to Europe because of some kind of connection with the anti-aging miracle drug and an underground, subversive group."

"What kind of a group?"

"I don't know."

"I need more detail about what Porter's actually doing."

"Man, you can't expect miracles. But I can tell you he eats breakfast every morning at Sammy's Diner on Peachtree Street in Buckhead before heading downtown. Be good! By the way, here's a headshot of him."

Chapter Nine—Nelson Porter

Monday, July 8, 7:23 a.m.

Tim sat alone at a booth sipping hot coffee at Sammy's Diner. It was an old establishment, quaint, a little dingy, but it specialized in a great southern breakfast menu.

Twenty minutes passed; then thirty minutes were gone. Tim was about to give up when a man walked through the door who looked familiar. Tim pulled out the photo to be sure and concluded that it was positive identification. Nelson Porter had average features with a pale complexion, sandy brown hair, and appeared to be in his early forties.

Tim watched Nelson Porter sit down at a booth on the opposite side of the room. He noticed that the CIA operative was a snappy dresser who wore a dark blue blazer and white silk pants with cuffs at the ankles. His tie was a metallic blue with small gold dots embroidered on it.

The man did not seem particularly sinister or menacing. Tim watched quietly for a few minutes as Porter asked for a cup of coffee and ordered breakfast.

Initially unsure about the best way to approach the man, Tim decided to be blunt. "Excuse me. I'm looking for information about a missing woman."

Porter reacted with a cold stare. "How would I know anything?"

"In your line of work, you have reason to know about these kinds of things."

"I'm in real estate. My name's Preston Powers."

"No, you're not. You're Nelson Porter, CIA operative. Don't be so modest."

The man's face turned a bright shade of red as he grimaced and rubbed his chin. "Who are you?"

"My name is Tim Jennings and I need your help."

Porter motioned for him to sit down. "How do you know who I am?"

"I keep my ear to the ground and my nose to the air."

"I would suggest that you not be such a wise guy if you want any help. Now what's your problem?"

"My fiancée disappeared awhile back and I believe that she somehow became involved in a criminal enterprise, but with no bad intent on her part. This group probably has knowledge of a drug that supposedly will stop the aging process. Do you know anything that will help me?

Nelson Porter grinned, but his reaction morphed into a wicked stare at Tim. "I oughta shoot you on the spot."

"Sure! In cold blood in view of dozens of people."

"I can justify anything I do. It only means there's a lot of paperwork."

"All I'm trying to do is find the girl I love," Tim said.

"You're breaking my heart. Listen, most of the information I deal with is classified and even if I had something to give you I couldn't because my job and national security might be at stake. And besides, I don't even know you. You come waltzing over here asking for information that you might regret knowing later."

"Are you telling me that you have knowledge of an anti-aging drug?" Tim asked.

"I'm not telling you anything."

"All I ask is that you assure me that she is alive."

There was a long pause.

Porter took a sip of coffee. "What was her name?"

"Nancy Proctor." Tim showed the man Nancy's photo.

"Who was your father?"

"My father? Edward Jennings. He was the U.S. Attorney for the Northern District of Georgia back in the late seventies and early eighties. He's deceased."

"I thought so because I saw the facial resemblance and remember seeing pictures of you in his office."

"You knew my father?"

"As a fresh graduate out of law school, I worked for the law firm of Jennings, Trautwick, and Hasty for two years."

"You worked for my father?"

"I sure did," he said. "I really respected him."

Tim seized upon the opportunity. "My father got to know Nancy before his death. He was very impressed with her and he wanted the best for me."

Nelson Porter looked out the window. "I don't have anything to tell you."

"I'm not asking you to stick your neck out, but give me assurances that she's alive and any general information I can go on."

"I can't make a decision like that on an empty stomach," Porter said as the waitress approached to take his order.

She jotted down an order of three scrambled eggs, two sausage patties, wheat toast, and a big glass of orange juice.

Impatiently, Tim waited. "You've got to help me," he said as the waitress walked away.

Porter looked at Tim for a long time. "Be at the carrousel in the food court at North Point Mall tomorrow at noon."

Tuesday, July 9, 11:52 a.m.

Tim Jennings walked briskly through North Point Mall, a very popular retail center in the northern suburbs of Atlanta. Along the way, he dodged two boys with nachos and a mother pushing a stroller.

As he stood in front of the carrousel, Tim was reminded of one of his early dates with Nancy. They went to Six Flags over Georgia, the popular amusement park. Tim wanted to be bold, brash, and daring as he tried to impress the young lady. He asked her to ride all four roller coasters with him but she flatly refused. He asked her to ride the log flume and she declined. He insisted on a trip to the haunted house, but she begged off.

Finally, Tim asked Nancy Proctor what attraction she wanted to ride.

"The carrousel," she said. "I've loved riding them since I was a little girl."

"Good to see you again, Mr. Jennings."

Tim turned around to find Nelson Porter standing beside him. "I didn't see you coming."

"I know. You seemed to be in a daze, staring at the merry-go-round."

They walked a few feet and sat down on an uncomfortable metal bench.

"We must make this brief," Porter said. "I am sticking my neck out for you. This is very abnormal and if it weren't for your father, I would not be talking to you. Anyway, you did not hear this from me, do you understand? You must not betray my confidence!"

"I won't ever mention your name to anyone."

Porter looked over his shoulder and quickly back at Tim. "We in the Agency do not appreciate it when people betray our confidence."

"I understand. Now what can you tell me?"

"A woman matching her description has been seen in connection with our investigation of the anti-aging drug."

Tim's face went pale. "Where was she? What was she doing?"

"I don't know. She was seen in the U.S. I can tell you that but our investigation has taken us to Europe as well. She was seen in Germany and Denmark recently," Porter said.

"Tell me more," Tim demanded. "Is she working with Saul Marino? What about the underground organization?"

"That's all I know," Porter said. He walked away.

Tim squirmed on the hard bench. He struggled with the possibilities, wondering if Nancy might have developed a split personality. In all the years that the couple was together, she never so much as expressed an evil thought to anyone.

Later in the evening, Tim sat in his office and watched a steady rain pelt the nearby window.

The police had not concluded their analysis of the video that Tim had given to them for their investigation. He pulled his disc copy of the incident from a nearby shelf, placed it in the DVD player, and fast-forwarded it to the section where the woman appeared. Tim blew the woman's image up on the screen with his video editing equipment.

She looked like Nancy.

The rain fell outside as Tim stared motionless at the screen.

Wednesday, July 10, 9:16 a.m.

Tim walked briskly up the staircase leading to the main entrance of the Atlanta Police headquarters.

"Detective Grover is off today," a receptionist said.

Tim asked to speak to Howard Welch.

"Yes, he's here." She paged him over the intercom.

Welch came to the outer office.

"What do you want?"

"I want to see Marino."

"What for?"

"It's very, very important."

"I don't care how important it is. This ain't visiting hours."

"Don't tell me you can't get around it."

"Yeah, I probably could but I won't for one simple reason. He's not here."

"You're kidding me," Tim stammered.

"No. He got bailed out by his attorney. There will be a preliminary hearing on the charges next week."

"I can't believe it. He should not be walking the streets!"
"Hey, keep it down!" Welch demanded.
"What about Petrie?"
"Same deal. He's gone, too."

Tim's attempt to talk to the two men had been thwarted. He had planned to drill them about Nancy to see if they knew anything.

Sunday, July 14, 9:22 a.m.

The doorbell rang.

Tim swung open the door.

"Church!" Tiffany announced. "You promised to go with me regularly."

"When did I do that?"

"The other day. You got a lot out of church when you went on Wednesday night even though you won't admit it."

Tim felt very low because he had made a promise to attend regularly with her but he was in no mood for church.

"Hurry up and get ready. We need to leave in fifteen minutes," she said.

"I'm too tired and I have a headache."

Monday, July 15, 8:34 a.m.

As Tim pulled out of his driveway, a black Buick Century drove up and blocked his path. Nelson Porter jumped out of the vehicle.

Porter grabbed Tim by the shoulders and pulled him out of his car.

"What are you doing? Trying to talk to Petrie and Marino? You might blow the entire operation. Stay out of it. Do you understand?"

"Yes. Yes. I understand. Now get out of here before I charge you with assault."

"There's much more involved here than you realize," Nelson Porter said angrily through clinched teeth. "Forget about all this."

Tim noticed an airline ticket in the front seat of Porter's vehicle. It was imprinted with the words 'Copenhagen, Denmark.'

Tim jumped into his vehicle, sped out of his driveway, and caught up with Porter who had not traveled very far down the road. To avoid notice, Tim allowed two vehicles to stay between them.

Tim remembered that Petrie had mentioned Denmark during his comments about the anti-aging formula. He figured that something significant must be developing or Porter would not have been so angry.

The vehicles traveled through downtown Atlanta and eventually to Hartsfield/Jackson International Airport. To remain undetected, Tim parked his vehicle far away from where Porter had parked.

Porter walked through the main entrance with Tim following at a safe distance. Tim broke into a jog to the Delta ticket desk. He was relieved to find out there were tickets still available for the only flight to Copenhagen that morning.

In the crowded terminal, Tim paused for a moment to consider the situation and what he was about to do. He was carrying his passport but did he really want to drop everything and go on a potentially embarrassing wild goose chase? The answer was a hesitant 'yes.'

After purchasing his ticket, Tim was processed through the security station. He reached the gate for the airplane with merely minutes to spare. As Tim approached the ticket attendant, he thought about the fact that he was leaving a laundry list of loose ends in Atlanta. There were bills to pay, business matters to look after, a dog to feed, and a girl to appease. Tim knew that what he was doing was crazy, ridiculous, and probably a waste of time, but he was desperate to learn if Nancy was alive.

As he entered the plane, Tim saw Porter putting his carry-on bag in a compartment above the seats, his back turned.

Tim breathed a sigh of relief as he walked to the back of the plane. He would be seated far enough away from Porter to go unnoticed.

Tim flopped down in his seat. To his left, there was an old woman with gray hair. She wore a frumpy-style, out-of-date dress and was studiously at work on a crossword puzzle. To his right, a man in his early twenties sat, wearing worn blue jeans and a pull-over sweatshirt that was much too big for him.

Ten minutes later, the airplane was off the ground and Tim was on his way to Europe, with no idea what may lie in store for him.

Chapter Ten—European Adventure

Tim awoke.

The gray-haired lady slapped Tim in the face. A big jolt of turbulence had ruffled Tim out of his sleep and sent him into the woman's lap.

"Get off of me!" she grumbled.

"Sorry."

"How many more hours?" Tim asked the young man seated next to him.

"Til what dude?"

"Til we get to Denmark?"

"I got me a couple of those hot Danish babes waiting to greet me so I hope it's not too long," the young man laughed.

"What? Do you live in Denmark?" Tim asked.

"Man, I live anywhere I hang my head."

"Then you're a wanderer?"

"Wanderer, free-spirit, malcontent, you name it."

"In other words, you don't have any purpose," Tim scoffed.

"Hey dude, don't get so brutal. What are you after yourself anyway?"

"My love!"

The plane touched down in Copenhagen. Tim waited until Nelson Porter had left the plane then he disembarked. He watched Porter walk out of the main terminal exit and hail a cab.

Tim walked up behind Porter in fear and near panic with no native currency, no sense of direction, and nowhere to stay.

The taxi came to an abrupt stop and Porter slid into the back seat.

Tim ran up to the taxi, stumbled at the curb and scrambled into the back seat before Porter could close the door.

"What are you doing here?" Porter shouted as the taxi drove away. His face turned crimson red.

"Going my way?" Tim laughed nervously.

"What are you doing here, you sorry punk?" Porter shouted.

"You're going to lead me to my woman."

The taxi driver shouted out in a thick German accent. "No free here. You pay, too."

"You imbecile!" Porter said with fury.

The vehicle screeched to a stop. "Out! Out! Out! Or pay now!" the cab driver said.

"Relax," Nelson Porter said. "Take us to the hotel and I'll pay for his trip."

"Thank you," Tim said.

"I'm not doing you any favors," Porter said. "I'll figure out what to do with you when we get to the hotel."

"I'm not letting you out of my sight," Tim said. "I'll camp out in the lobby."

"Keep your mouth shut for now," Porter said. He looked at the driver. "Let's go."

Ten minutes later, Tim and Nelson Porter walked into the lobby of a huge, historic hotel. The lobby was grand with illustrious chandeliers, remarkable wood paneling, and carpeting with stately patterns.

"You don't have any luggage?" Porter asked.

"Sure don't."

Porter checked into the hotel at the front desk.

As they rode up to the eighth floor in the elevator, Porter glared at Tim. "Our nation's security doesn't mean anything to you?"

"Listen, I'm as patriotic as the next guy. I don't want to hear any of that kind of talk."

"Did you expect to be able to tag along with me?" Porter asked. "The only thing to do is to buy you a plane ticket back home. You can rest up for a while in my room then it's back to the airport."

When they reached the room, Tim stretched out on a thick, spacious couch. "All I want to do is to find the girl I love."

"I've told you everything I know about it so you're grasping at straws."

"I don't think so because I'm convinced that woman you talked about in Atlanta is Nancy. You can lead me to her."

"You thick-headed dolt! Don't you know that you could end up getting me killed?"

"I don't take what you do lightly. I know it's dangerous but that's why we need to work together."

"Do you really think that we could work together?" Porter mused.

"Sure why not? I'm more motivated than you are to stop Marino. After all, that's your assignment, isn't it? To get the goods on his operation and then pin him to the wall?"

Porter walked into the bathroom and shut the door. Tim grabbed Porter's briefcase, flipped through it, finding a notebook with handwritten notes in it.

In the most recent entry, Tim read: "Bremerhaven location: Jennings' girl seen there."

Tim was prepared to confront the man as he came out of the bathroom but instead was leveled by a devastating forearm thrust from Porter to the bridge of his nose. Tim dropped to the floor, out cold.

When Tim regained consciousness, he found himself in a barren, small room with white concrete walls. He sat in a wooden chair with a flimsy card table that held a glass of water within arm's reach.

The big steel door in the corner of the room opened and two men entered.

Neither man was smiling.

"The Agency is not pleased with your annoying persistence and demands that your interference cease immediately," one of the men said.

"Excuse me, but who are you?" Tim demanded.

"You don't need to know our names. We're with the Central Intelligence Agency."

"I'm afraid your big mistake was when you decided to leave the friendly confines of the U.S.A.," the second man said.

"Our assignment is to make sure that you are situated," the first man said.

"What do you mean by that?"

"It means that you must be detained for a while," the second man said.

"What? You're kidnapping me? You can't do that."

"You will not be allowed to leave," the first man said.

"What are you saying? I can't even go back to the States? That's outrageous."

The men walked out of the room.

Tim found himself overseas with no friends to call on and no one back in the States even knew where he was. He stood up from the chair, pacing nervously. Random thoughts and images filled his head. He thought about a day five and one half years ago.

It was an average morning that was slightly enhanced by Tim's desire to get tickets for a concert appearance by the band, The Moody Blues. The concert was to be held at the famous Fox Theatre in the midtown section of Atlanta. The Fox was one of the last of the fabulous old movie palaces. It had been refurbished to a splendid state recently, making it a grand location for a concert.

The line was lengthy at the Fox's ticket booth but Tim was willing to wait. When he got close to the window, he heard a pleasant voice from the ticket window attendant. The voice was soothing, almost hypnotic in its calming effect. Eagerly, Tim waited in line to meet the body that went with the voice.

When he made it to the front of the line, Tim saw a young woman of twenty standing behind the ticket window. She had the most captivating smile Tim had ever seen. Her long brunette hair was shiny, framing her delicate, lovely facial features, high cheekbones, and a cute button nose with light, thin eyebrows. Her eyes were green. Tim looked into those eyes for several seconds. Her eyes radiated a warmth and friendliness that Tim had never quite seen before, causing him to stare at her for a long time.

"May I help you?" the girl asked.

Tim simply looked at her.

"May I help you?"

Tim hesitated, then rambled, "Yes. Yes. I'd like a ticket to the Moody Blues concert."

"Would you like B. A. L.?" the girl asked.

"B.A.L.? What does that mean?"

"Best available location."

"Yes. Give me the best. The B.A.L." he said with a wry smile.

"Two tickets?" she asked.

"Only one."

"That's no fun."

"Why? What do you mean?" Tim thought she had a twinkle in her eye.

"It's no fun to go to a concert alone. You should get two tickets."

"But then who would go with me?" he asked hopefully and invitingly.

She smiled ever so slightly. "Why that would be up to you, wouldn't it?"

Tim wondered if the comment was an opening.

"Hurry up because I don't have all day to wait," the man standing in line behind Tim shouted.

"O.K. I'll take two tickets."

"Thank you," the girl said. The ticket transaction was completed.

Tim stood in his tracks, not knowing what to say. He wanted to ask her to go to the concert with him but he felt awkward.

"Thank you," she said again.

He waited for her to say more but the girl did not say anything else. Tim realized that perhaps he had been duped into buying an extra ticket.

"She probably does that same routine twelve times a day," Tim muttered as he walked away from the ticket window.

As he approached his car, Tim looked at his watch. The ticket window would close in forty minutes, so he decided to wait and get his date.

Tim sat quietly in the Cubby Hole Coffee Shop on the other side of Peachtree Street as five o'clock approached. He peered hopefully through the shop window as a slight misty rain fell, observing the line for tickets dwindling.

Eventually, the last person purchased his tickets and was gone. Soon the girl walked out of the ticket booth. She walked with a graceful, nimble gait. The wind kicked up and tossed her dark brown locks up and down on her shoulders.

Tim stood up from his table, walked out the door, and transformed his trek into a jog as he crossed the road. He caught up with the girl in an adjacent parking lot as she fumbled with her keys.

"You see, I've got an extra ticket and I was wondering if you would like to go to the Moody Blues concert with me."

She turned around quickly. "Are you talking to me?"

"I sure am. You doing anything tomorrow night?"

"I don't date customers."

Tim laughed. "This customer wouldn't be stuck with an extra ticket if you hadn't sweet talked him into buying it."

She looked at him for a long time. "I've really got to go."

"But I wish you'd say yes." Tim looked at her with very sad eyes, the most dour of faces.

"O.K., but it's only because I work here and I'll be getting off work about that time."

Tim's heart skipped a beat. He smiled widely and practically jumped off the ground.

The following months were a romantic journey. Tim fell head over heels in love with the woman named Nancy Proctor. She was elegant and Tim had never dated a truly elegant woman. She conducted herself with a quiet class and sophistication that made Tim feel important.

Tim would often stare at her as they walked together at Piedmont Park. A sense of comfort overwhelmed Tim when he was in the presence of Nancy. He had never appreciated a woman like her.

The cold, dirty room seemed to close its walls around Tim as the minutes dripped along slowly. Finally, the first CIA agent opened the door and walked in with a tray of food.

"Eat this meal then you're free to go. I would strongly suggest that you head home. Please get out of the country and don't try to locate Mr. Porter. You'll never be able to find him anyway."

Chapter Eleven—Alone in Denmark

Tim had a small amount of cash with him that he could convert to the native currency. Fortunately, he carried two credit cards with him at all times so he had access to some resources.

"I was called away on business for a few days," Tim lied to Tiffany over his cell phone. "Please feed the dog and tell Bud to look after the office until I get back." The brevity of information and short nature of the call would certainly not help their relationship, but Tim did not want Tiffany to worry.

As he walked through downtown Copenhagen, Tim wished for all the world that he could play the role of tourist.

He found a small bed and breakfast type lodge. In the lobby, he encountered an old, gray bearded man standing behind the front desk. He was approximately five feet in stature with a tangled and matted beard. His nose was distinctly crooked with round, framed wire glasses sitting on it.

As Tim approached the desk, the old man looked intently at him.

"You are an American?" he asked in broken English. "You are an American?"

"Sure, I'm an American. How could you tell?"

"We can tell. We can tell," he laughed.

"I am an American without much money in my pocket. Do you take credit cards?"

"No."

"Would it be possible for me to stay here tonight? I'll pay you double tomorrow when I have money wired to me?"

"From the States?"

"Yes."

"You mean the U.S. States?" the old man asked.

"Yes."

"I will let you stay for one night to sleep."

"I may need another night to ensure that the money gets here."

"I will allow it."

Tim smiled.

"You must tell these famous American stories to me and my family at dinner every night," the old man said.

"How many folks are we talking about?"

"Eight."

"Can I eat dinner with you?"

"My son, you have not to worry. I will feed you. How you say? Three round meals a day."

"Three square meals. That's very nice of you."

With his lodging situation resolved, Tim felt a sense of relief. All he had to do was to come up with some fantastic yarns about life in America.

Tim's room was quaint and rustic, situated on the second floor, overlooking the busy street below. The walls featured wood paneling, adorned with portraits of mountains and rivers. However, the bed looked a bit too small but a reading chair in the far corner with an accompanying gooseneck lamp looked very inviting.

Tim stretched out on the bed thinking about his plight, realizing that a few days ago, he never would have dreamt that he would be located in Copenhagen, Denmark with little resources, searching for his fiancée and trying to outwit some organized criminal figures.

Tuesday, July 16, 7:31 a.m.

At breakfast, the old man, Mr. Hertzel, introduced his family.

"The children are such fine students. The English of theirs is so good they might one day live in America," the man said.

As they finished eating their breakfast, a beautiful young woman walked into the room. Her long blond tresses hung lazily down her back. She had big, bountiful lips, violet blues eyes, and delicate facial features that were spoiled by the frown on her face. Her dress was pale green and pedestrian.

"Who is that?" Tim asked.

"That is our cleaning lady," Mr. Hertzel informed him.

Later in the morning, Mr. Hertzel asked Tim to join him in his study.

"You know," the man said as he motioned for Tim to take a seat in one of two huge suede chairs with oak arm rests, "I admire you. How is it said? 'Yankees.' You are high spirited and free spirited persons," Mr. Hertzel said. "What is it about your people? You are always discovering things like the Moon and the bulb of light."

Tim cocked his head and laughed. "We do our best."

"Why are you here?" Mr. Hertzel asked. "What made you come to Denmark?"

"I'm searching for someone I love dearly."

"Is it a female?"

"Yes, it's a female," Tim laughed. "Perhaps you can help me."

"Eh, how you mean?"

"Have you ever heard of Dr. Herman Bron Wagonheimer?"

"Dr. Herman Bron Wettenheimer?"

"No, no. Wagonheimer."

"I do not know of the man."

"You've never heard rumors about a scientist performing experiments on people during World War II, and apparently the effort secretly continued after the war."

"There are legends and fables in this land in almost every corner. There are many such stories."

"Sir, with all due respect, I believe these reports have some basis in fact."

"What did this mad scientist do?"

"It is believed that he was experimenting with anti-aging drugs of various sorts."

"Anti-aging drugs? You mean old people become new people?"

"Something like that."

"Vikeeta. Vikeeta. Come quickly!"

Tim sat up uncomfortably in his chair. "I don't think that's necessary. We don't need to stir up the entire household."

His wife appeared at the doorway.

"Vikeeta, our friend says that he has discovered the secret to young life."

Tim sighed. "I never said that."

"I have been getting wrinkles," the woman said. She glanced quickly at a mirror on the far wall.

Tim bit his lip. "Well, I'm afraid I can't help you."

"But what do you know?" Mr. Hertzel asked.

"I know practically nothing as I was hoping you had heard of the scientist," Tim said.

"I do not know this man."

"He worked in a little town in Germany."

"I do not know German scientists or German history."

"I'm going to have to go to Germany. I'll hitchhike if I have to do it."

Mr. and Mrs. Hertzel's facial expressions turned to bewilderment.

"You know." Tim extended his thumb to demonstrate the motion of a hitchhiker.

They stared at each other blankly.

"Please rest for the day and leave in the morning," Mrs. Hertzel suggested.

"Yes, please," her husband said. "It is a long trip."

"I appreciate your concern." Tim noticed that the cleaning woman had walked into the room and was staring and smiling directly at him. "O.K. I'll stay another day."

The young cleaning woman continued to smile at Tim.

Later in the afternoon, Tim lay prone on his bed, realizing that he knew nothing about Denmark, or Germany, but he knew that he intended to survive. He grabbed a sheet of paper, jotted down the items that he would need, putting a weapon at the top of the list, followed by a radio and a flashlight.

"Is your housekeeper still here?" Tim asked Mr. Hertzel over dinner.

"She works from 9:00 until 4:30," Mr. Hertzel said.

Tim frowned. "Please pass me the bread." He looked all around the table at his hosts. "I'm on a mission. I've got to find someone and it has got to be soon."

"How do we help?" Mrs. Hertzel asked.

"I need to get to Bremerhaven, a town near the German coast."

"Ah yes," Mr Hertzel said. "I will give you map."

"Is there any type of public transportation?"

"If you mean a motor bus? The answer is no."

"Then I'll have to hitchhike."

The children all looked at him with wide-eyed curiosity.

"It means sticking your thumb out and getting the attention of a passing motor car," Tim said as he protruded his thumb out to demonstrate.

The smallest children mimicked the action, giggling joyfully.

As Mrs. Hertzel passed apple strudel around the table, the children peppered Tim with questions about American culture.

The housekeeper walked into the room.

Tim watched as she gracefully and almost artfully assisted Mrs. Hertzel in cleaning off the table.

As the woman went into the kitchen with an armful of plates, Tim commented, "I thought you said that she was not working this late. What is her name?"

"I don't know why she came back to our home at this hour," Mr. Hertzel replied. "Her name is Gretchen."

"Gretchen what?"

"Only Gretchen."

Gretchen entered the room again. She wore a gray and black, checkered blouse with a loose-fitting skirt.

Tim watched curiously as she cleaned off the table, moving gingerly. Her motions, the act of wiping clean the table with a cloth, were smooth and deliberate.

"It is not good for you to travel by foot and by thumb in a strange land," Mr. Hertzel said. "I would like to drive you but I cannot stay away from the inn."

"I'll be fine."

"I will take you."

Tim whirled around in his chair. Gretchen stood before him, smiling pleasantly.

"We have not formally met. My name is Tim Jennings. What is yours?"

"Gretchen, but you know that."

Tim smiled. "What's your last name?"

"You can call me Gretchen. That's enough."

"O.K.," Tim laughed. "But what would possess you to offer a perfect stranger a ride?"

"I do not work tomorrow and I will visit my mother who lives near Bremerhaven."

"Great. I'll go with you." Tim turned to Mr. Hertzel. "Well, you can't beat that, chauffeured by a pretty girl."

"This is true," Mr. Hertzel agreed.

Tim turned back to thank the young woman, but she was gone.

Chapter Twelve—The Old Factory

Wednesday, July 17, 8:23 a.m.

Tim packed his belongings and said his good byes.

He asked Mr. Hertzel to come out in the front yard. "I would feel better with a weapon for protection.

"Will you find danger?"

Tim scratched his head. "Yeah, I'll probably find danger. Do you have a pistol? I'll buy it from you."

Mr. Hertzel hurried into his house and came back with a small pistol. "You can have it as my going away gift. I will give you a box of bullets." He handed Tim the pistol and the bullets.

Within minutes, Gretchen drove up in a sparkling sky blue Mercedes Benz convertible with the top down.

"I like this girl," Tim laughed.

"Let's go," Gretchen said.

Once they had cleared the Copenhagen area, they drove through rural farmland over a landscape with beautiful, rolling hills of deep, rich, green grass.

Tim looked at Gretchen, wondering why a young woman would volunteer to drive a stranger from a foreign land across the countryside. He caught himself once again staring admiringly at her.

Tim had promised himself that his eyes would not wander, believing that he was on the trail of his only true love. All else would be a distraction. And Gretchen, the woman with one name and two beautiful legs, was definitely a distraction.

She glanced quickly in his direction, their eyes meeting momentarily. She blushed as Tim rubbed his chin awkwardly in a moment of nervous embarrassment.

Usually feeling at a disadvantage with women, Tim wanted to speak but did not know what to say. He finally blurted out, "You're a pleasant companion, er, driving companion."

She winked at him.

His commitment to Nancy kept Tim from flirting with Gretchen. Instead, he bit his lip, turned his head, and stared at the mountainside outside his window.

"Nancy was my fiancée," Tim said openly. "I wish you could meet her." His comments were for her benefit as well as his own. "Quite a woman, down to earth, yet she was vibrant and different. What's the word I'm looking for?"

Tim looked in her direction but Gretchen did not respond. Her lily white skin glistened against the afternoon sun.

Gretchen spoke little during the drive as one hour became two, then two and one half hours. Finally she spoke. "Don't worry," she said stoically. "I'm not trying to seduce you and there's no need to be defensive. I'm only being kind to you."

Tim's face turned red.

Pleasant discussion ensued on matters ranging from American music to international cuisine. Eventually, the conversation turned to the nation of Denmark.

Denmark is actually a group of islands clustered closely together in the North Sea. After leaving Copenhagen, the two travelers and their vehicle were transported by ferries over water on two legs of the journey, at which point they were on the mainland of Denmark. Subsequently, they traveled south into Germany.

Late in the afternoon, Gretchen pulled over to the side of the road. "I will take you down the small road up ahead where we will be near Bremerhaven."

"Don't dump me out."

"There is an inn on this road where you will stay."

Before he had time to protest further, Gretchen had pulled her vehicle to a stop on the side of the road where Tim waved goodbye. He walked down a narrow dirt road for a mile and one half before he reached the lobby of a very old and run down inn.

When Tim entered the front door, he found a gray-haired woman staring at him from the front desk.

"Do you speak English?" Tim asked.

"Yes."

Tim knew that a large percentage of Danish people spoke English and he hoped that was also true for the natives that he encountered in Germany.

"Do you know how close I am to an old factory that was used by the Nazis during World War II?"

"Why must you know?" she growled.

"I'm looking for research purposes."

She walked to the nearest window and pointed to a mountain range on the nearby horizon. "The factory is there. Old factory but I would not go."

"Why not?"

"Death is in the air."

Thursday, July 18, 8:32 a.m.

An open field lay before Tim as he walked off the grounds of the inn. Soon he was at the base of a small mountain range with uneven, rocky terrain.

After forty minutes of climbing the rocky surface, Tim found himself standing on a large, jutting rock.

Gazing down into a valley, he saw a huge seven-story building made of bricks and concrete. There were glass windows on each floor except the ground floor, but most of the windows were broken. The building was approximately the length of two football fields with two distinct wings. On the west wing, Tim observed what appeared to be a huge storage facility, or a warehouse. The entire place had the look of abandonment.

Tim ran down the uneven embankment, stumbling several times. On the final stumble, he did a summersault to the base of the hill. He picked himself up and walked to the front doors of the building.

The doors were firmly locked, so Tim decided to break a second story window if he could reach that level and enter through it. He needed to find something to assist him in his climb to the second floor.

Tim walked down to the warehouse, a trek of approximately an eighth of a mile. When he arrived at the warehouse, he found the entrance was slightly ajar. He swung the big, broad wooden door open.

Warily, Tim poked his head in while swinging the huge doors open. Sunshine flooded the warehouse floor.

A disturbing and brutally revolting stench hit Tim's senses like a bomb. His nose practically withered as the smell entered his nostrils, forcing him to reel back in stunned nausea.

It was the smell of death. Tim wanted to run away, and in fact, he started to run but stopped. Resolutely, he took off his jacket and wrapped it around his face. The cloth was thick enough to block most of the odor.

The warehouse was empty with nothing, not so much as an empty cardboard box, inside, but the stench lingered.

Tim walked back to the main building, jumped up and grabbed the ledge of a second story window. Dangling with both hands like a sack of potatoes, Tim tried to pull his body up to the window but could not pull it off. He tried a second time and a third time. Finally, he burst out in a primal, uncivilized groan and pulled himself up to the window ledge.

Tim coiled into a fetal position and thrust his body through the fractured window as shards of glass fell upon his torso in a shower of debris. He was in a room with barren walls with an assortment of old chairs and desks, piled up on top of one another all over the room. A musty, moldy smell covered the entire room as spider webs dangled from the ceiling and all over the furniture. The wood paneling on the floor was uneven and faded in several sections. The ceiling was marked by numerous water spots.

Tim walked into a hallway, hearing the creaking of the floorboards upon each step. Eventually, he reached a stairwell. As he descended the stairs, Tim saw a rat scurry a few feet in front of him. As he rounded the corner, he spotted two more rats.

A door was at the bottom of the stairwell. Tim turned the doorknob, swung open the door and reeled back as scores of rats, dozens upon dozens, came running from the other side. They were big, feisty, and agile. As the rodents swarmed around his ankles, Tim felt a distinct bite.

Falling back on the floor, he recoiled in pain as the rats swarmed all over his body. He picked himself up, ran up the staircase, and furiously slammed the door shut.

Completely unnerved by the experience, Tim felt sick to his stomach. He worried about the bite.

As he gathered his composure, he looked out a window and saw a little feeble man staring back up at him. He appeared to be very emaciated with an unkempt appearance, highlighted by stubby whiskers and stringy, dirty, gray hair. He wore scruffy jeans and a plaid shirt full of holes.

Their eyes met for a moment, then the man ran away from the building. Tim thought about giving chase but he knew that by the time he scrambled out of the window and down the wall, he would have no chance to overtake him.

Tim continued his tour through the abandoned warehouse as he looked for any clues to help him in his search for Nancy. He overturned desks, walked through spider webs, and kicked over boxes.

After a long search of the building, Tim decided there was nothing of value for him in the place, so he went back to the window and eased his way out. When he reached the ground, he noticed an open door at the far end of the building. As he got closer, he saw that the door had an unsecured padlock on it, and a thick chain.

He peered in the door and noticed a bulb in a light socket hanging from the ceiling. He pulled on a chain switch and the light illuminated, giving him a clear view of small cages stacked one on top of another. There was a big table in the middle of the room and a bundle of test tubes filled a box on the corner of it.

His curiosity piqued, Tim approached a desk located on the far side of the room. He rummaged through the drawers but found nothing but a few blank sheets of paper and assorted pencils.

A rustling noise came from outside the building. He peered out the door to see three huge men on horseback emerge from the underbrush. One of them wielded a long piece of lumber that appeared to be a crude club.

"All clear on the perimeter search. Let's head back to the compound," one of the men said in English. "A bus load of new recruits is on the way. Let's go."

Tim watched as the three men galloped away on their horses. He decided to walk in the same direction.

Chapter Thirteen—Rusty Shaw

Tim walked for at least a mile until he reached a dirt road that he followed until he saw a tall fence with an electronic gate. There was a small security guard shack to one side of the gate.

A big passenger bus rumbled up the dirt road and stopped about fifty feet from the gate. Tim crawled on his hands and knees through the underbrush to get a closer look at the bus. He watched as approximately twenty-five well-groomed, neatly dressed, young men stepped out of the vehicle.

"I wish they would have told us more about the jobs that we are applying for. It sounds like the pay and benefits are excellent," one of the young men said. "But they should not be so mysterious."

"I'll do anything for what they are going to pay," another man said. The accents sounded distinctly American.

The bus driver stood in front of the vehicle as he motioned for the men to walk in single file toward the gate. When they reached it, a security guard emerged from the shack, holding a clipboard and pencil in his hands.

Impulsively, Tim scrambled out of the bushes and fell in at the end of the line.

"Let me account for everyone," the security guard said.

Tim realized he was in trouble when he saw the printed list tacked onto the guard's clipboard, knowing that he would not be allowed admittance when he shouted out his name.

When he reached the security guard, Tim stuttered and stammered. "Ah…. ah…. ah."

"You must be Rusty Shaw," the security guard said. "The last unchecked name."

"Yes! Yes! That's me," Tim said as he tried to mask his surprise. Apparently, one of the men had been a no-show. Tim took advantage of the opening. "I'm looking forward to the interview."

"All clear to enter the compound," the security guard shouted to the bus driver.

Tim boarded the bus along with the other men, sitting uncomfortably as it entered the compound. Immediately to the left, he saw an old factory that had been slightly refurbished. He could almost sense gloom in the air. Only two minutes inside the gate and he was already feeling very unsettled.

The bus stopped in front of a dormitory building where they were met by a middle age man in a dark suit.

"You will wait in the lobby. The applicants that survive the first round will be staying overnight here," he said.

Tim sat down on a cushioned chair in the lobby, wondering what had happened to the real Rusty Shaw.

A few minutes later, the middle age man reappeared. "Everyone that you meet here is bilingual. For your benefit we will speak in English. You will have an orientation session in the conference room behind me in five minutes."

As soon as everyone had assembled in the room, a tall, gaunt, old man entered and stood in front of the group. He wore a gray suit that was probably a size too big for him.

"Welcome to Empowerment Pharmaceuticals," the old man said in a German accent. "You have the opportunity to embark on a mission that will forever change the world, and along the way, your life as well!"

"Apparently, not your average, run of the mill job," someone seated behind Tim whispered.

"Let us learn about you," the old man said. The men were told to stand up when it was their turn and talk about themselves.

Their occupations ranged from a manager of a retail store to an attorney to a construction laborer. Half of the men were American citizens, the other hailed from countries in Europe. None of them were married.

When it was Tim's turn to speak, he hesitated momentarily. Then he blurted out the first thoughts that came to mind. "My name is Rusty Shaw. I am an accountant and I live in Dallas, Texas, and I'm single."

"Big D!" Someone shouted from the back of the room.

When the introductions were complete, the old man smiled. "Interesting group. I wish we could keep all of you, but only the cream of the crop will stay. I would like to introduce myself. Dr. Vog is the name." He pointed at one of the young men in the third row. "What brought you here?"

The applicant was caught off guard. "Oh, everything the ad described. High salary, the chance for adventure, and a contempt and dislike of the United States government."

"What?" Tim reacted quietly under his breath.

Dr. Vog distributed sheets of paper to the group. "All persons should sign this contractual agreement immediately and return it to me."

In the fourth row, a participant stood up and asked, "Shouldn't we hear more information about the organization and our job descriptions?"

"In due time, my friend, in due time," Dr. Vog said.

"I agree with the guy," a short, stocky man said. "We need more information."

"Is it a binding contract?" another person asked.

"Yes," the old man said. "If you're serious about the task at hand, you will join us."

"I'm not obligating myself under these circumstances," a man said boldly.

"Very well," the old man said. "Trust is the issue. You will be taken care of if you sign. Otherwise you are free to leave." He smiled broadly.

A third of the men stood to their feet and walked out of the room.

"Read the contract gentlemen," Dr. Vog said to the other men. "I will be back shortly. Don't forget to sign it."

The remaining men in the room looked at each other in various states of bewilderment. Eventually, they read the contract.

It started with standard language for an employer and employee relationship. It included a section that was explicit in its demand of allegiance to the organization. There would not be dialogue with "persons or parties not affiliated with the organization relevant to official business of Empowerment Pharmaceuticals, to include family members. Termination of the contract would be made entirely at the discretion of Empowerment Pharmaceuticals".

"We are literally signing our lives away," Tim said to the young man seated next to him.

"I can always back out," the young man said.

"No. You cannot! Read the contract," Tim said.

"In this day and age, contracts don't mean anything."

"Somehow I have the feeling that this one does," Tim said. "Why do you hate the U.S.?"

"I'm involved because I want a change in my life," the young man said. "I need completely new scenery."

"Are you an American?"

"Yes."

"Why do you hate your country?"

"I don't hate my country, not really. Didn't you read the ad? It meant 'the government' not the country itself. I guess you'd say I'm a mercenary. For the right price, I'd hate anything."

Tim looked around the room and watched as everyone else was signing the contract. From a legal standpoint, Tim was not sure that the language was enforceable but practically speaking, he knew that if he signed it, he was obligated to something that scared him, or should scare the real Rusty Shaw. Yet the situation piqued his curiosity.

Dr. Vog returned. "Everyone turn in your contracts."

Tim signed the document and passed it forward.

"Excellent, excellent," the doctor said. "No cowards in this group."

"Are you the leader of this organization?" someone asked.

"No, I am not. You will meet our inspirational leader later in the day. I am his chief of staff and senior advisor."

"At least, tell us something about the leader. What's his name?" the same person asked.

"His name is Mr. Jon Actund. The genesis of the organization, Empowerment Pharmaceuticals began many years ago in the youthful mind of Jonathan Actund," the old man said. "A very unique young man! His parents were simple farmers who lived in the small quaint coastal town in Denmark known as Nymindegab where Jonathan was born."

"A natural leader was Jonathan," Dr. Vog continued. "A brilliant mind, a child prodigy. Instead of playing with building blocks as a tyke, he mastered mathematical equations. Later, Jonathan would spend lazy, hazy summer days not in the enjoyment of kickball and fishing, but in reading the philosophical works of Socrates, Plato, Marx, Engels, Lenin."

"As he progressed through school, Jonathan developed his leadership skills, honed his debating prowess, and studied philosophy, history, and government hungrily."

"As the years passed, Jon Actund attracted a small cadre of young followers who were very devoted to him. When Mr. Actund was nineteen years old, his parents divulged to him that they owned five hundred acres. Jon had been led to believe that they only owned a quarter acre and the small, modest home.

Within six months, Mr. Actund's parents were dead as a result of an automobile accident. Their son inherited the entire five-hundred acres. Eventually, he sold the land to a huge company that planned to build a furniture factory at the location and Mr. Actund returned a tidy profit."

"What a buildup," someone seated behind Tim whispered.

"With a huge nest egg to fall back on," the doctor continued. "Mr. Actund decided to do what came natural to him and became a motivational speaker, traveling all over Denmark."

"What did he talk about?" one of the men asked. "How did he inspire the people?"

"That will become obvious when he speaks to you at dinner tonight. As I was saying, he traveled all about the country. As you can imagine, his followers and admirers increased in numbers."

"I bet he has an ego bigger than this room," Tim said to the person sitting next to him.

"The admiration people have for him has been quite amazing," Dr. Vog said. "It occurred to Mr. Actund that he could draw upon his popularity to perhaps influence people philosophically and politically. He wanted to create a pool of true believers."

"How many true believers does he have?" someone asked.

"Look around you throughout the compound. Enough people to make a dream come true."

"How many women work in the compound?" one of the men asked.

"Enough women to make the environment interesting," Dr. Vog said.

"Where are they?" Tim interrupted. He was hoping for a lead on Nancy's whereabouts.

"Don't distract me from the topic," Dr. Vog said. "As young Jonathan studied the Danish government, he discovered sloth, greed, and arrogance. Mr. Actund has no patience for arrogant politicians."

"I can't stand the fat cats," a young recruit declared.

"Silence!" Dr. Vog shouted. "If there is one thing that we demand, it is structure and orderliness, and no mindless chatter. Continuing, Jon Actund understands the United States. He understands capitalism and he has seen the greed and avarice. He has worked long and hard to recruit a pool of talent that will attack the foundation of the U.S. and topple it. It is very personal to him. He despises the influence of the U.S. in the global community."

Low whispering murmurs erupted all over the room.

"What are we going to be?" someone in the audience asked. "The grunts?"

"No. Quite to the contrary," the doctor replied. "Most of our talent is young and ambitious and will play important roles, but we do have some senior members, including myself. All of you have the potential to move up quickly in our ranks."

"What do we have to do?" someone asked.

"You must be obedient and gain our trust because there will emerge from your group a remarkable few who lead us into destiny." Dr. Vog looked at the men thoughtfully. "We demand physical discipline, proper training, and good eating habits."

Tim could not believe what he was hearing.

"In the next few days, there will be a battery of aptitude, intelligence, and personality tests administered. Once we determine your profile, you will be assigned an occupation. Immediate training will commence. I must stress that you will be on time and complete all of your assignments."

"Does that mean homework?" someone moaned.

"Yes. There will be a strict 11:00 p.m. curfew when everyone must be in their rooms."

"You're making it sound like boot camp," one of the men protested. "I'm thirty-five years old and don't need to be told when to go to bed."

"Here you do," the old man said. "Here you do."

"We've got to have recreation and fun. What about that?" a different person asked.

"We must have priorities so wine, women, and song are put on the back burner," Dr. Vog said.

"Hey, don't keep us from the ladies," a good-looking, slender, brunette man said.

"Ah yes! The tender gender," Dr. Vog said. "In due time, my friend. In due time."

"How long will that be?" the good-looking man asked. "It may take weeks to bus the girls in here anyway. We're out in the middle of nowhere. Is it too late to back out?"

Dr. Vog shook his head. "There is no turning back."

"But if I want to leave, you can't keep me here," the good-looking man said.

"Doc, what do you say?" another man asked. "That would be kidnapping."

"The word 'kidnapping' is very subjective," Dr. Vog said. "Please don't use that word."

"But what's the answer to the question?" Tim asked. "You can imprison people?"

"We've a schedule to keep." The doctor ignored the question. "As we progress, the big picture will crystallize for you. But at this time, concentrate on the here and now. That is enough for now. You are dismissed to your rooms. Please be back in the main dining hall in this building at 7:00 p.m. this evening."

Chapter Fourteen—
The Mysterious Jon Actund

When Tim entered the dining hall, he saw five long tables with fine china and silverware neatly placed on them. All the recruits appeared on time and everyone was seated as several well-tailored waiters began their duties.

"What do you know about Jon Actund?" Tim asked a waiter.

The waiter turned a pale red color. "He is our leader, very intelligent and caring. He is inspirational and has amazing ways of seeing straight into your heart and piercing your soul."

"You've experienced this yourself?" Tim asked.

The waiter walked to another table and did not answer the question.

Dr. Vog entered the room. "Enjoy your meal."

"I will lead us in the blessing," a young man said as he enthusiastically rose to his feet. "Heavenly Father...."

"We will have none of that!" Dr. Vog said. "Praying to a mythological being is a waste of time and it will not be tolerated."

"But you can't arbitrarily eliminate religion from our lives," the same young man said.

"Yes we can and we have," Dr. Vog said.

The young man walked toward the doctor in an agitated state, wanting to protest, but he was restrained by another recruit.

As the evening progressed, the group engaged in light-hearted conversation. Tim heard stories of football games gone by, deer hunting lore, talk of old girl friends, and favorite school teachers.

Tim noticed that Dr. Vog had left the room. Soon he returned with a tall, strikingly handsome man who was probably in his mid-thirties. The man had dark black hair with streaks of gray and wore a stylish white European suit.

There was a confidence in the way the man walked with his purposeful gait.

"I would like to introduce you to Mr. Jon Actund," Dr. Vog said.

Actund shook hands with the doctor and quietly gazed at the audience as he spoke. "Welcome to your destiny. You are all young men, hearty in spirit and inquisitive in thought. As you learn, understand that you will play a role in changing our world forever."

"How will we do that?" someone asked.

"You must take baby steps first, my friend. As you progress, the big picture will crystallize for you, but tonight concentrate on the here and now." Actund strode briskly about the room, stopping at one table, leaning over and taking a carrot stick from the plate of one of the recruits.

"Please have more," the recruit said.

"I don't need your permission to eat a carrot. I'll eat the entire plate and your potatoes, too, if I please."

"Yes. Yes sir," the recruit stammered. "I meant no disrespect."

"Priority number one," Actund said. "I demand respect because if there is no respect from the bottom up to the top then our foundation is weak. Discipline is crucial and motivation must be sustained to the highest degree. I guarantee you that I will remain motivated and that drive will filter down to you. How many of you were rebellious in your school days?"

Approximately one half of the group raised their hands.

"I admire a person who will swim against the tide and take the unorthodox approach to life… to zig when others zag and zag when others zig."

Actund looked out a nearby window. Suddenly, he turned around and faced the group.

"Let's give Dr. Vog a hand," Actund said.

The crowd's response was tepid but Actund clapped his hands together loudly and enthusiastically. Most everyone followed his lead.

Dr. Vog stood to his feet and acknowledged the applause by waving his hand.

"A touching moment," Tim said under his breath. "The old coot's popular."

Actund gave the 'thumbs up' sign to Dr. Vog. "You are beloved," he said to the old man. He turned back to the crowd. "Dr. Vog is the type of person we are looking for, my friends. He is faithful and also a deep thinker."

"What type of doctor is he?" someone asked.

"A skilled surgeon, a brain surgeon," Actund said.

"Did you retire?" the same person asked.

"Dr. Vog has not retired. In fact, he is busier than ever," Actund said.

"I no longer perform brain surgery, but I am busier than I have ever been with my involvement in this grand movement," Dr. Vog said.

"Before any rewards come your way, there must be sacrifice," Actund said.

Dr. Vog pointed at a short, prematurely bald man. "What would you die for?"

"Me? Well I think I would die for my parents."

"Would you sacrifice your life for a philosophical movement?" Dr. Vog asked.

"To be honest, no, I don't think so," the bald man said.

"What about the rest of you characters?" Actund asked. "Who would die for their principles?"

"You mean in defense or preservation of our principles?" Tim asked.

"Yes, that's what I mean," Actund said.

"I would. Of course, I would," Tim said.

Actund looked Tim in the eye. "What we have here is a crusader. I like that."

"I was only being honest," the bald man said nervously. "Talk is cheap. When reality hits, people look out for number one." He looked around the room for positive affirmation from the others but no one responded.

"Everyone here will look out for number one and number one is me," Actund laughed. "I'm your leader so get comfortable with it."

"Everyone is forced to follow your philosophy?" the bald man asked. "Is that what you are leading up to?"

"As time goes by, you will appreciate what the organization is working toward. You will believe!" Actund declared.

"Will we get to go to Copenhagen or any other town for fun?" the good-looking man asked.

"There will be rewards along the way for the strong and the obedient," Dr. Vog said.

"But we distract ourselves too much with the trivial," Actund said. "When I was a child, I attended the circus with my parents. We sat under the big tent. There were children to the left of me and children to the right of me. A big, colorful and noisy clown came out on the stage. The boys and girls giggled and snorted but I simply scoffed and sneered."

"What's wrong with clowns?" someone in the crowd shouted.

Actund's face turned red. His countenance became dark.

There was dead silence in the room.

"A clown? Think of the symbolism and picture the audacity," Actund said. "The sad existence of a clown! A person dresses in ridiculous outfits and puts absurd makeup on his face, then his worth is measured by the chuckles he can coax out of children."

"As I was saying," Actund continued. "There were children to the left of me and children to the right of me. Their little hearts and minds were content, overflowing with silly emotions. I realized at a young age that everything in life should have purpose and reason. A clown appeals to the most trivial of emotions and serves no practical purpose. In your life, don't be a clown. Have purpose and meaning so you don't eat up space. Make an impact on this world by your devotion to Empowerment Pharmaceuticals."

Several of the men whispered to each other. Tim wondered if they were discussing the mental stability of the speaker.

"As we forge ahead," Dr. Vog said. "Learn to trust this man."

"I want to trust him," a recruit said. "I believe we all want to trust him, but please explain Empowerment Pharmaceuticals. Will we be involved in sales or management?"

"Before we describe the organization, I would request that you keep these three principles in mind at all times," Actund said. "Number one: Trust me. Number two: Lose your selfish instincts. Number three: Divorce yourself from all emotional ties to the United States."

Whispers filled the room.

"Who among you will not commit to these core principles?" Actund asked.

The crowd was quiet.

Finally, a brave soul stood to his feet. He was a short, frail young man with curly hair and thick, black-rimmed glasses.

"Are you trying to…. quote…. brainwash us?" the young man asked as he motioned with his fingers as if he were making quotation marks in the air. "That's very Cold War."

"I'm not brainwashing," Actund said. "I don't have time for that nonsense. You better follow these principles or you won't be needed."

"And we all want to be needed, don't we?" Dr. Vog asked.

Most of the group responded with affirmative nods of their heads.

"Wouldn't you prefer that we believe in the cause in our minds and hearts rather than having it scared into us?" the young man asked. "Besides what does all that philosophical talk have to do with selling pharmaceuticals?"

"Mr. Big Shot," Actund said. "The man with all the answers. I think we'll call him Mr. Big."

"I meant no disrespect."

"You are violating the first principle already," Actund said. "You do not trust me."

"I have a right to state my views," the young man said defiantly.

"Sit down!" someone from the back of the room shouted.

"I don't think I'm the only independent thinker in the group," the young man said.

Tim was tempted to rise in support of the rebellious man but he sat in silence.

"It would appear that you are outnumbered, my friend," Dr. Vog said. "It is time to leave." He walked to the door, opened it, and motioned with his hand. A tall, muscular man, dressed in camouflage fatigues, entered the room as Dr. Vog pointed at the vocal recruit.

The muscular man approached the recruit, grabbed him by the arm, and dragged him out of the room.

Tim could not hold his tongue. "What happens to him?"

"It does not matter," Actund said. "We must look forward and not behind." He stared Tim down. "Now that we have eliminated the problems," Actund continued. "We can resume our orientation."

"You have been carefully selected based on your applications and the screening questions that you answered before you arrived here," Dr. Vog said. "None of you have families, no wives, no children, no debts to creditors, no contractual obligations."

"You're free as a bird," Actund said. "It would be fantastic if you could now all set your minds at ease and follow the first principle and trust me."

"You are in a very unique situation," Dr. Vog said. "You should appreciate how fortunate that you are."

"We know from your applications that many of you have had horrible experiences at the hands of organized religion," Actund said. "Please share your stories, any and all."

A slender recruit stood to his feet. "I am Herbert Ragsdale. Back in the States, my parents rode me night and day, forcing me to live their way. No parties, no booze, no women, no cruising. They ordered me to go to church every Sunday and Wednesday. I got a double dose of preaching and Bible thumping every week. Most of the people sitting there in that church were hypocrites, especially the preacher. He cheated on his wife and stole money from the church treasury. The hypocrites! They are all over the place."

Tim listened as several other recruits told similar stories.

One long-haired man topped them all. He related a story about working for a television evangelist who solicited money from his viewers and spent the funds on his own lavish lifestyle.

"Our mission is complicated," Actund said. "But I will state upfront that one of our priorities is to eliminate religion from the world."

Tim's eyes widened and his mouth dropped open.

"We know the pain that religion has caused individual people," Actund said. "And we are disturbed by the influence that such mythology is having in our culture. Too many government leaders are allowing religion to impact their decisions. In the U.S., the situation is worst of all."

"You want to do away with all religions, including Christianity?" Tim asked. He tried to conceal his anger.

"Especially Christianity," Actund said. "More harm has been inflicted on society by Christianity than any other philosophy in the world."

"The Do-Gooders turn my stomach," Dr. Vog said.

"To rely on an imaginary God to provide someone hope and faith is sad," Actund said. "People should rely on their own talents, abilities, and power. That's why we are all atheists."

"Is that realistic?" one of the young men asked.

"Yes," Actund said sternly.

"Everyone must understand our commitment to this goal," Dr. Vog said. "Everyone here will play a role."

Tim wanted to shout in protest but he kept his composure. He looked around the room. Based on their facial expressions and body language, it was difficult to gauge the true reactions of the recruits to what they were hearing.

"The evening is complete," Dr. Vog said. "Everyone go back to your rooms. I would suggest that you seriously contemplate our opposition to religion because we are dead serious. If you don't feel that you can work with us, then I want to know about it in the morning."

"But what about our mission?" Tim protested. "Don't leave us hanging. Are we putting a new drug on the market or expanding into third world countries or something?"

"In due time you will learn our mission," Dr. Vog said.

Tim turned to asked Jon Actund the same question, but he was gone.

Chapter Fifteen—The Face Off

Friday, July 19, 7:45 a.m.

Tim was the first to arrive at the dormitory lobby, and by 8:00 a.m., there were only seven men gathered.

Dr. Vog walked through the main entrance of the dormitory and greeted the young men. "I hope everyone had a pleasant evening."

"What happened to the other guys?" Tim asked.

"They decided that they did not want to participate," Dr. Vog said. "Such is life!"

"Where are they now?" Tim asked.

"They are divorced from the program."

Tim feared the worst, as outlandish as it might seem.

"We are the 'Magnificent Seven'," one of the men said.

"Don't get so self-absorbed," the doctor said. "I am not surprised that we find ourselves with a faithful few. Everything is unfolding as anticipated."

"What now?" Tim asked.

"Each one of you will individually be summoned to meet with Mr. Actund today." Dr. Vog handed each person a sheet of paper.

Tim was scheduled to meet with Actund at noon over lunch in his private quarters.

At the end of a winding driveway, Tim stood in front of an impressive looking house. It was in better condition than any other building on the compound. Jon Actund called it home.

Tim rang the front door bell. A tall gray-haired man appeared at the door who introduced himself as Actund's butler, and ushered Tim into a beautiful dining room.

"Mr. Shaw, you are American?" Jon Actund was seated at the head place of the long dining table.

"Yes, I live in Atlanta." Tim cringed slightly. The night before he had announced that he hailed from Dallas, Texas. He feared that the slip up might give away his false identity.

"Ah, yes. A lovely city that I enjoyed during my visit to the Olympics."

"I'm glad to hear that."

"I hate your cities," Actund said.

"I understand."

"Americans are imperialists who try to bully their way all over the world. Your greed and decadence is disgusting while the average man, the low class worker, gets stepped on in your country."

Tim listened as the man continued his diatribe. He rambled on for another five minutes about his perception of the evils of America as drool formed around the edges of his mouth. His face turned red and his eyes seethed.

Tim applauded politely. "Very well said. Bravo. Bravo. I've been stomped on by the system more times than you can imagine."

"What has America done to you?" Actund asked.

"I have been humiliated many, many times." Tim did not know what else to say.

Actund smiled and motioned for Tim to follow him. They walked down a long hallway and into a nicely furnished office with modern furniture.

"I am sure that you are well diversified in your revenue streams. What else do you do to generate income?" Tim asked.

"You Americans have an expression. 'Filthy rich', I believe it is."

"But how did you get so filthy?"

"I am a salesman."

"Of what?" Tim asked.

"Of whatever the market will bear."

Tim's mind conjured up numerous illegal and unethical situations that the man might be involved in. His quest for information about Nancy could lead him down a road of no return. "I admire a person who can react and adapt," Tim said. "But why be so mysterious about what you do? I'm sure you are a pillar of the community."

"Are you interested in changing the world?" Actund asked.

"Not today, but possibly tomorrow," Tim smiled slightly.

"I will go down in history."

"That is fantastic and makes me want to learn more about the organization."

"To learn more requires a commitment on your part."

"What kind of commitment?"

"Let's eat first," Actund said.

They walked back to the dining room.

"How much are you worth?" Tim asked.

"If you only knew what was at stake here and the reason our organization exists!"

"Then let's get right to it."

Actund picked up a handful of grapes from the table and tossed one into his mouth. "I need enthusiastic young men for the organization."

"I want to help your organization."

Tim was seated at the end of a long table across from Actund. The table had the finest linen, plates, and utensils that one could afford, with two waiters on duty to cater to their needs.

"What do you enjoy most in life, my friend?" Actund asked.

"Many things."

"The best things in life are a loose woman, all the money you want, and of course, the power that goes with it."

"And so you've got it all, but it sounds to me like you're being very hypocritical."

"Why do you say that?"

"I say it because you've been criticizing Americans all day for their greed and selfishness and here you are behaving the same way."

"No, no, no. You don't understand. I am earning my good life and I'm the leader of a revolution."

"You've got a lot of self-confidence, don't you?"

"I'm a leader so I have to demonstrate my confidence because I have grand plans for Europe, the United States, and then the world. I am entitled by virtue of who I am and what I am leading."

A waiter entered the room with the main course of the meal, a rib-eye steak with scalloped potatoes, onion rings, and asparagus.

Tim despised the man but he enjoyed mooching off of him. "Most people would be taken aback by your confidence."

"I could inspire people to walk through burning buildings for me."

"But they have to believe in what you're trying to accomplish."

"What I'm doing will change the world."

"What are you doing?"

A sly smile came over Actund's face. "You have yet to demonstrate to me that you are capable of joining the team."

"What do I have to do to convince you that I'm ready, willing, and able to contribute to your program?"

"In time, you will be accepted or discarded, but only I will know the time." Actund took a toothpick from the table and slowly and meticulously picked at his teeth. "I have numerous theories about mankind that would pique your curiosity. Mr. Shaw, how well do you know your fellow man?"

"What do you mean?"

"We need stronger people in this world, people with focus and drive and sacrifice."

"You are already building a team. Where did you get these people?"

"They are eastern Europe's finest. I've assembled numerous scientists, physicians, and scholars. We have the best in business managers, engineers, psychologists, social workers, and teachers. The best and the brightest as your people say."

"Well, I'm your man." Tim gulped as he continued the charade in the blind hope that he could find Nancy, or at least information about her.

"I demand your loyalty. By the way, the food that you ate contained a lethal dose of poison."

Tim trembled.

"You see, young man, I am in complete control."

"You're mad!"

Actund stood, walked to a desk, pulled open a drawer, and produced a small vial of liquid substance. "In my hands, I hold the only hope that you have of survival. If ingested, it will kill the poisonous invaders and spare your woe begotten soul."

"Give it to me!" Tim shouted.

"No need to get tense." Jon Actund looked at his watch. "You have all of ten minutes to decide your destiny. The poison will finish you off about that time so you must decide if you will join the effort with your first gesture to be to turn over all the important information you have on yourself."

"What do you mean?"

"I want your social security number, all your credit card numbers, and any other important numbers like bank account numbers."

"So you want to steal all of my money? You can have it!"

Actund leaned against the wall. "This is not about petty larceny, but it is about you becoming a living, breathing full fledge partner in the organization."

Tim was frantic. "My time's running out. Give me that liquid!!!"

Actund scratched his nose and grinned. "Produce the information!"

"I don't have the bank account numbers with me but I'll give you my credit cards." Tim was sweating profusely. "Show me some mercy." He slammed his fist on the table. A saucer and glass of water fell off the edge, causing pieces of glass and porcelain to shatter all over the floor. "I can give you my Social Security number."

Slowly, Actund walked to the door. "I have no more time to waste on you," he said. "Incomplete."

Tim jumped up from his seat and lunged at Actund, grabbing the man by the shoulders. "Let me have that stuff!!!" Tim tried to put a chokehold on his neck but found himself turned upside down and hurdling through the air. Actund had flipped him aside like a rag doll.

Laughing uncontrollably, Actund stood over Tim as he lay sprawled on the hardwood floor. Tim's anger grew into a rage as he sprang to his feet, grabbed a wooden chair from beside the dinner table, and hurled it at Actund. The chair caught him on the arm with a glancing blow.

The vial of liquid was visible in Actund's pocket. Tim reached for another chair, rushed Actund, lifting the chair over his head as he stopped within inches of his tormentor. He brought it down on the man's head, breaking it into several pieces on impact. Actund's eyes became groggy and his knees buckled under.

Actund fell to the floor on his stomach, unconscious. Horrified that the vial might have been crushed, Tim attempted to turn him over.

One of the servants entered the room. The squat, middle-age woman, weighing no less than two hundred pounds, reacted wildly when she saw Tim crouched over her employer. She shouted at him in German as Tim jumped to his feet. The woman picked up a broom from the corner of the room, ran at him, waving it frantically.

Tim grabbed the broom from the woman and easily pushed her aside. Doggedly, she lunged at Tim with clinched fists but he pushed her away once again.

Tim crouched down beside Actund and managed to pull the vial from his pocket as two security guards stormed the room and drew their weapons.

"Put your arms straight up in the air," one of them demanded.

"Gentlemen, I'm only trying to save my life," Tim pleaded. He lifted the glass container, swallowed the substance and then thrust his arms upward.

The two guards surrounded him, one of them handcuffing Tim while the other one frisked him for weapons, discovering the pistol.

Tim was led down a dark, dingy hallway, directed to walk down a rickety staircase, at which point a security guard motioned for him to enter a big, empty closet. A massive door slammed shut behind him.

With no windows or lighting, Tim found himself in complete darkness.

As he sat down on the floor, Tim was relieved to find that he felt physically fine. Apparently, the liquid substance had negated the poison. But he had to come to grips with the fact that he was dealing with a mad man.

Two hours passed.

There were voices coming from around the corner, followed by an abrupt opening of the door. Tim adjusted his eyes to the streaming light that came from the outside.

A figure walked through the doorway, standing silently over Tim. It was Jon Actund.

"You're a very resourceful and determined young man. Good attributes to be sure, but surprise to you! I'll have you know that there was no poison. It was a ruse to test your strength and ingenuity. You are a strong young man but the truth is that you heisted colored water from me."

Tim threw up his arms in anger. "This is unbelievable."

"You were engaged in a test of survival and you passed with exceptional style and determination."

"After what you have done to me, will you let me out of this cage and finally tell me everything about your organization?"

"Do you feel like being a part of history?"

"Yes."

Actund pointed at Tim. "I am leading a legion of people who are tired of the oppressive ways of the United States... that cowboy mentality... plundering and elbowing its way through the rest of the world."

Tim listened intently.

"Our strategy and our weapons will be different," Actund said.

"Are you talking about an all-out war?"

"I'm talking about doing whatever is necessary to topple the giant, but we will definitely have new resources at our disposal."

"What do you mean? Weapons? Money?"

"What's the most important resource?" He did not give Tim any time to answer. "Human resources."

"So you have a lot of talented people working with you."

"That is a true statement, but we are working to make our people stronger and more talented."

"Are you Communists or Socialists?"

Actund laughed and put his hands on his hips. "You might say that we are a mixture of both, a combination of neither, and a sprinkle of something new."

"I'm trying to understand but you are making it difficult," Tim said.

"In time, you will understand. Of course, you tell me that you are anti-America but I'm not sure how sincere that statement is from you," Actund laughed. "As a practical matter, it is of no consequence."

"What do you mean?"

"You do not honestly believe that after pouring out my heart to you that I am going to let you simply walk away?"

"No, I don't, so whether I like it or not, I'm stuck. Right?"

"You're a smart one!'"

"So what happens next? I stay in this meat locker?"

"We have a lot of work to do yet you are not ready to fully engage. However, I could use you close by my side."

"Why?"

"I like your spunk… your tenacity!"

"And you will give me work to do?"

"Ah, menial tasks at the outset. However, you are going to assist us in the ultimate goal… the complete control of the world."

"Thank you." Tim felt sick to his stomach.

Chapter Sixteen–
Meeting the Inner Circle

The banquet hall was an elaborately decorated room with two massive bay windows bordered by rich, red silk curtains. The walls and the ceiling were painted a bright golden color. The dinner table, made of mahogany wood, was decorated with a long beautiful tablecloth that appeared to be embroidered by hand.

Four men sat at the table with Jon Actund. One of the men appeared to be pushing ninety years old, looking very frail. The second man sported a crew cut hairstyle. He had two visible scars on his face and wore a pale green suit with a red polka-dot tie. The third man probably was no more than twenty-one years old, with blond hair. Dr. Vog rounded out the group.

Jon Actund motioned for Tim to come forward. "Please join us for dinner."

Warily, Tim sat down in the nearest chair.

Actund pointed to the elderly man. "This is Vernon de Jour, valuable because of his historical perspective, among other talents. Next we have Eric Stroller." He pointed to the young man. "He is my nephew."

The crew cut man introduced himself. "Mr. Lugar, defense and security specialist." He stared intently at Tim.

"I'm pleased to meet everyone," Tim said. "So that means I'm hired?"

There was silence.

"I do most of the talking when we are together as a group. You will find that there is economy of dialogue," Actund said. "We are a serious team that only infrequently invites newcomers to meet with our group. Mr. Shaw, you appear to be head and shoulders above the other applicants."

"And you've all read my application," Tim asked.

"Only I have read your application and your questionnaire," Mr. de Jour said. "As well as starting the preliminary stages of an investigation into your background. I must say that you look somewhat different than the one photograph of you that I found. Of course, I do not have good eyesight anymore, but I believe you have lost weight."

"Yes, that is true," Tim said. "And I am proud of it."

"Mr. de Jour is a good judge of people," Actund said. "So I have given him the responsibility of heading up our program to fill key personnel positions."

Tim found himself fortunate that the others had not studied his application or seen the photograph and therefore had no reason to be suspicious or catch his verbal inconsistencies. Clearly, however, he was living on borrowed time.

"Well, I'm pleased to be in the company of such a splendid group of men," Tim said. "But if you don't mind my asking, when do we talk about drug sales? I mean legal drugs. After all, you produce and sale pharmaceuticals. Right?"

"I would call it our day job," Actund said. "Our primary reason to work together as a group is the establishment of the new order. Our personal ambitions and pleasures are nothing."

Tim bit his lip and nodded his head.

"You are about to embark on a journey that will one day place you at the center point of history, so please appreciate this moment."

"Yes," Tim said.

Actund motioned for Tim to stand. "You will recite our oath of allegiance."

"Isn't this a little premature, at least, until you have completed your review of my application?"

"Don't worry," Actund said. "You will have a place with us, no matter what. If it is further down the personnel ladder, so be it, but we expect more from you."

Tim stood to his feet. "Don't you have a Bible?" he asked innocently.

Everyone in the room laughed.

"We don't waste our time with Bibles," Actund scoffed.

"I'm not talking about reading it but we need to use it to put my hand on during the oath."

"We don't want that book here for any reason!" Actund shouted.

"I'm sorry," Tim said.

"Repeat after me," Actund said. "I, Rusty Shaw, do swear and affirm that my allegiance and faith shall be vested in the Empowerment Brigade. The goals of said organization shall be my first priority. Nothing shall interfere, including family."

When he finished the oath, Tim felt like he had sold his soul to the devil.

"Dinner is served," one of the servants announced.

As the meal was spread on the table, Actund motioned for Tim to come to the head of the table and sit by him. "Our man of the hour!" he proclaimed.

A chair was pulled up and Tim, feigning enthusiasm, sat down with the other men.

"A toast to young Rusty!" Mr. de Jour said.

They all drank from glasses of wine.

"So we're called the Empowerment Brigade?" Tim asked.

"Yes!" Actund said.

"So how many chicks are you dating?" Eric Stroller asked. "I'm curious."

"What?" Tim asked. The comment was not expected.

"I am sure that you know many American babes!" Eric said. He smiled broadly

Tim shook his head. "I know a few."

"Eric, you have too many bad habits," Actund interrupted. "You cannot be distracted by women because we have important work to do!"

"Women are a useful commodity at certain times…. eh…. eh…. eh?" Mr. Lugar laughed. He jabbed Tim in the rib cage sharply with his elbow. "In fact, I've had many lovers."

"How are you going to overcome a military force with thousands of men and the resources of a multi-billion dollar budget?" Tim asked.

The old man, Mr. de Jour, smiled calmly. "Brute force is not the only way to subdue the enemy. In due time, you will understand."

Tim was beginning to lose his patience. "Don't you think you ought to give me more details about your goals? You indoctrinated me with oaths!"

"This is a systematic process," Actund said. "Never attempt to get ahead of the program."

"Tonight, we should simply relax. And enjoy each other's company," Mr. de Jour said. "My compliments to the chef. This basted goose is superb!"

"Rusty. Tomorrow, I'll take you to the caverns near here… about a mile away," Eric Stroller said in a low tone of voice. "It's a fun place to explore because there are many old souvenirs from World War II lying about."

Tim glanced at Actund. "I'm still on a leash… correct?" Are you going to trust me to go skipping through the countryside?"

"The area of which he speaks is entirely within the borders of our compound," Actund said.

"But like I was saying, it's a fun place to explore and there's an underground pond, too," Eric said.

"What kind of World War II artifacts are out there?" Tim asked.

"Old bullet casings and strips of clothing and other things like that," Eric said.

"There is a strong professionalism and good work ethic in our ranks," Actund said. "The dedication to our goals is evident in everyone you work with here. Some of us have been working for years to reach this stage so we must not allow incompetence to interfere with the mission. To that end, you will be on a trial basis for two weeks if your background search is satisfactory. Then it will be determined if you continue in upper management or a low level position. At that point, you will get a detailed briefing on our program with background information."

"So I belong to you at that point?" Tim asked.

"No, you belong to us now," Actund said flatly. "Do not fail in your duties!"

"But what if I do fail?"

"I suggest that you don't," Actund said.

Tim felt a cold shiver run down his spine.

Chapter Seventeen–
Confiding in Each Other

Monday, July 22, 4:02 p.m.

The two young men met on the back veranda of the main living quarters. Eric led Tim out to the edge of the landscaped backyard where they plunged into the underbrush. The first several hundred feet were a land mine of vines, bushes, and scattered foliage. Eric practically skipped through the brush as Tim dragged himself along, stumbling three times.

Soon they were walking through an open field, scattered with daisies and lilies and bugs that flew in waves throughout the area. Eric caught a bug in the eyeball while Tim endured an insect in each nostril.

About fifteen minutes later, they came upon the beginning of the hills where the landscape turned to a rugged patch of rocks, sand, and dirt. There was a chalkiness to the soil that kicked up a dusty haze as the two men walked.

Eric was wearing custom-made German hiking boots and Tim wore running shoes that he borrowed from someone. The shoes were not ideal for the terrain as he stepped on a rock awkwardly and twisted his ankle.

"Ughhh," Tim screamed, flopping to the turf in pain.

"American dude, are you hurt?"

"I twisted my ankle."

"We will wait until you are better. Rest it for a few minutes."

"I hope it doesn't swell up on me." Tim decided to make the best of the situation by seeking information. "Tell me more about Actund."

"Uncle Jon is strict like a father… You see, Rusty, he raised me."

"I don't doubt that he cares about you." Tim did not want to come across as being too inquisitive or disagreeable, but he needed answers.

"You do not know him," Eric said.

Tim moved his ankle in a circular motion as the pain started to subside. "It feels a little better."

"You do support our team, correct?"

"I do support the effort," Tim lied. "I am only curious about the man."

"I am very much similar to my uncle and I am supposed to succeed him in command one day."

"I don't believe that you are anything like him. Where does he get his drive and motivation?"

"He is a born leader." Eric picked up a rock and hurled it across the gully. "It sounds like you do not admire my uncle!"

"No. No. I admire the man just like you but I want to understand him so I can serve him more productively." To test his ankle, Tim walked slowly and gingerly back and forth across the rough ground. He flexed his leg out in front of his body. "How do you feel about killing people?" Tim asked.

Eric's face turned white as he looked down to the ground. "No problem at all. I could do it anytime of the day or night," he said in an unconvincing tone.

"I don't believe you because it's not in your makeup."

"You ready to walk?"

Tim tested his ankle. "Yes… I'm fine."

They walked to the top of the next ridge.

"This ridge coming up is the best. It's the highest for miles around," Eric said.

A glistening, cool mountain brook lay across their path. Tim and Eric skipped through the water as a flock of birds soared over the hillside. The chirping of the birds and the steady humming of the wind instilled a sense of peacefulness to the area.

When they reached the summit, Tim looked out upon a panorama of scenic beauty and majesty, decorated by a light, misty fog that nestled over the setting. He found a tree, sat down on the ground, and leaned against it.

"This is fantastic, so peaceful, so serene. When do we need to go back?"

"In about one half hour."

"Where are all the military artifacts? We better start looking."

Eric Stroller shook his head. "There are no artifacts."

"Then why did you lead me all the way up here? What kind of stunt is this?"

Eric approached him.

Tim took a step back, turned around, and peered down at the rocky, wooded surface below. It was several thousand feet to the bottom.

Eric reached for his jacket pocket.

Tim's face turned red.

After a moment of fumbling, Eric pulled a plastic canteen out and unscrewed the top. He drank from it, quickly and lustily. "I was very, very thirsty. Would you like some water?"

Laughing nervously, Tim said, "Yep, give me a swig."

They sat down on an old dead tree that lay stretched across the ground as the clouds above floated about in a soothing, steady pattern. An unusual number of butterflies fluttered in the sky and a sweet fragrance of flowers accented the scene.

Anxiously, Eric tossed pebbles over the side of the mountaintop.

"So why did you drag me all the way up here if there aren't any artifacts?" Tim demanded. "What's going on here?"

"My uncle has ears everywhere… but we should be safe here."

"What do you need to tell me?"

The young man lowered his head. "My uncle is a madman!"

Tim stood to his feet. "I don't understand. I thought your uncle was the most wonderful, awesome, man you ever knew and all that rubbish."

Tears welled up in Eric's eyes. "I say that type of thing out of fear. It's a programmed reaction."

"Why are you telling me this?"

"Because it is a true fact and I find you to be a good person… a man of common sense… an American man."

"I do appreciate you confiding in me."

"We must stop the man. He is determined to the rule the world… literally. He has a desire to topple the free and good governments of the world and he does not care what or who he must remove to accomplish his goals." He looked about anxiously. "I brought you up here because this is the only area on the complex that I do not believe he has wired with listening mechanisms, so we should be safe." Eric continued to look about nervously.

"Don't worry because he can't harm you here," Tim consoled him. "Besides, he is probably going to tell me everything in a few days anyway."

"Possibly but he will use you to his good advantage and then probably discard you. I fear for your long term safety."

"But he can't go around hiring people and then killing them off."

"There have been a few men before you who have vanished because they had no more usefulness to my uncle."

"How do I know that this isn't some kind of loyalty test? If I side with you, the next thing I know, I might be in trouble."

"No… No… That is not possible because I am being honest with you."

"Prove it!"

"I have no way of proving it. You must trust me."

Tim looked the young man in the eye. He could see the sincerity in Eric's face. "I believe you."

"Uncle Jon is planning to strategically place his allies and sympathizers in important positions in the government."

Tim frowned. When you say 'government', what exactly do you mean?"

"I mean the whole world, the entire globe."

"That might be his grand scheme," Tim said. "But he's gotta start somewhere. Where? Here in Germany and Denmark?"

Eric bristled with tension. "Yes, and he's further into his goals than you would believe. I am frightened for my native people!"

"How is he putting these folks into the high government positions?" Tim asked.

"He has many friends already in government who may or may not be personally in support of what he's doing, but they owe him for previous favors. Of course, he is recruiting new people."

"It's not realistic."

"My uncle believes that is possible. When Germany and Denmark are conquered, he will pursue England next, then all of western Europe," Eric said. "Then he will get a foothold in the United Nations. If that happens, there will be no stopping him."

"You don't realistically believe he can dupe and manipulate that many people, do you?"

"Uncle Jon does not have to conquer every individual. He must only position himself to be riding a wave of power and popularity."

"Tell me more about his political and social philosophy. I'm confused about it."

"I am not very clear as to his entire philosophy but I know that he wants to harm the United States."

"So it's the 'hate the U.S. philosophy'!" Tim said. "How does he expect to become so popular?"

"I only know that he has been conducting experiments… or I must say his lab scientists have been, which Uncle Jon has said will revolutionize life as we know it in a positive way."

Tim perked up. "Well, what did he tell you about these experiments?"

"Not much of anything. Only a small group of people know about it and are involved in it but the result of these experiments when they come, it seems, will be the key development to the entire program."

"Does it have anything to do with an anti-aging formula?"

"I do not know."

"What do you really expect me to do about all of this?"

"You are an American and you say that you want to work for him and against your country. I hope that is not true because I believe that you only want a good job."

"You're right. I'm basically a mercenary," Tim lied.

"You care about your country! You must! Leaders in your country should be warned."

Tim shook his head. "But what about all the employees who work for him? This is a legitimate pharmaceutical company on the surface. How many people in the company don't even know what your uncle is doing?"

"Many."

"They would feel the same way as you. I bet most of the people that are a part of his scheming don't believe in it in their heart. Band together and then go to the local authorities."

"Mr. Shaw, there are two types of people who work under Uncle Jon. The first group is the uneducated and poor who only care about food on the table. I would describe the other group as intellectuals and elite, at least in their own minds. They are totally devoted to what my uncle is trying to accomplish, so I stand alone."

"I suppose that I am flattered that you have singled me out for assistance."

"When I met you, I knew that you were different. As a matter of fact, I do not understand what Uncle Jon is trying to accomplish by bringing in an unknown American. He is very difficult to predict." Eric looked at Tim in an odd way. "And what are you trying to accomplish?"

Tim was hesitant but he decided to trust him. "Have you ever been in love?"

Eric blushed. "I am in love as we talk. The girl's name is Zanzibar."

"Well, I am sure that as time goes by, the two of you will develop a bond so tight that you will be inseparable. That's the kind of relationship that I had with a woman who I lost, but I am on her trail. The trail has led me here. Have you ever heard of a woman named Nancy Proctor?"

"No."

"My real name is Tim Jennings and now I've told you some very sensitive information."

"I will not tell."

"I'm counting on it. My only recourse is to be patient and observe."

"But why don't you ask him about where the woman is?"

"I can't do that because I have to earn his trust and now I'm counting on your assistance!"

"And the negative opinion of America was a charade by you?"

"Buddy, I'm a true blue American. I love baseball and Duke Wayne movies!"

Eric looked envious. "I admire America and I would like to visit the nation."

"When we get all of this mess behind us, I'll give you the grand tour of the United States."

Eric looked out upon the horizon at the mountain tops as darkness crept in. "You do understand that you and I would be in danger if my uncle ever found out about our discussion?"

"Oh, I understand. That's why we must trust each other because I'm hoping that you can help me find out some information on Nancy."

The young man shuffled his feet and looked to the ground. "I will try."

Tim showed the photo of Nancy to him. "Have you ever seen her?"

"No."

Tim scratched the nap of his neck. "You should write down all of your recollections of the Empowerment Brigade and what your uncle has done to organize it. We'll meet again, but in the meantime, we will quietly observe everything. And at some point, perhaps decide to bring in outside assistance."

Darkness engulfed the top of the mountain as Tim and Eric slowly began their descent.

Tuesday, July 23, 5:54 p.m.

"How was your day?" Tim asked.

"I have not learned anything new," Eric said. "What have you learned?"

"Only that the employee training manual for the pharmaceutical outfit is boring."

"I am concerned for your safety. If you cross the wrong people, you will pay with your life."

"I've got more lives than the Cat in the Hat!" Tim laughed nervously.

"And you may need them all!"

"I'll be fine."

"I have talked to one of the workers at the plant in Bremerhaven. He tells of beautiful women," Eric said. "They are technicians and researchers. Two or three of them are standouts and they have American accents."

Tim's eyes widened. "You have a plant at a separate location?"

"It is a medical supplies plant. Syringes, bandages, and other things, but in the basement, there is more. Planning and research for the Empowerment Brigade happens there. The surface activities are a source of income for my uncle's goals."

"Take me there… please!"

"That would be much too difficult a task. I have arranged for my friend to take quick photographs of the lovely ladies and then deliver them to me. I should have the photos soon."

"Nancy could be one of them," Tim said. "Did the man say what the women looked like?"

"He did say that there are two skinny brunettes. Is that not what your woman is to you?"

"She's definitely a slender brunette."

"I would like to look at the other ones," Eric said.

Tim paced on the lawn with nervous energy. "How long have these women been working at the same location?"

"I do not know but I think it would be best to wait for the photograph identification before we get any other information."

"I suppose we don't want to stir up suspicions. Are you sure you will be able to keep track of this employee friend of yours?"

"Yes," Eric said. "He is not going anywhere."

Chapter Eighteen—Courage to Worship

Saturday, July 27, 7:14 p.m.

"I've had my nose in the employee manual all week. What do you do around here for fun on a Saturday night?" Tim asked.

"There is not fun of any sort on this facility. You should know that by now," Eric said.

"No kidding," Tim said. "But do you ever have any town passes or anything like that? Are there towns around here?"

"There are two small towns nearby but no one gets a pass to leave."

Tim shook his head in anger. "So we're terminally entombed here?"

"No. If there is a true emergency, a person can be transported to the hospital. But of course, we have our own health clinic."

"This is absolutely amazing," Tim said. "We live in our own little world."

"That is very accurate because we have all the necessities of life in our boundaries."

"So you never leave this place yourself?"

"I am trusted to leave the compound," Eric said.

"Good."

"I am able to monitor the outside world… go to the picture shows and my favorite restaurants and buy a newspaper."

"What are you trying to do? Make me jealous?" Tim laughed. "We can't even watch TV or listen to the radio."

"I am only making the point that we can use my freedom to our advantage."

"Absolutely. You're right and as a matter of fact, be ready at all times to head for the hills if we need some help." Tim looked around his tree-lined surroundings. "We might as well be on the North Pole as far as I'm concerned, because I can't leave."

"I am frightened. We do not know what danger lies ahead," Eric said.

"I feel the same way, but tomorrow is Sunday. Nothing significant will probably happen until next week," Tim said. He learned on the first day that each employee was entitled to one day off during the week. Tim chose Sunday because he felt comfortable with continuing his routine that he had followed back home. Tim had taken Sunday off for several years but there was no religious significance to his decision.

"Do you go to church much back home?"

Tim stood up and stretched. "No, I'm not very faithful. My current girlfriend is the only reason I go to church… when I do… to make her happy."

"Denmark and Germany are not very religious countries. Of course, I am not intelligent on these subjects but I am currently exploring my spiritual inner being."

"Well, I hope your exploration goes well."

"I must hide my spirituality from Uncle Jon because he detests religion."

"It's sad," Tim sighed.

"An old gentleman leads a chapel service in this facility each Sunday morning."

"Does Actund know about it?"

"It's a secret. Uncle Jon would shut it down if he knew."

"How many people attend each week?"

"Not very many, because of fear. The workers fear that they will be severely punished if found at the service."

"I admire the old man for his conviction," Tim said.

"Why don't you attend the service?"

"I would blow my cover once and for all. When does it start? So I can stay clear of the place."

"11:00 a.m."

"Do you go?"

"No. My uncle would explode."

Back in his room, Tim flopped on the bed and stretched out. As darkness fell upon the compound, Tim wondered how such a place could exist. Anger brewed from within as he thought about the poor people huddling secretly to worship, so he decided to support them by attending.

Sunday, July 28, 9:45 a.m.

After tumbling out of bed, Tim staggered to the kitchen where he pulled a banana and an apple from his pantry. He regretted that he did not have any formal clothes but he was fairly sure that no one else would be dressed formally at the chapel service either. Thoughts drifted to Tiffany attending her family's Southern Baptist church decked out in one of her flowered, brightly colored summer dresses.

The weather was overcast and gray as Tim walked to the chapel service. He made his way to the sixth floor, entered the room, and was greeted by strange looks and glares.

Seven men and five women, all middle-aged and older, were seated in chairs that were aligned in neat rows. The people, most of their faces taut, wore drab, plain clothing. A silent tenseness hung in the air as Tim sat down on the front row.

Ten minutes passed before an old man with slicked back black hair emerged from an adjoining room. He wore a dark blue suit with a light blue dress shirt. When he saw Tim in the front row, an expression of concern came over the man's face.

In making opening remarks, he spoke in German, yielding the floor quickly to a hefty woman. She let out a stirring German rendition of 'Amazing Grace.'

Tim looked at the shriveled, elderly woman sitting next to him. "No translation necessary," he said admiringly of the song.

An offering plate was passed but Tim had nothing to give.

The preacher began his sermon and immediately his German-speaking voice, underscored by forceful hand gestures, boomed throughout the room.

He was ten minutes into his sermon when the door burst open. A group of men wearing camouflage uniforms, pistols at the hip, black jump boots, dark glasses, and red berets rushed in. The leader of the squad approached the preacher and struck him with his fist.

Tim lunged at the leader but was held back by two of the other thugs in camouflage. Twelve men had entered the room, whereupon they started shoving the people around like rag dolls. Several of the older attendees fell to the floor, suffered kicks by the guards, then were dragged by their shirt and coat collars out of the room. An elderly woman was dragged by her hair through the threshold.

Tim was the final person forced out. Immediately, the guards threw him and the others up against a hallway wall.

The leader shouted in English, "Take their Bibles!"

His associates seized the Bibles.

"What are you going to do with these Bibles?" Tim asked.

The leader stopped in his tracks, approached Tim and swiftly elbowed him in the stomach, then followed it with a knee to the groin.

Buckling over, Tim looked up and said, "Answer my question, you skunk!"

Ruthlessly, the leader raised his boot high enough to lift it over Tim then forcefully brought it down squarely on his head. His sense of focus and equilibrium compromised, Tim shook his head to numb the sharp pain and to get his bearings back.

"Do not interfere with my purpose," the leader shrieked.

"Your purpose is to deny these citizens the opportunity to worship as they please! Wake up! We're not in the dark ages anymore. People aren't supposed to be tormented for their faith."

"We will have nothing interfere with the mission," the man said.

The women sobbed.

Tim noticed that every Bible, book of devotion, and inspirational tract had been collected and stacked up in a big pile.

"What are you going to do with these Bibles?" Tim asked.

"So you want to see what we are going to do with the books?" The man motioned for two of his colleagues to spring into action. They grabbed Tim, led him outside and into the backseat of a car. He was driven to a back alley that led to a field where he was dragged out into the dirt.

"You disappoint me, Mr. Shaw. Why must you make such mischief?" Jon Actund approached from behind. "I do not have much patience for people who do not follow rules."

"What am I doing out here?"

"I was told that you wanted to know our plans for the Good Book," Actund laughed. He pointed to his left to a big stack of Bibles on the ground.

"I was disturbed moments ago when I found out that your name was on the list of what we call 'weakling worshippers.' You have so much potential but, alas, everyone has an Achilles heel," Actund said. "Apparently, religion is your weakness."

"What should we do with him?" the leader of the thugs asked.

"We make him watch," Actund said. "Then we give him one more chance." He snapped his fingers then stepped back several paces.

The leader produced a cigarette lighter from his jacket pocket, flipped the switch, lit one corner of a Bible and watched smugly as flames shot upward. He repeated the act with several other Bibles, creating an eventual huge inferno of heat.

His teeth gritted, Tim watched as the thug openly laughed at the sight of the Bibles aflame. The mass of fire was so intense that Tim had to step a few feet back to avoid the heat against his face.

"I realize that old habits are difficult to break," Actund said. "But please, no more faith in mythology because we only accept reality here."

The flames burned well into the day.

Monday, July 29, 7:30 a.m.

Tim's thoughts were flush with anger and despair. He had surprised himself with his actions of the previous day. Never a religious man, he was now taking bold stands in a foreign land for Christianity. Tiffany's impact on him had possibly been greater than Tim had imagined or wanted to admit. He knew that she had been praying for him as well.

Tim always regarded himself as a good person, but he never wanted to be restricted or tied down by religious rules. Regardless, Tim believed that nobody should deny people the opportunity to gather and worship God or study the Bible.

Tim met with Eric over breakfast in the main cafeteria of the compound.

"Why are you down?" Eric asked as they sat at a table in the corner of the room.

"I am in a sad mood, my friend, because I don't like what happened here yesterday."

Eric leaned forward over his meal. "What happened?"

"The chapel service. I enjoyed it until about the time that your uncle's henchmen came rushing in and threw everyone out!"

Eric put his face in his hands. "Tell me more."

Tim described the event in vivid detail. "I don't like seeing Bibles burned. How do you think they found out about the meeting?"

"I don't know but I do know that the closer my uncle gets to his goals, the more ruthless he will be. He does not want any competition for loyalty, and he feels threatened by religion."

"I feel threatened by him." Tim looked all around the dining area. "I don't see any of the people that were at the service. I hope they are all right."

"They're probably in the hole."

"The hole? What's that?"

"When my uncle is very, very angry, he will banish the offending person to a deep dungeon type room under the main building. There's no light, no water, and no beds. Just cold, concrete and a few rats."

Tim thrust his fist down on the table. "And he would do that to those old people?"

"He has never discriminated when it comes to the hole."

"But how long do people stay in the hole?"

"Please lower your voice," Eric cautioned.

"Sorry."

"A long time."

"He's a madman!" Tim charged.

"He has intimidated everyone at this facility."

"We can't let those old people waste away in that dungeon."

"What do you propose to do?" Eric asked.

"We gotta rescue 'em."

"You could not successfully complete a mission like that."

"I oughta be down there with them."

"I am so sorry," Eric said.

"Your uncle is gonna watch me like a hawk now. One more false move and I'm in serious trouble," Tim declared. "But I gotta have more information so I can know what your uncle is attempting to pull off in the near future. Help me with some intelligence and gather me some facts. For example, what are those lab technicians doing all day? Get me some answers!"

"You should not be too aggressive because your secret intents would be known."

"That's why I'm asking you for help because you are family."

"It is not easy living here. There are no pretty women for me to admire, no pizza, and no cable TV."

"I guess that you haven't heard anything yet from your friends at the factory?"

"Not yet but we will soon. And I look forward to meeting her because I know that she is a fine American woman."

"Yeah," Tim grinned. "But I've got first dibs on her."

Chapter Nineteen—A Flicker of Hope

Tuesday, July 30, 5:57 p.m.

With great anticipation, Tim hurried to the backyard patio after Eric had called to say that he had learned that one of his friends at the factory was coming to the compound to make a delivery.

"What have you heard about Nancy?"

"My friend was not there when I called, but they told me that he was on the way in the factory truck to make a delivery. Let's go to the loading dock and talk to him."

They walked along a winding dirt trail around the property.

"How well do you know this guy?"

"Very, very well. We like to party together when we go to Copenhagen."

Soon they reached the loading dock of the warehouse at the far side of the building complex. A rickety old dark gray truck rolled up the road. It was badly in need of repairs. Most of the paint was peeling off, the roof of the cab sank in the middle, and the top of the storage bed was slightly askew.

"That's my friend. That's Rechard," Eric said.

The truck came to a screeching stop as the brakes made a hissing and scratching sound. A tall, husky, almost bald, young man climbed out of the cab of the truck wearing bib overalls and walking with a stride that resembled a bag lady pushing a grocery cart.

"I must unload before we talk," the man said to Eric.

"How much you got?" Tim demanded.

"Who is this?" the man asked.

"This is my friend," Eric said.

"Let's help him unload," Tim said. He walked to the back of the vehicle.

"Absolutely not," Rechard said. "I have very valuable china and glasses that should not be damaged under any circumstances. I need to do it myself so please step off of the line."

Eric grabbed Tim on the shoulder. "Please do as he says because he may not cooperate otherwise."

Tim grimaced. "The wait's been so long."

They stood by at the curb for at least fifteen minutes as Rechard unloaded his haul. Eventually, he completed his task with sweat drooling off his eyelids and glistening on his forehead. He reached into the cab of the truck and pulled out a soda.

"That tastes divine," the man said as he gurgled down a swallow of the beverage and walked over to the anxious young men. "So you are the American?"

He waved the open bottle of soda in Tim's direction, imploring him to drink from it.

"No, thank you. You have seen a woman matching the description of my fiancée, haven't you?"

Fumbling in his shirt pocket, Rechard produced the copy of the photograph of Nancy that Eric had sent to him.

"Well… Was that the woman you saw?" Tim asked.

Rechard smiled. "Lovely woman." He looked admiringly at the photograph. "Lovely young woman."

"Give me an answer."

"Yes. This is the same woman," Rechard said.

Tim waved his fist through the air in triumph as he hugged Rechard while patting him on the back. "I knew it! I just knew it!"

Rechard chuckled under his breath.

"What more can you tell me? How often do you see her?" Tim asked.

"I do not see her very often."

Tim rubbed his chin. "When was the last time you saw her?"

The man paused for a moment. "It was yesterday… No. Two days ago."

"Listen man," Tim shouted at Eric. "We gotta bust outta this place and head for that factory and find Nancy."

Eric looked to the ground. "I do not know if we can do it."

"You may not be able to get me off this crazy place but you could go find her for me."

Nervously, Eric looked all around the area. "Rechard, you may finish your routes. Thank you for the information."

As the truck pulled away, Eric walked back toward the main building. "Please be very careful. Rechard does not know the truth about the organization. Be careful who you speak in front of…. please."

"Well, he should know about it."

"He's not on the main facility and he has free access to the outside. That's why they haven't told him," Eric said. "That's the reason that they want me to spend time with you… to make sure that you don't talk too much."

"But I'm anxious to get this nightmare over."

"This will not be easy."

"We can do it with your help and then we'll all go to the United States together."

"But we cannot shrug our shoulders and walk away from the Empowerment Brigade as if it did not exist," Eric said.

"Look me in the eye," Tim said. "There's a lot that you have not told me about your uncle's plans. Now tell me the whole story."

"I don't know the whole story, but I do know that he has been systemically organizing and strategizing for years."

"Give me some details. What's the master plan?"

"I told you what I knew on the mountain. He is afraid that I talk too much so he does not include me in his private meetings. But I hear a little bit here and a little bit there. The United Nations is one of the important goals," Eric said. "My uncle has numerous friends and sympathizers in that organization. He is closer to accomplishing his mission than you believe."

"I simply do not believe it. The leaders of those countries aren't that crazy."

"It is actually the ambassadors that vote at the U.N. for their countries," Eric said.

"Well even if you get the ambassadors to go for his scheme, that does not mean that the actual heads of state will follow suit," Tim scoffed.

"Don't be surprised if he has an impressive list of presidents and prime ministers in support of him."

Tim laughed. "The U.S. alone could stop any United Nations plot attempt. Not to mention England, Canada, and several other normal countries."

"But if my uncle gathers enough countries with their militaries, and then gets U.N. approval, that would give him even more troops. U.N. troops. Some of the small countries will be swayed to join with the majority in a vote."

"Get out of town!"

"What do you mean, 'Get out of town'?"

"It's just a slang expression."

"We could be on the verge of World War III!" Eric said.

"Totally improbable scenario! What's behind his philosophy? Hate?"

"He has a hatred of the U.S. The main reason that he wants a one world government is because he wants to doom your country."

"So he doesn't necessarily believe in communism or socialism. He just hates our freedom and what our country stands for. Is that it?"

"Partly but I think he also has personal reasons, although he won't tell anyone what they are."

"This is scary," Tim said. "But there is no way that he can pull it off."

Eric sighed. "I hope you are right, but regardless of the final outcome, my uncle has motivated himself to pursue this goal and fight to the end, so there will be bloodshed!"

"We better make sure there's no bloodshed," Tim said.

"I do not know precisely how far he is toward the planning and implementation of the goals, but I am afraid that Uncle Jon is close."

"How many people does he have working with him here and at the other place?" Tim asked.

"I do not know, but many of them need a job or a feeling of self-worth," Eric said.

"Now don't go and start getting philosophical and making excuses for this sorry bunch of people."

"What should we do, my friend? What should we do?" Eric asked.

"The only logical thing to do. Go to the German authorities!"

"Are you ready to do it now?"

"No! Of course not!" Tim's face turned red. "You know what my primary objective has always been!"

"Yes. Finding your lovely woman."

"I've got to get her safely back to American soil before I call in the authorities cause I don't want her to get caught in any crossfire or hostilities, or for her to disappear with Actund and some of his people."

"I admire your dedication to the woman."

"Level and tell me what kind of research is going down at that other site? What do they have Nancy mixed up in?"

Eric shrugged his shoulders. "I do not know."

"Let's get back to my original question. How are we going to get Nancy out of that facility?"

"You are not permitted to leave the premises here," Eric said.

"We're gonna make our own rules."

"You are about to put us both in a very dangerous situation."

"We gotta follow through on this thing."

"Let me find out more about Site II and then we will make plans," Eric offered. "Will that be acceptable?"

"Yes, but let's not waste much more time."

Wednesday, July 31, 8:44 a.m.

Actund sat behind a huge wooden desk with a very solemn expression on his face as he peered at Tim from behind a pile of papers.

"Sit down, Rusty. Please do sit down," Actund said.

Tim sat in a big black leather chair with armrests. "What can I do for you?"

"How do you like your new home?"

"I'm happy and content."

"We will all be happy and content," Actund said. "As long as you have no more indiscretions like your meeting with the religious fanatics, but I know that old habits are hard to break."

"It was a moment of weakness," Tim said. "But surely you can understand."

"Our cause is very important." Actund sipped from a big mug of coffee. "So no more mistakes. Do you understand?"

"Yes." Tim looked into the cold eyes of Actund.

Chapter Twenty–
An Uncomfortable Place to Live

Thursday, August 1, 12:08 p.m.

Eric took a bite out of his sandwich. "I've arranged everything with my contact so we should be ready to go." He looked around the room. "What are your plans after you find her?"

"You will join us as we travel to the American Consulate's office in Copenhagen and report Actund's scheme."

"I fear for my uncle's life. The authorities might do harm to him."

"He has to be stopped as soon as possible," Tim said. "And you don't want to be around this place when they come down on him."

"Do you believe the civilian police or the military will come?"

"If I were a betting man, I would say both of them are gonna be involved."

"I am concerned that the members of the Empowerment Brigade will take up arms and fight the authorities," Eric said.

"I don't doubt that at all, and that's why we need to be out of the way! When do we leave for Site II?"

"I will come to your room tonight and inform you."

A few minutes after the sun went down, Eric arrived.

"Sit down. Please!" Tim pointed at the chair in the corner.

"You have very good living quarters."

"It's not bad," Tim said. "Now when do we leave?"

"We will leave… How do you say it? Covertly… Soon… Sometime next week."

"Why do we have to wait that long?" Tim fumed.

"It works out best for my contact. We will travel in a truck," Eric said. "I must inform you that you will be hidden in the back of the truck underneath a covering."

Chapter Twenty-One—
In Need of Comfort

Friday, August 2, 12:03 p.m.

Tim decided to take a walk to clear his head. He could not dismiss the fact that there were innocent people at the compound who were merely pawns in Actund's schemes. The realization that he would need to carry the burden and much of the responsibility in stopping Actund had weighed heavy on him. Tim was not sure if he had the courage or conviction to withstand the coming days. He felt very inadequate and, in some ways, very selfish and shallow, too shallow, perhaps too weak, to make it through the situation.

Miraculously, Eric had befriended Tim, but it was a strange relationship. He was the only living relative of a madman that had to be stopped, as well as the person who probably held the key to Tim finding the only woman that he ever truly loved.

In his room that evening, Tim thought about the love that Tiffany felt for him, admitting to himself that he had not treated her fairly. Tiffany was a woman of prayer. A tear formed in his eye, as he pictured her on bended knee praying fervently for his safety.

He pulled a tattered photograph of Tiffany from his wallet, his favorite shot of her. In his private thoughts, Tim confessed that he was not worthy of a tenth of the love that she demonstrated towards him. He felt shallow and cold.

Tim looked anxiously about for his Bible. He always kept it in the trunk of his car, a convenient place to retrieve it for his trips to church with Tiffany. When he reached for his overnight bag from the trunk of his car at the airport, Tim saw the Bible and tossed it inside. It was a Bible his mother had given to him.

As he opened the Bible, three items fell out from within the pages and tumbled to the floor. Tim picked up one of them, a card that his mother had given to him on his seventh birthday. The next item was an original Topps trading card featuring Hank Aaron. The last keepsake was a special letter that Nancy sent to him one week before her disappearance.

The young man clutched the Bible, wishing that he had been more attentive in Sunday school. His mother was very adamant about his attendance, but he had no enthusiasm. However, Tim did remember a few verses. He turned the pages to the Book of Romans and read the twenty-eighth verse of the eighth chapter: "And we know that in all things God works for the good of those who love Him, who have been called according to His purpose."

Tim read it twice as a sense of comfort and peace overwhelmed him. Suddenly, he had a resolve to recognize the blessings in his life and to remember that his current trials and experiences would only make him stronger.

As Tim put the Bible down on his nightstand, he felt an even stronger sense of loss than before, that he could not attend any worship services on the compound. His bitterness toward the leaders of the Empowerment Brigade grew.

Chapter Twenty-Two—
Inside the Empowerment Brigade

Monday, August 5, 9:00 a.m.

Jon Actund stood before seven individuals in his conference room. Seated at the table were Tim, Eric, Lugar, Vernon de Jour, and two new individuals.

"I would like to introduce Mr. Van Clamm," Actund said as he pointed to a fat man. "He specializes in explosive devices."

"He will have to get that fat stomach off," Lugar said.

"And we have Dr. Patel, an esteemed doctor and scientist," Actund said. "He is a native of India."

"I am pleased to meet everyone," Dr. Patel said.

"This morning, gentlemen, you are about to share in the most wonderful of discoveries... the final chapter in a timeless quest for mankind... the reshaping of human existence is close and within our grasp," Actund said.

They walked down a long hallway. As they reached the end, they were met by one of Actund's security staff members.

"Sir, come right in. We've been waiting for you," the security guard said. He reached into his pocket and produced a plastic card, scanned it over a rectangular pad on a thick, steel door that immediately opened.

The group walked into a long dark concrete corridor with small red light bulbs spaced evenly along the wall. It seemed to Tim that they had walked at least a half mile at a descending incline when they came to a big iron gate with three security men posted in front of it.

One of them pushed a button on the wall and the gate swung open. When they were all on the other side of the gate, Actund assembled the group around him. "We will enter the military hardware depot first," he said.

He led them through a nearby door into a gigantic warehouse. It was filled with military weapons and equipment of all kinds, including tanks, Humvees, various surface-to-air missiles, and a wide array of spare parts, as far as the eye could see.

Actund climbed to the top of one of the tanks. "This impressive selection of military toys has been assembled because of hard work, dedication, and a strong network of contacts throughout the militaries of the world. Of course, it was very costly to fill this room but it will be worth it. You see, I've had experts in weaponry and military sciences assisting me. We've studied what is already on the market in the hope of improving upon it. I am proud to tell you that we have made significant progress in the design stages of some fascinating new military hardware.

"This is amazing," Tim said. He noticed deactivated land mines and specially rigged jungle warfare traps.

Like the Pied Piper, Actund led them into an adjoining room that was actually partitioned off in halves. A Plexiglas wall was split directly down the middle of the room. On one side, there were pipes and vents that were visible in the ceiling, and a huge thermometer and other barometers and gauges.

"Who knows what we use this room for?" Actund asked.

"Chemical weapon experiments?" Tim asked.

"How right you are, my friend," Actund said with a very broad smile. "As most of you are aware, chemical warfare is the wave of the future." He swerved and bobbed his body as if he were surfing in the ocean. "I am proud to report that we are in the final stages of a chemical weapon that will absolutely curl your toenails, literally."

A locked door on their side of the room caught Tim's attention. Through its small window, he could see four prison style cells with iron bars. "What are those cells for in there?" he asked.

"To house the volunteers for our experiments," Actund said.

"You put volunteers in prison cells?" Tim scoffed. "That's a nice spin to put on it." Tim knew that he was digging his own grave.

"You ask too many questions, my young friend," Actund said. "We will be prepared for chemical warfare." He motioned for the contingent to follow him back to the main hallway.

The next stop for the group was an experimental baby nursery where they were shown rooms with toys, educational devices, and cribs. The biggest room could best be described as a giant playpen. In the middle of the room, a chair sat atop a sturdy, cement post. It looked similar to a lifeguard's station at a swimming pool. A young woman sat on the chair as she looked out over the assembled toddlers, twenty in all. Two teen-age girls walked the floor, ready to attend to the children's needs.

"So there are children here," Tim mumbled under his breath.

"What are those rooms for, those small rooms over there?" Eric asked. He pointed to a series of six doors that were visible at the far side of the big playpen.

"Let's go take a look," Mr. Van Clamm said.

Mockingly, Actund knocked on the closest door. "Is anyone in there?"

There was no answer so he opened the door. "This is quite simply a diaper room." The group peered in to see a tall table and two clothes hampers. "Not every stop on this tour will astound you. There is no getting around the basic necessities of life."

Before they left the nursery, Actund referred to the walls themselves. "You will be interested in knowing that these are the finest, state-of-the-art, walls in existence." Approaching a wall, he thrust his closed fist into it with great impact. To the group's amazement, his fist penetrated into the deceptively soft wall.

Out of curiosity, everyone felt the wall, finding softness to the touch. It felt like rubber with an essence of cotton, yet the material was incredibly resilient.

"I will hasten to add that the materials used to make this wall are non-toxic, and in fact, very much edible. Of course, such would be a worst case scenario, if a child tore a piece of this wall off and began to chew it." Actund pulled a small sample of the wall off, put it in his mouth and chewed. "Mmmm… cherry flavor."

"Extraordinary!" Mr. Van Clamm proclaimed.

Next on the tour, the group found themselves in a wing of the underground complex with several classrooms. "In these rooms, we will teach all the major foreign languages of the world," Actund said. "I have assembled an impressive array of instructors and linguists to teach the tongues of the earth. Initially, we will limit the classes to our upper level administrative personnel. Eventually, many more people will get exposure to the languages." Actund smiled confidently. "The education of our people is of utmost importance."

Chapter Twenty-Three—
The Fountain of Youth

The group walked a long way through a dim corridor, finally encountering a huge steel-framed door with big, round cast iron bars and a small window in the middle of it. Instead of a doorknob, there was a small panel with numbered keys on a pad.

"Why more security?" Eric asked.

"The reason we have layered security is because the area that we are about to enter is so important to our success and we could not allow for the possibility that anyone with dubious intentions could enter this room," Actund said. "I can assure you that the work going on behind that door will one day change, and I might emphasize, one day very soon, will change the face of this earth."

Actund turned his back to the group long enough to punch in a numeric code on the keyboard which, in turn, sprung open the door, allowing them to walk into a spotlessly clean laboratory.

Awaiting them was Dr. Vog, dressed in a gray business suit. "I am getting older, just like you and alas, I can only look back with wistful fondness on my days as a young man. I vividly recall my late teenage years as I played football with my fellow chaps on crisp fall afternoons, and the winter evenings when I cast my attention on a certain woman or two, only to have my heart broken before Christmas. Do you remember that feeling? You two young men." He pointed at Tim and Eric. "You've had those experiences recently, haven't you?"

Tim and Eric looked at each other incredulously.

"The eternal quest, the desire to stay young is Man's greatest challenge," the doctor said.

"What type of medicine do you practice, sir?" Dr. Patel asked.

"I am a retired brain surgeon, but as a secondary discipline, I am also a gerontologist," Dr. Vog smiled. "I have graduated from some of the finest schools in the Western Hemisphere, studied and researched at the European Institute on Aging in Brussels, completing concentrated studies on hormones. You will be interested in knowing that there are three hormones that effect muscle strength and fight disease. One of my goals has been to discover a balance between these hormones and hopefully find a way to make them complement each other to the physical body's advantage. In other words, no more muscle loss or easy susceptibility to disease."

"My wife only cares about looking young with no more wrinkles," Mr. Van Clamm said.

"Yes. Vanity, sweet vanity," Dr. Vog said. "Everyone wants to look as young as humanly possible. You happen to be talking to the man who has patented an anti-aging cream, containing the appropriate strain of alpha-hydroxy acids. It will bring fascinating and quick results. The skin is smoother with better color and reduced sallowness."

Dr. Vog walked to a blackboard, picked up a piece of chalk, and began to write. He wrote the following: DEHYDROEPIANDROSTERONE (DHEA).

"You may be wondering what that word means," Dr. Vog said. "It is a potent anti-carcinogen."

"Well, that explains everything," Tim quipped under his breath.

"Both sexes synthesize male and female hormones from DHEA. It appears to retard diabetes, reduce cardiovascular disease, and enhance memory." Dr. Vog picked up a tray of pills. "These little pills are available only by prescription, produced by only one manufacturer… .legally I should say." He looked at Actund and winked.

"What is this going to do for us today?" Dr. Patel asked.

"How would you like to look as youthful twenty years from now as you do today?" Dr. Vog smiled.

"Keep talking," Tim said.

"I would like to continue with my praise for DHEA. It is currently being used for chronic fatigue syndrome and is heralded for its ability to strengthen the immune system in AIDS patients. It can do wonders, especially when you use it in collaboration with other drugs. I am thinking about estrogen now." Dr. Vog walked over to a pot of coffee and poured a big helping into a mug.

Actund took the opportunity to address the group. "I hope you appreciate your rare place in history, learning about a major medical breakthrough."

The doctor returned to the center of the room. "Estrogen is quite an animal in its own right, full of benefit, so women are lucky. I'm sorry that I'm not a woman sometimes. Estrogen helps to prolong life, decreasing the likelihood of heart attacks and strokes."

"I would still rather be a man," Lugar said. "Cause that way you can look at the ladies." He elbowed Dr. Patel in the ribs.

"Let's move on. How many of you are familiar with the molecular clock?" Dr. Vog asked.

Eric spoke up. "It's when women can't have babies anymore."

Dr. Vog almost growled. "No. You are thinking about the biological clock. You see, everybody, male and female alike, has a molecular clock. When cells cannot replicate, heart disease is a natural occurrence. A weakened immune system is a sure thing as well, and the clock eventually stops." He paused for dramatic effect. "So we must recognize the challenge and develop the best way to create a perpetual, never-ending clock."

"You mean living a lot longer," Mr. Van Clamm said.

"Exactly!" Dr. Vog concurred. "You are not as dumb as I previously thought. Soon we will unlock the key to everlasting life."

"Won't the world get a little crowded?" Tim asked.

Dr. Vog smiled in a somewhat agitated way. "People will still die because the body will never be indestructible. As long as people drive like maniacs on the highways in their motor cars, we will have death. As long as love triangles develop in American mobile home parks, we will have death. As long as young urban boys crave expensive sneakers, we will have death. As long as war abounds on earth, we will have death."

As he gazed thoughtfully at the group, Dr. Vog continued. "Through experimentation, we are getting oh so very close to eradicating old age. With the proper formula, we will reinstate the timing mechanism of our molecular clocks, thus ensuring that healthy cells will replicate. Weak cells will die, most notably cancer cells, so the possibilities are tremendous."

"Very, very interesting," Dr. Patel said. "When are you going to turn the information over to the world? The press? The medical community? You're stored away in this hole, but you're obligated."

"We are not obligated to anyone," Actund said. "We are being very deliberative and cautious in our research and our release of information. I must stress that you gentlemen are the chosen few, but you cannot and will not divulge any of this information to anyone until I give permission."

"We understand completely," Mr. Van Clamm said.

"I trust that you young stalwarts realize that I am very, very serious about complete and total discipline in terms of communication to the outside world," Actund said. "Continue Dr. Vog."

"Thank you. The fundamental element of our physical bodies is the genetic material we call junk DNA. These little fellows are found at the ends of chromosomes. The end segments, compared quite effectively to the plastic tips on the ends of shoestrings, are called telomeres."

Dr. Vog paced across the floor. "When these cells divide and make copies of themselves, the telomeres on each chromosome get a bit shorter. We call this activity replication. My friends, it actually starts when the fertilized egg begins to develop into a fetus and continues throughout life."

"You could become quite a pioneer and well regarded in professional circles," Dr. Patel said.

"I know that what I am seeking will be a revolutionary difference that will astound the world. If telomere loss could be selectively stopped, then of course, your chronic diseases such as atherosclerosis, arthritis, and dementia might be arrested," Dr. Vog said.

"Next thing you know, it's the best way to defeat cancer," Mr. Van Clamm said.

"I believe you are quite prophetic," Dr. Vog said. "Cancer cells all produce an enzyme that prevents telomere loss, allowing tumors to grow totally out of control. Now you see, my friends, if telomere loss were promoted in cancer cells, these cancers would die. We are getting so close."

"If you're going to cure cancer, I would suggest that you be ready to answer questions from every reporter in the known world," Tim commented.

"All in due time. The world has survived this long without a cure. There would be no compelling reason to disclose a cure immediately," Actund interjected.

"The telomeres eventually are gone, but when that takes place the cells don't necessarily die," Dr. Vog continued. "They simply get old and feeble and function poorly, very poorly. We call it replicative senescence."

"This is exciting stuff, boring, but exciting," Mr. Van Clamm said. "I might never be an old man after all. It's gonna change the world but imagine… no more mall walkers… or Sunday afternoon drivers who forget to turn off their turn light switches."

"Yep, and what about the senior discounts at Shoney's? Hey, Piccadilly's cafeteria would cease to exist," Tim said. "You're about to shake up the world."

"Industry and commerce the globe over will be changed," Dr. Patel said.

"That's right. No more laxatives, dentures, or bifocals," Mr. Van Clamm said.

"Droll," Dr. Vog moaned.

"We recognize the impact that such a development will have in society in general. That is why we must ensure that our crusade is in place before we attempt to change the makeup of the population," Actund said. "We will effectively deal with the situation. Dr. Vog, please continue."

"As I was saying, the telomeres are the key element so we must study all we can about the subject. There is an unidentified substance that steps in and suppresses any further production of telomerase, the main ingredient of the telomeres. Then, starting with the first cell division, the ticking sands move us closer to replicative senescence. So we must develop a way to allow the enzyme telomerase to remain active and continue to restore the telomeres."

"You're starting to lose me, but I wish you great luck," Mr. Van Clamm said.

Chapter Twenty-Four— A Debate

"Intriguing," Dr. Patel said. Of course, you are swimming upstream against the natural order. The intrinsic dimension has to come into play, because nature has deemed it best to have humans reproduce, nurture, die, and leave their offspring to be stewards of the earth. Now we will come in and totally turn the world upside down!"

"Dr. Patel, you sound so disapproving," Dr. Vog said. "I believe you are a willing participant in our program, are you not?"

"Yes, of course, but I had not anticipated this development."

"Surely, you have no difficulty becoming enthusiastic over the prospect of ending aging as we know it?" Dr. Vog mused.

"Theoretically, we all find it to be wonderful, marvelous, and extraordinary, but I am a pragmatist." Dr. Patel rose to his feet. "When we begin to talk of eliminating aging and ultimately banishing death itself, we must consider the ramifications, both good and bad."

Everyone stared at Dr. Patel, transfixed by his monologue. Jon Actund was particularly intent on listening to his comments.

"We must take stock of our resources," the man from India continued. "When I say resources, I am talking about food, water, and the materials that allow us to survive. Minerals, coal, iron… the essentials that society needs to maintain prosperity and to simply keep us warm, healthy, and contented. These items are not in an endless supply."

Eric interjected. "Are you saying that we'll run out of those important things?"

"Yes, in essence, that is what I am saying. The population will boom throughout the world. Of course, we are already overrun in population in some parts of the world. For example, my native land and other regions are suffering from starvation epidemics. Young children are dying in the streets, clean water supplies are limited, and pollution that fills our skies will become suffocating."

"In this world, no one has a monopoly on the resources around us. The fittest will survive," Actund said.

"I recognize Darwin's theory of survival, but I do not believe that he had any notion of what we are talking about… an abnormal effort to saturate our planet with people," Dr. Patel said.

Dr. Vog was clearly becoming agitated. "You talk in such negative tones that I am afraid that you do not understand whether or not you are coming or going. We will be better off if we can find cures to so many of our diseases and our ailments in the world. We must strive for immortality. In our rapidly changing world, we are all on a collision course with death, so just think of all the people who could be spared to live and contribute."

"The only way to conquer death is to trust God and hang on," Tim chimed in.

"An interesting topic for discussion," Dr. Vog said. "I can tell you that no one can survive simply based on their faith in a greater being because that's fairy tale material. Let us determine what is reality based and what is fable and tradition. Young American, I know that you have a logical mind. Use it!"

Jon Actund shot an annoying glance at Tim as he stood. "We are close to perfecting our formula." He looked all of them in the eye, one by one. "My friends, you may never die.

Do you realize the awesome impact of such a statement? And no one else in the world knows about such a magnificent development, so you should all feel wonderful. Dr. Vog, please continue."

"Disease, injury, hunger, and other stresses hasten the replication of cells, and some of the telomeres wear down sooner than others. We must halt telomere loss at all costs, then we will have conquered disease." Dr. Vog paused, scratched his forehead, then continued. "Cancer, that ominous monster, the debilitating messenger of doom... Cancer cells have turned off the process which suppresses telomerase. You see, telomeres are restored in the cancer cells which are eternally active."

"You do understand the potential here, gentlemen," Mr. Van Clamm said. "An entrepreneur would love to get his hands on this concept! Overcoming cancer, doing away with death, and make bundles of money."

Actund looked warily at the fat man. "I am aware of that possibility. In fact, we have already encountered a difficult situation with a man who, by all counts, is a leader of an organized crime syndicate. He has tried to steal our aging research findings through intimidation, dishonesty, and covert activities."

"Where is he from?" Mr. Van Clamm asked.

"Not surprisingly, the man is from the United States," Actund said. "His name is Saul Marino."

Tim looked to the floor.

"So this Marino wants to sell your secrets to the highest bidder?" Mr. Van Clamm asked. "How low!"

"As I was saying, I have conducted a series of tests, chemical in nature, with conclusions that there are indeed many, many telomerase in cancer cells," Dr. Vog said. "And in normal cells, you will find none so if we stop that elusive, mysterious suppressor of telomerase, then we have really accomplished something special."

"You have obviously spent countless days and months in study and research on this matter," Dr. Patel said. "Are we close to a resolution?"

"Very, very close. In fact, I have developed experimental drugs that totally stifle and suppress telomerase on most tests. I am struggling for consistency in the experiments though," Dr. Vog confessed.

"What have you seen?" Dr. Patel asked.

"I would rather not say. The experimental phase is never easy because the products that you create are not very consistent. It is obviously a trial and error period."

"What are you saying?" Tim asked.

"I am only going to say that I have used the utmost discretion in my attempts to reach our goal," Dr. Vog said.

"How long have you been experimenting?" Eric asked.

"Thirty years. I have carried on this effort as a tribute to my father. He was a key player in conducting these experiments in the 1940s," Dr. Vog said. "Soon we will have a permanent youthful, vigorous legion of young warriors who will lead us to total control of the world."

"How is everybody going to discover the Fountain of Youth at the same time? It seems like there would be complete chaos as far as the balance of society," Dr. Patel said. "It is a fascinating subject with so many unanswered questions. Will your youth formula salvage the outward appearance as well?"

"You bring up an interesting point," Dr. Vog said. "Of course, our first and most important goal is to increase longevity of life, to prevent the major ailments that overtake us as we get older. These ailments serve to impede and eventually end our lives. I'm thankful that we have people who have experienced so much in their lives. I think of my own Grand Mama Leone." The doctor's eyes moistened. "The knowledge, the experience, and wisdom that come with age is amazing. But too often, the senior citizens become slow in their faculties. The mind becomes faulty. When their memory and adequate communication skills diminish, they become nonproductive, so we are striving to have the best of all worlds, physically sound bodies with young appearances, yet these people will attain experience and knowledge as they grow older."

"So what is the answer to my question?"

Dr. Vog crossed his arms. "We are so close in our research. We are creating a formula that will preserve the appearance of the person at the time implementation of the medication begins. Unfortunately, there is no possibility of retroactivity in appearance, so our favorite seasoned citizens will benefit internally but not externally."

"You can't have everything," Mr. Van Clamm said.

"Many years ago, European scientists dabbled and experimented in the finest of laboratories," Dr. Vog said. "They had a notion to create the perfect human specimen. Secretly, they developed a medical formula that would… when perfected… stop the aging process. Speculation abounded that they completed and documented an anti-aging formula. We believe that they actually used the formula on a small group of people. We have proof that the aging of these people was stopped. Seventy years has passed, yet these people have not aged in any significant way."

"Are you telling me that they are walking around in society?" Mr. Van Clamm asked.

Dr. Vog glanced at Actund. "We have had the stories confirmed."

"Fascinating!" Dr. Patel said. "Truly remarkable."

"Neat!" Mr. Van Clamm said.

"What is the evidence?" Tim asked flatly.

"Photographs, eyewitness accounts, and letters," Actund said.

"Then why are you doing all your experiments?" Tim wondered. "Repeat what they did."

"We don't have the entire formula," Actund said. "We are missing at least one element or step in the process, but there is a strong possibility that a bound notebook with the anti-aging formula recorded in it exists somewhere."

Chapter Twenty-Five—Background

"The formula was lost," Dr. Vog said. "But we know that it was in the possession of various parties through the years in Europe."

Actund picked up the story. "There was a Belgium mercenary group that snatched it and had it for a long time. Eventually, an organized crime syndicate from Italy stole the formula."

"What would these two groups do with it?" Eric asked.

"What else?" Actund said. "Make money by selling it to doctors, scientists, for a dollar or two. The Italians had the formula for a very short time when their syndicate leader traveled to New York in an attempt to sell it."

"What era was this?" Tim asked.

"Doctor, when was it?" Actund asked.

"It was circa 1955," Dr. Vog said.

"The good old 1950s," Actund continued. "It was quite a time.

"There was a big rumble of sorts between two ethnic gangs. The Italian leader somehow ended up in the middle of it, but I don't care to tell you the details. Let's simply say that this Italian syndicate leader wound up in the bottom of a lake somewhere in upstate New York. The stronger of the two gangs ended up with the formula in their possession."

"Then what happened?" Eric asked.

"This hapless band of cut throats was so immersed in their petty criminal activities that they did not realize what they had their hands on," Actund said.

"Idiots!" Lugar said.

"Eventually, somebody with knowledge of medicine and history recognized the significance of the information. Instead of telling the gang leaders, they took the formula and ran back to Europe with it. However, that person was murdered. I believe he was basically a mole, a snitch, a mercenary," Actund said.

"Was he working for someone? Eric asked.

"We don't know, but we recognize that he was our missing link for a very long time. Our researchers had the most difficult time tracing the formula back to Europe on its return voyage," Actund said. "But then an enterprising young book nook was able to piece together the facts."

"A great deal of time and effort has been put into it," Dr. Vog said. "A great deal of elementary detective work came into play."

"We recognized the importance and carried on," Actund said. "Despite the rumors we heard that the CIA of the U.S. government was trying to find the formula."

"That was not the half of it," Dr. Vog said. "We all heard about traveling carnivals in Hungary and Austria. There was supposedly a sideshow with two people, a man and woman. They were in their fifties but looked like they were teen-agers. 'Baby Barbara' and 'Juvenile George' were all the rage in those countries. I actually have several newspaper articles about the subject."

"Don't that beat all!" Mr. Van Clamm said.

"There were attempts by doctors to examine these people, but the owners of the carnivals would not allow access," Dr. Vog continued. "They were a gypsy, nomadic-type clan, always on the move."

"This incident spawned a lengthy list of stories about ageless wonders. One story played off another, although most all of the stories could easily be dismissed as false," Actund said. "For example, there was a case in Hungary of a man who apparently reverted in his chronological appearance. He was fifty years old and he eventually looked like he was twenty, the change taking place all in the course of six months. A ridiculous story!"

"These stories have been passed down through the years," Actund continued. "I heard them so many times that I decided to assign a researcher to dig out facts. We determined that a German doctor by the name of Herman Bron Wagonheimer developed theories about aging and the body, mind, and soul."

"My father knew Dr. Wagonheimer. They were acquaintances," Dr. Vog said. "I explored the writings of the doctor and determined that he was serious about the issue. Dr. Wagonheimer was very secretive in his research. However, I was able to secure from my father's files several letters that he had received from the doctor. From the correspondence, I was able to determine a location where Dr. Wagonheimer conducted his research."

"But upon descending on the location in the small town of Shyle, we found out that the building had been destroyed in American bombing raids," Actund said.

"So we appeared to be at a dead end," Dr. Vog said. "But six months ago, I discovered that there was an assistant who worked for Dr. Wagonheimer. He was found in a Bremerhaven nursing home at ninety years old. He claimed that there were two early deaths in experimenting with the formula. Apparently, they suffered severe reactions to the composition of the drugs,"

"Disturbing," Dr. Patel said. "I hope that you have not jeopardized all that you stand for and represent as a medical professional."

"Absolutely not, because I always conduct exhaustive research on my theories. I have concluded that it is entirely possible to complete this project." Dr. Vog said. "In fact, I believe that Dr. Wagonheimer reached his goal and there are actually people in existence who have stopped aging. However, his assistant denied any knowledge of the possibility."

"Many years ago, a gentleman by the name of Ponce de Leon had some crazy ideas about the Fountain of Youth," Dr. Patel said. "I believe we have found our latter day Ponce." He pointed at Dr. Vog.

"This is fact-based, not fiction. I can assure you of that," Dr. Vog said. "It's one of the biggest medical breakthroughs in history."

"Do you think mankind is ready for such an enormous change?" Tim asked sincerely. "Community stability might be jeopardized. What if people make a run on the formula because they have a fear that the supply is limited?"

"Everything will work out," Actund said.

"But we must find the missing element to the formula," Dr. Vog said.

Actund led the men into the adjoining room where they saw a long row of unoccupied computer consoles. On the wall above the shelf, four wide screen television monitors were spaced evenly apart.

"This will be the command post and communications center," Actund said. "World-class, state-of-the-art technology will be at our fingertips as we orchestrate our plans." A half dozen clocks were posted on the walls, set for different time zones, with the name of a city posted beneath each one.

"You have invested a fortune into this room," Dr. Patel said. "Where is all the money coming from to pay the bill?"

"We have an impressive list of financial backers," Actund said. "They are leaders of all nationalities, coming from many businesses. We have retired people, young executives, and CEOs of major corporations, but they would like to protect their privacy."

"We have already taken the initiative to put in place media personnel who are sympathetic to our cause in strategic local television and radio outlets in cities in Germany and Denmark. We have done the same thing with important print media in the two nations," Dr. Vog said. "We must build early momentum and the media will play into our hands and carry our story forward."

"That is a very difficult task, to control the people with the pen and ink," Dr. Patel said.

"Money goes a long way towards creating a cooperative attitude," Actund said.

"You see, my friends," Dr. Vog said. "The American pop culture shapes so much of what the youth throughout the world believe. The young, innocent little minds are ready to believe anything that is presented as hip and modern. We will influence their entertainment."

"We will indoctrinate the youth," Actund said. "We will give it an innocuous name such as 'Young Champions for Justice.' I thought of it myself."

"And what would the lads accomplish? Dr. Patel asked.

"They would promote our goals to youth all across the land, chapters in homes and communities," Actund said. "Then these chapters would branch off into schools and universities as we incorporate plenty of wholesome fun and games into their curriculum. If we get an early jump on their time and their impressionable brains, then we are much better off for it."

"I am not sure that you can get through to these kids that easily," Eric said. "The kids in Europe and the U.S. are very apathetic."

"I am very much aware of how apathetic young people are today," Actund said. "That's why we need to try to indoctrinate through the entertainment medium."

"Are you talking about books?" Vernon de Jour asked.

"Books will be a part of it," Actund said.

"But Uncle, kids don't read books very often."

"The more cerebral ones do," Actund said. "But the vast majority go for television, music, and movies, so you will be interested in knowing that we have several contacts, actually sympathetic friends in entertainment, who will certainly be very enthusiastic about the prospect of helping with a revolution, while at the same time plying their craft."

"Brilliant," Mr. Van Clamm said..

"That concludes our tour," Actund said.

Chapter Twenty-Six—One-on-One

"We learned the whole story today," Eric said as he relaxed in Tim's room.

"Your uncle's nuts," Tim said. "It was scary and he has to be stopped. We need to be aggressive. Your contacts in the factory can get us in the building?"

"Yes, they can. I should have a layout of the factory by tomorrow."

"And the van that we are traveling in. We will be able to get away in it afterward?"

"Yes."

"What kind of security does that place have?"

"It is average business security," Eric said.

"What would happen if your uncle were taken out? Tim asked.

"What do you mean 'taken out'?"

"Eliminated, assassinated!"

"I don't want to think about something so dreadful."

"If it were the only way to stop this nightmare, what would you say?"

Eric paced in front of the window. "I would say that I don't believe that it would stop them. His top associates would carry on his dream and they would be more determined than ever! It could not help and we might even be worse off!"

"I don't think you can come to that conclusion so easily. His followers could lose focus."

"Are you thinking about assassinating my uncle?"

"No," Tim said. "I'm thinking about asking you to do it."

"You're crazy. I could never do that. He's my family!"

"That's all the reason it would work, because no one expects it," Tim said. "It might totally demoralize them. You could walk right up to him and get it done."

"I don't want to be a barbarian like they are."

Tim tapped his fingers on the wall next to his bed. "We have the ability to end this situation without allowing it to escalate out of control. Why don't we do it?"

Eric looked out the window. "My uncle is a sick man and needs help. He should be confined under the best of medical care. He needs spiritual help, too."

Tuesday, August 6, 7:00 a.m.

Awakened by the alarm clock, Tim fell out of the bed and onto the floor. He was so exhausted that he fell asleep upon impact.

When he heard a loud knock on the door, Tim sprang up from his sleep.

"I can't believe I overslept," Tim muttered. "I'll be there in a second." He grabbed his bathrobe from the dresser drawer and put it on, hurried over to the door and looked out his peep hole. Not surprisingly, he saw an angry Lugar standing in front of the door, red in the face.

"You should have been downstairs at 0800 for training. What is wrong with you?" Lugar shouted as he entered Tim's room.

"I'm sorry. I really am."

"I do not want a lazy freeloader to disrupt our plans. You have five minutes to get dressed and be downstairs for stretching."

The previous day, he had been informed in a vague way that he would be an apprentice or assistant to Lugar for a while.

"What are you going to train me to do?" Tim asked as he met up with Lugar outside.

"We must concentrate on physical fitness first and foremost," Lugar said. "And we'll work up a mighty sweat." Lugar shadow boxed with a furious intensity, then led Tim in a series of stretching, followed by a run.

When they returned from the four-mile jaunt, Lugar put Tim through a serious round of exercises and hand to hand combat techniques.

Lugar looked squarely into Tim's eyes and laughed. "You don't have what it takes to stand before a man and kill him. We should never deceive ourselves that you could become a faithful warrior." He rolled his eyes. "We're finished. Have a nice day." Lugar sauntered away.

Chapter Twenty-Seven—The Clones

Wednesday, August 7, 9:21 a.m.

"I am a pacifist so I would never participate in bloodletting," Mr. Van Clamm said in Jon Actund's office as Tim walked in.

Actund sat smugly behind his desk as he held court with the same group that he had entertained on the tour.

"But you're selling explosives that could be used by terrorists," Dr. Patel said.

"I believe in free enterprise, the right to sell, trade, export, and import. It keeps the world's economy flourishing. I'm only doing my part, while making a dollar or two."

"So you don't care that the product that you are marketing is an instrument of death?" Dr. Patel asked. "An instrument of mayhem!"

"The way I look at it is very simple," the fat man said. "A product in demand will sell so it does not matter if it is me or somebody else. I am only serving as a vehicle for good commerce."

"Please leave the poor man alone," Vernon de Jour implored. "He is a realist, a practical man."

"I'm not here to cause difficulty," Mr. Van Clamm said. "I try to keep difficulty to a minimum."

"Interesting discussion," Vernon de Jour said as he gnawed on his cigar. "We must have these… What do you call them?… Rap sessions?" He looked at Tim. "Is that what you call them, young American?"

"Yeah, that's what we call them," Tim said.

"We are the favored few," Vernon de Jour said. "We will be working very closely together so we must learn to open our feelings more and communicate."

"Yes. A splendid idea!" They all turned around. Dr. Vog had entered the room. "I agree that we must communicate effectively because it builds trust and camaraderie."

"It builds trust and cohesiveness," de Jour said. "So let us continue, Doctor, if you don't mind, for a little while longer."

"Yes, please do!"

"Who would like to speak?" de Jour asked. There was silence. He waited thirty seconds. "Then I will start. You must all realize that I am a self-proclaimed perfectionist. I demand that the best emerge in all of you."

"You are a neat freak, too," Lugar said.

"I suppose you mean that I demand cleanliness, true, so true."

"I know that you never let me get by with throwing cigarette butts on the ground," Lugar said.

"I readily acknowledge that I detest untidiness. Appearance is very important," de Jour said as he looked over the group.

Dr. Vog walked to the middle of the room, a somber expression on his face. "Now is the time for me to brief you on the next phase of our scientific and medical strategy."

"A new wrinkle," Tim said under his breath.

"I hope most of you are familiar with the cloning process," Dr. Vog said. "A clone is an exact genetic copy of a living thing, be it animal or plant. But it is not like an identical twin in that a true clone is a copy made from a body cell, not an egg cell. The early cloning attempts involved fertilized egg cells only. As the fertilized egg divided into more and more cells to make first a clump of cells and then an embryo, the scientist made it split in half, or twin."

"Should we be taking notes?" Lugar asked sarcastically.

"No! You should be keeping your mouth closed and listening," Dr. Vog snarled. He gathered his thoughts and continued. "My friends, each of these embryo twins had genes, or technically DNA, from two parents, but the cloning attempts never succeeded." Dr. Vog walked to the other side of the room. "But along came Dolly!"

"Who is Dolly? An old girlfriend?" Lugar asked.

"Dolly, for you uninitiated, was the sheep that was created by cloning in Scotland," Dr. Vog said.

"Yes. I remember," Eric said.

"The agricultural scientist, his name was Ian Wilmut, took genes from the nucleus of the udder of an adult female sheep." Dr. Vog paced back to the other side of the room. "The genes were put in an unfertilized egg cell that had no nucleus."

"This is getting way too technical for me!" Lugar said.

"That's why you're the muscle in the organization," Actund said. "Dr. Vog, please continue."

"Gentlemen. You must appreciate the significance of such a development."

"We do," Tim said. "But what does that have to do with us?"

"I provided that pretext in order to prepare you for my important announcement. For you see, my friends, experts have claimed that society is years away from developing a method of successfully cloning humans."

"I don't think society is ready for it. Forget about the scientific research," Eric said. "The ramifications that it would have on society would be disturbing."

"I would like to inform you that our scientists and doctors have successfully cloned a human being."

Stunned silence filled the room.

Tim finally spoke. "If this is true, it will be revolutionary for the world. You must have recruited some of the best scientists in the world to pull this off!"

"We have assembled as stellar a lineup of doctors, scientists, and technicians as has ever been documented in one place working on the same project," Dr. Vog said flatly.

"It poses many questions of an ethical nature," Dr. Patel said. "And what about the failures, the failed experiments with human life?"

"It was a very difficult experience," Dr. Vog said. "There were failures along the way that should be left unmentioned."

Dr. Patel cocked his head, turned up his nose, and said, "I have read a great deal of information on the original sheep cloning. There were almost 300 failed attempts to produce the embryo that became Dolly the lamb."

"What are you saying?" Eric asked.

"I am saying that the failed attempts were very unpleasant," Dr. Patel said. "Some of the embryos died in laboratory dishes. Some of them were born dead after implantation in the wombs of surrogate mother sheep."

"That's not too bad," Lugar said.

"But that's not the whole story!" Dr. Patel said. "There were deformities and wickedly, grotesque defects, missing body parts. The researchers had to destroy many of the poor creatures."

"Yes! But such are the sacrifices of science," Dr. Vog said calmly.

"But we can go too far, and I am afraid that you have!" Dr. Patel said. "I do not even want to conjecture." He lowered his head. His thick lens eyeglasses slid down his nose. "I do not want to speculate on the gruesome failures that I am certain came out of the experiments. Human beings, mind you!"

"Science can be trying," Dr. Vog said. "It is not for the squeamish!"

"We are not talking about getting sick to the stomach," Dr. Patel said.

Dr. Vog walked to a small freezer in the corner of the room, pulled out a frosty, cold beverage and took a sip. "I make no apologies for what is destined to go down in history as one of the greatest medical and scientific breakthroughs ever!"

"But were there failed experiments?" Eric broke in.

"Yes," Dr. Vog said. "But everything was taken care of."

"I do not believe that you comprehend what is happening," Jon Actund said. "You are the first individuals other than the participants to be informed of the news, the monumental news, that we have successfully cloned a live, breathing human being!"

"I was simply making the point that I am hoping we did not diminish the final result because of callous actions leading up to the breakthrough," Dr. Patel said.

"The field of science is not without its faults and drawbacks," Dr. Vog said. "Quite obviously, the failed experiments resulted in living creatures that were so unprepared to live a viable life that they were destroyed, but the good news is that down the hallway, the most darling baby boy is playing in the nursery. Shall we look in on him?"

Dr. Vog motioned for the entire group to follow him. He led them out of Actund's office and down the main hallway. Two lefts and a right turn later, they found the nursery. The group observed two young women in white blouses and light blue pants looking down into a crib. A baby of about six months sat in the crib, playing with a bright red rubber ball while looking at a mobile that hung from the ceiling.

"This is the baby that will change the course of history," Actund said.

"What is his name?" Mr. Van Clamm asked.

"We call him Atlas or Atlee for short," Actund said.

"Atlas? Why?" Tim asked.

"We call him that because he has the weight of the world on his shoulders," Actund said.

"We could almost say that he is a messiah child," Dr. Vog said.

"It looks like a very healthy baby," Eric said.

"Are we to believe that Atlas has had no fevers, rashes, coughs, or pain?" Dr. Patel asked.

"He is a normal child, so, of course, he has had fevers and hiccups and the like. That is very normal," Dr. Vog said. "But we expect him to grow up to be a healthy, prosperous man."

"Are you preparing a literal baby factory in our midst?" Mr. Van Clamm asked. He shook his head in amazement.

"We are perpetuating and promoting our way of life," Dr. Vog said.

"Please explain how this development fits into our overall agenda," Tim requested. "It's one bombshell after another."

"The ability to produce the finest citizens possible is essential to ensure success in our revolution," Actund said. "As soon as we discover the missing element of the anti-aging formula, we will be able to produce the ultimate citizen of the revolution. Combine the youth and vitality offered by the formula with the multiplicity of possibilities of the cloning process, and you can see what will happen. We will have the ability to create the perfect human specimen at our fingertips." He smiled brightly.

"Of course, the most healthy, intelligent, disciplined warriors will result in a victorious revolution," Dr. Vog said. "Our laboratory scientists will succeed; no doubt about it. A cloned colony of people who do not age and are descendants of the brightest, most viral, well-rounded specimens in existence will make our sustained success a certainty."

"This disturbs me, Uncle Jon," Eric said. "Do we really want robots living among us?"

"They will not be robots," Dr. Patel said. "A key point that should not be overlooked is the fact that these individuals will not be created as full grown adults. The babies will be subjected to the normal environmental and societal conditions that shape a personality."

"What do you mean?" Eric asked.

"I am saying that the people that come in contact with the child, mostly his parents, will play a major role in shaping the individual's persona, as well as where the person lives, education, and extracurricular activities, too," Dr. Patel said.

"We are planning to create a pristine, controlled environment," Dr. Vog said.

"So this little tyke is the first of many little warriors to come," Mr. Van Clamm said. "I can envision an enormous commune with huge day care centers serving as the hub of all activities. There will be gigantic warehouses that will be stocked to the ceiling with diapers and Gerber's baby food. Stuffed toys galore with choo-choo bars and cocoa sweets will fill everyone's cupboards with plenty of replenishments in reserve."

"Indeed, this is a well-organized effort and there is no question that we can be best prepared with long-range planning," Vernon de Jour said. "Some of us will have departed the friendly confines of this earth by the time our project has tasted its ultimate fruit, but the legacy that we leave will undoubtedly be profound."

"As far you know, is this baby healthy?" Tim asked. He looked around the room at the others.

Dr. Vog smiled. "This baby is as healthy as a horse, as you Americans say, or at least as healthy as a pony!"

"Of course, you can't be entirely sure about a baby's health because it is in his growing, formative months that you can determine a lot about his overall health. The body structure and organs should be watched very closely in the first two years," Dr. Patel said.

"Who do you think you are? That baby expert, Mr. Spock?" Lugar asked.

"A word to the wise. Humor is best when it is factually correct," Dr. Patel said. "Keep that in mind, my friend."

"This baby looks normal, but only time will tell for sure," Tim said.

"That is precisely why we will keep perfecting the product," Dr. Vog said. "Tinkering, dabbling…. perfecting." He smiled broadly.

"We are confident that the baby is physically normal," Actund said.

"Unlike your early specimens, correct?" Dr. Patel implored. "What did you do with the dead carcasses?"

Dr. Vog and Jon Actund stared at him with steely eyes of anger.

"Are you going to set up a breeding farm?" Eric asked.

"You'll probably have a platoon of surrogate mothers," Mr. Van Clamm laughed. "Ready to donate the services of their wombs to further the cause."

"You might laugh, but the opportunity to become a part of history, plus a hefty salary, will attract many healthy young women," Dr. Vog said. "I'm wondering if we might want to clone the best athletes, brightest musicians, and most brilliant artists to elevate the culture of our society.'

"We might very well do that," Actund said.

"I am proud of your accomplishments," Vernon de Jour said.

"I might be proud if I was convinced that this program was being used for benign health care research as well," Dr. Patel said. "For example, burn victims could benefit greatly with skin grafting. However from a strictly scientific standpoint, it's almost pointless to indulge in cloning."

"And why is that, my foreign intellectual friend?" Dr. Vog asked.

"It is because we learn nothing new! No new science is developed at all!" Dr. Patel said.

"What do you mean?" Lugar asked in a confused stupor.

"Science is a discipline that evolves and expands based upon new findings that break molds and develop outside of conventional documented parameters."

"In other words, it's not new in theory on paper but in reality, we are breaking new ground in a new, never attempted manner. If you don't like the way we use the science, that's your problem, Dr. Patel!" Actund said. "You are too abstract, but I'm a practical person."

Chapter Twenty-Eight—The Headache

"We will be dining in the private facility down the hall," Actund said. "Everyone please convene there in five minutes. Everyone but you, Dr. Patel."

Dr. Patel trembled slightly as his face went flush and his eyes turned red.

A few minutes later, Tim sat down next to Eric in the dining room.

"Should we wait for Uncle Jon?" Eric asked.

"No," Vernon de Jour said. "The other three gentlemen will not be joining us."

Tim whispered to Eric, "I don't think we'll see Dr. Patel again. He wore out his welcome."

"This entire cloning episode is intriguing to me," Mr. Van Clamm said. "I mean we'll be able to create the best basketball team in the world by cloning Michael Jordan five times."

"How about five Heather Locklears?" Lugar joked.

"Or Ursula Andress," Vernon de Jour chimed in.

The meal included a basted chicken with yellow rice and squash.

"I need five of me to eat all of the food that we are served at the compound," Mr. Van Clamm said as he went for a second helping of everything.

"You know, if we sliced you up into little pieces, we could clone you and have enough Santa Claus actors to satisfy every Western Hemisphere shopping center's need at Christmas time," Lugar said.

"That wasn't very funny," Mr. Van Clamm said as he stuffed a fork full of rice into his wide mouth.

"Well, we aren't exactly at Disney World," Tim said. "This place isn't supposed to be funny."

"This cloning situation is really going to change everything," Eric said.

"Yeah, we're sitting on the most fascinating and important story of the last one hundred years," Tim said. "The media doesn't know anything about it."

"No one needs to know about this development outside of our small group," Vernon de Jour said. The veins on his forehead bulged. "Is that clear?"

Everyone shook their heads affirmatively.

"I know my friends here won't talk to the wrong people," Lugar said. "Because if they do, they'll have me to contend with and they know it."

"The thing that concerns me is that cloning technology can do some good things for a lot of people, medically speaking. We don't need to deprive people who are in desperate situations any modern advances which may be available, do we?" Eric asked.

"You have a very good point, young man." Dr. Vog said. "We are doing humanity a very good deed by developing the cloning technology."

"But if no one knows about it until years and years down the road, then so much good that it could have accomplished is wasted," Eric said.

Vernon de Jour sipped from a glass of dark red wine. "We are revolutionaries, not humanitarians."

"But you gotta try to help your fellow man whenever you can," Tim said.

"We can't lose our focus," Dr. Vog said as he sat down to eat.

"Speaking of humanitarians, where's Dr. Patel?" Tim asked, knowing that his question would stir angry emotions.

Dr. Vog and Vernon de Jour exchanged uneasy glances.

"Well… Should we forward his mail or what?" Tim asked snidely.

"That is not your issue," Dr. Vog said. "I suggest we change the subject."

"Gentlemen," Mr. Van Clamm said. "You do understand one of the fringe benefits of our clone phenomena, don't you?"

"What's that?" Lugar asked.

"We can create the most beautiful women in the world… many times over… a whole factory full of them."

"Practically speaking, we will be able to rear young women who excel in beauty pageants, the ultimate super models," Eric said. "We would be able to market them and hire them out."

"I like what I am hearing," Mr. Van Clamm said. "We would create many nationalities, personalities, and redheads, blondes, and brunettes. It will be fantastic. If you really wanted to do it, a program of this type could be quite profitable. It could include a mail order bride service on the Internet."

"How about harems at bargain rates?" Lugar laughed.

"Polygamy is illegal in most countries," Mr. Van Clamm said.

"Not all countries, my friend. Not all," Lugar said.

"It will be very difficult to keep the outside world from finding out about this medical breakthrough," Mr. Van Clamm said. "Somebody will try to get the word out and the media will descend on this place like a swarm of locusts. They'll be clamoring, climbing, and digging to get in and come up with a story." Mr. Van Clamm looked at Dr. Vog. "You may have outsmarted yourself. Your entire cover might be blown prematurely."

"We are a humble pharmaceutical company," Dr. Vog said.

Chapter Twenty-Nine—On the Road

Later in the evening, Tim and Eric met beside the nature pond.

"We all set?" Tim asked. Both young men wore black pants and black shirts.

"As ready as we can be."

They walked along the dirt trail that led to a fence behind the big warehouse. At the big wooden fence, Eric pushed open a loosened board, allowing the two of them to squeeze through. They encountered a long row of big oak trees.

Crouching down behind the trees, they watched a truck roll up to the loading dock of the warehouse. Two bedraggled workers came out of the building and unloaded boxes from the truck while the driver, Ollie, stepped out of the cab.

When Eric and Tim reached the back of the truck, Ollie helped them climb into it, instructing them to hide under old dusty, ragged shipping blankets.

Ollie started the truck, its engine humming at an idle pace. The truck inched along slowly until it cleared the outer perimeter gate. It picked up speed, chugging along at a steady pace on the desolate highway.

It was a twelve minute drive to their destination. When the truck reached the gate to Site II, Ollie applied the brakes.

"Show identification," a security guard said as he emerged from his little shack.

"Here it is but I am a regular driver," Ollie said. "Here is my checklist with all my cargo."

"We must search the vehicle," a second security guard said. "Please get out of it so we may complete the search."

As he listened to the discussion from the back of the truck, Tim's body tensed up. He shot a glance at Eric who was also afraid.

"This is a waste of time," Ollie said.

"Please cooperate," the second guard said. "Turn the engine off."

Ollie turned the ignition key to the off position, climbed out of the cab, and feigned a sigh. "There is no problem and you are wasting my time."

"We've started doing random checks," the second guard said. "Now I will get in to examine the dashboard and under the seats. My associate will examine the back."

Tim could hear them unlatching the hinged back door of the truck and tossing away the sides of the tarp that sheltered the bed of the vehicle. The young American could do nothing but remain as still as possible underneath the burlap blanket.

A beam of light shone through the blanket.

"What is underneath that blanket?" the first security guard asked.

"It's a sack of old clothes," Ollie said.

"Move out of the way and let me check."

"That's not necessary," Ollie said.

"Move out of the way," the first security guard said.

Tim decided to go on the offensive. He sprung up from the floor, threw off the blanket and hit the security guard square on the chin with a forearm thrust. The man had no time to react, crumpling down on impact, knocked out.

"What is going on back there?" the second guard shouted as he ran to the back of the truck, his M-16 rifle positioned across his chest.

Tim had grabbed the other guard's M-16.

"Drop it," the second guard ordered as he saw Tim on one knee in the bed of the truck.

The unconscious security guard began to stir.

Tim took advantage of the distraction, jumped from the truck, and lunged at the second guard, driving him back on his heels. As the guard fell back, he fired off a round, hitting the side of the truck.

Tim fired his weapon, catching the man on the shoulder. He fell to the ground and immediately rolled underneath the truck.

Eric emerged from underneath the blanket with his pistol aimed at the groggy first security guard.

The second security guard scrambled out from underneath the front of the truck, stumbling into the shack at the gate. He pushed a button, creating a shrill, high-pitched alarm sound that pierced the night sky over the complex.

Within thirty seconds, a sedan station wagon and two Jeeps drove rapidly toward the main gate from inside.

"I give up!" Ollie, the truck driver, said. "I'm not a fighter." He walked away from the truck.

In desperation, Tim grabbed the first security guard by the back of his shirt and slung him out the back of the truck. "Ride shotgun," he shouted to Eric. Tim slid into the cab of the vehicle, started the engine, and accelerated straight into the metal fence that blocked their entrance. A section of the standard metal chain-link fence collapsed upon impact. Several additional sections folded like an accordion as the truck pushed forward.

In pursuit, the station wagon headed straight for the truck. When it was fifteen feet away, its driver applied the brakes. The car skidded wildly for about fifty feet then fishtailed and careened off the side of the truck.

The impact jarred Tim's hands from the steering wheel long enough for the truck to run up against the curb. The station wagon flipped over several times and crashed up against a small tin building.

Shaking it off quickly, Tim continued to drive with the two Jeeps close behind. Suddenly, he made a sharp turn onto a gravel road. A few hundred feet up the road, Tim stopped the vehicle and looked to the left and to the right. There were two buildings of very similar appearance one hundred feet down the road on both sides.

"What building is Nancy in?" Tim shouted.

"It's on the right," Eric said.

Chapter Thirty—Trapped

Tim accelerated the vehicle. "When I stop, we'll get out together. You lead the way! And I'll cover us from behind."

"There's security in the building," Eric said.

"Then I'll shoot our way into the place!"

"This is crazy!" Eric shouted.

"Tell me about it," Tim shouted as they bailed out of the truck. The two Jeeps were fast approaching.

They ran toward the building as fast as they could.

"Where's your friend?" Tim shouted.

"Here he comes," Eric said.

Rechard, the man who identified Nancy, approached. "What is all the commotion?"

"They are chasing us," Eric shouted.

"Too dramatic," Rechard said. Multiple rounds of gunfire struck Rechard's face and upper torso. He fell to the ground, dead.

"My friend!" Eric cried. "He's dead."

Straight up the road, the Jeeps had stopped and the occupants had fired off the deadly shots.

In a frenzied moment, Tim grabbed Eric by his collar and dragged him towards the building as a spray of bullets whizzed past them. They found a small unlocked door to enter. Inside, they encountered a darkened corridor with a flickering light that illuminated it.

Tim opened a door at the end of the corridor and was immediately confronted by a security guard. The guard drew his pistol at point-blank range but before Tim could react, Eric tackled the man around the waist.

As the man escaped Eric's grasp, Tim shot him with the M-16.

The man fell, lifeless, to the floor.

"Where do we go now?" Tim shouted.

They entered a small room.

"You killed a man," Eric said as he wiped perspiration from his brow.

"No kidding," Tim said. "But don't ask me how I feel because I don't have time to think about it."

"Follow me," Eric said as he pointed to a staircase in the far corner.

At the top of the staircase, they encountered another security guard with pistol raised.

"Stop!" the guard demanded.

Tim fired his weapon at the man, killing him.

They could hear the footsteps of a large group of people running up the staircase, so they scrambled into a break room filled with candy and soda machines.

"We're cornered," Tim said. He looked around the room. "Let me see if there is any way to get out." He scurried about on his hands and knees, finding no air condition vents or ducts. However, the ceiling panels were square, light weight, and appeared to be easily removable.

Atop a table, Tim stood on his toes and reached up to the panels, pushing one of them out of place. He looked at the space above the ceiling and found no opening, vent or crevice to squeeze through and get out. "There's no way out from up there," Tim said.

A voice speaking over an intercom system jolted their focus. "The building is being evacuated. Please leave immediately. All employees leave the building."

One minute later, the door to the snack room burst open and eight armed security guards surrounded the two young men. They grabbed them both by the arm, heaving them to the floor.

"You will please treat us with respect," Eric said as one of the guards burrowed his knee into Tim's back. "I am the nephew of your leader… Jon Actund."

"Keep your mouth shut!" the lead security guard said. "Don't give us any trouble."

Chapter Thirty-One—Incarceration

Tim and Eric were taken to an adjoining building where they were led into a small room with folding chairs and a small table.

"Why would our leader's nephew be involved in this chaos?" the leader of the security guards asked.

"Because I was trying to observe your facilities up close without being identified so I could report back to my uncle with a confidential assessment of the facility," Eric lied. "But your aggressive goons at the gate overreacted and well, it's a tragedy."

"Could that be true?" one of the guards asked.

"I'm afraid that you are all in serious trouble," Eric said.

"Fear not, gentlemen," the leader said. "If he is really who he says, then he is safe and healthy. They gunned down two of our men and we have no bloodshed on our hands. Confine them until we confirm everything we need to know."

They were led to a cell in the basement of the building.

"We're lucky they haven't killed us yet," Eric said.

"Thanks for sticking with me! You're a good friend," Tim replied.

Nearly three hours passed. Finally, one of the security guards came walking down the hall. "You have a visitor."

Jon Actund strode angrily towards the cell.

"Hello, Uncle Jon," Eric said meekly.

"What do I see before my eyes? My only blood relative behind bars. I don't understand," Actund declared. "Explain to me what happened!"

Eric lowered his head.

"Your nephew is a fine young man who was trying to help me," Tim said.

"You have gotten him in trouble," Actund shouted, his face turning a crimson red. "I know who you are, Tim Jennings! We checked your identification in your wallet."

"Your nephew has done nothing wrong," Tim said.

Impulsively, Actund reached into the cell between the bars, grabbed Tim by the shirt and pulled him closer.

As Tim tried to reach in between the bars, the security guard intervened and stood between the two men.

"I'll tear your heart out!" Tim shouted.

"I'll take your heart, dice it, and sprinkle it in my lunch salad," Actund countered.

"I decided to help him of my own free will because he's looking for a woman he loves," Eric said.

"At this facility?"

"Yes," Eric said.

"I don't care about your excuses," Actund said. He pointed at Tim. "You have dragged my nephew into this killing spree."

"Uncle Jon, I chose to help my friend," Eric said.

"Did you come here to find the woman and for no other reason?" Actund asked Tim.

"I love her," Tim said. "Your organization makes me sick."

"I believe, gentlemen," Actund said to the two security guards standing on duty, "that we have a subversive on our hands! You expect us to believe that you are a lovesick puppy? Who are you affiliated with… the American government?"

"I am a proud American but I am not with the government!"

Eric shook his head in disbelief. "You are ruining any chance you had of getting out of here alive," he whispered to Tim.

"Stay out of this!" Tim said, his upper lip quivering.

"But we still have a chance to find Nancy."

"I'm not getting out of here alive. It's too late."

"What are you whispering about?" Actund demanded.

"Let me do the talking," Eric said as he turned to his uncle. "He is a man in love and he has been frustrated. I am sure that you can understand how he is feeling because you lost the only woman that you ever loved."

"I am angry!" Actund said.

"It could have easily been me that killed your guards," Eric said. "I don't believe in your philosophy and my heart and mind cannot support it."

His eyes filling with tears, Actund shouted, "You do not believe such talk. This scoundrel is brainwashing you."

"No sir. I'm afraid that's not true. I support freedom and love and togetherness," Eric said.

"You have all of those opportunities with me," Actund said as he gripped a cell bar. "I am your only family and I give you freedom and joy and everything you will ever need."

"But that is not the point," Eric said. "I want there to be peace in the world."

"There will never be peace in the world. Our obligation is to create a society of strong leaders who can manage to keep order and foster prosperity."

"But Uncle Jon, there is no natural attrition. You will breed a new brand of people from your laboratory theories… master manipulation."

"Our people will ensure long term order in the world," Actund said. "Let's get my nephew out of the cell with this vermin and give him a good meal."

"What do we do with the American?" the lead security guard asked.

"Leave him here for now. I will make a final decision on his fate tomorrow." Actund snapped his fingers and pointed at his nephew, then walked away.

The guards opened the door of the cell. One of them pulled out his revolver and pointed it at Tim. "No sudden moves please."

The other guard led Eric out of the cell.

As he stared up at the ceiling, it seemed to be closing in on him so he turned on his side. A small spider scurried over Tim's pillow in front of his face. The minutes droned by slowly, inching along.

Eventually, a doctor came to visit Tim. A man with gray, curly hair and dark, sagging circles under his eyes, the doctor seemed solemn.

"My name is Dr. Brillo." He reached for his medical bag and pulled out a syringe with a long needle.

"What is that for?"

"It will make you rest," the doctor said as he grabbed Tim's arm, found a vein, and pressed on the syringe.

Tim gritted his teeth in pain. Within thirty seconds, he was uncontrollably fatigued and losing consciousness. He was out cold within another ten seconds.

Tim awoke, still in the cell, but he was strapped into a gurney with restraint belts and stripped of all his clothing except for his underwear.

"What's going on?" Tim cried as he struggled to free himself, nearly tipping the gurney completely over on its side.

Dr. Vog led a group of people into the cell, two men in white coats and two women who appeared to be nurses.

"It is so good to see you," Dr. Vog said.

"What are you doing to me?" Tim shouted.

"You are about to serve the program in ways you never imagined," Dr. Vog cackled.

"What you are going to do with me?"

One of the men wheeled the gurney out of the cell and pushed it down the hallway.

"Your value to us will be extraordinary, a living cadaver, so to speak, for experimentation. The final insult to your inability to support us," Dr. Vog said as he walked alongside the gurney. The group of people followed close behind.

He was pushed down several hallways and into a dirty loading dock area. An ambulance drove up and two attendants got out of the vehicle and loaded Tim, still strapped on the gurney, into the back of the ambulance as Dr. Vog climbed into the back.

The ambulance set out down the road.

Taken to the main compound and sent to a clinic, Tim was released from the gurney as armed security guards stood next to him. A nurse took a hypodermic needle and gave Tim a shot in the left arm, causing him to feel a strange sensation surge through his body. It began in his toes and made its way to his legs, a fiery and piercing sensation. Tim's knees buckled as he wobbled and stumbled to the bed. His stomach churned and his chest heaved while a spinning sensation developed in his head as his eyes rolled back. The entire room seemed to spin in circles as Tim's eyes diluted and watered; his vision a blurry mess. With his entire energy sapped, Tim passed out.

Ten minutes later, Tim awoke in a vile, agitated state. With no rational thoughts going through his mind, he jolted up from his bed. Two bulky assistants entered the room, grabbed Tim by the arms and held him on the bed. A nurse opened her medical kit and produced a hypodermic needle.

"This will reverse the effects of the other dosage," the nurse said as she embedded the syringe into his skin.

Within a minute, Tim was quiet and still as his faculties returned to normal.

With little time to reflect on the experience, Tim was sent to a small gymnasium with free standing weights, various athletic equipment, and basketball goals at both ends. The two assistants stopped in front of a long table attached to a keyboard panel with numerous buttons.

One of the bulky assistants turned to Tim. "Get down on the table."

Tim stared warily at the table. "What's this all about?"

"We are conducting experiments for the good of the organization," the nurse said. "Please cooperate."

"I'm not getting on that contraption!" Tim turned to walk away, but the two men grabbed him, picked him up off his feet, and threw him on the table.

They clasped restraints around his wrists and ankles and a waistband around his midsection. Then they connected six wires at various points on his body, stretching his arms above his head.

"What are you gonna do?" Tim moaned.

The nurse pressed a button.

Tim felt a riveting torrent of shock surge through his body, a sensation like hundreds of sharp needles piercing his skin. The pain was sharp and excruciating.

"Help me!! Stop this, please!!!"

The nurse stared at Tim with a cold glare, looked at her watch, and let thirty seconds elapse. She gave a casual nod to one of the assistants and he turned the machine to the 'off' position.

The machine transitioned to a slow purring stop as Tim sensed his muscles recovering, his tendons unwinding, and his entire body relaxing.

"The drug should have dulled the pain more than it did," the nurse said.

As she spoke, Tim looked across the room and saw two huge glass chambers. The nurse pointed at the chambers and gave instructions for Tim to be tossed into one of them.

Within one minute, Tim felt a cold steam engulf him from the roof of the chamber. A digital temperature gauge on the outside flashed '52' degrees Fahrenheit. Then it was '45', '30', '20', '12', '0', '-5', '-10', and finally, '-20'.

His teeth chattered as his skin started to turn blue.

The glass that imprisoned Tim developed a thin layer of frost. He huddled in the corner, folding his arms and legs into the fetal position as he began to shake uncontrollably. With icicles forming on his eyebrows, he could not control his impulses or muscles. There was a quivering in his biceps and spasms in his abdominal muscles. In a short time, Tim began to lose consciousness, falling down, face first on the floor.

As he was about to black out, the door of the chamber swung open and the two assistants walked in. They dragged him out of the chamber, shaking him until the color in his face came back. One of the men slapped him on both his cheeks until Tim sat up on his knees.

As the nurse approached, she gazed at him sternly with no sympathy on her face at all. "Let's get him on the examining table."

Tim was hoisted on a table, his vital signs checked. His pulse was very low and his heart rate unstable. His vocal cords were nearly frozen, his eardrums numb, and there was no feeling in two of his fingers.

"I'm probably catching pneumonia… Give me a flu shot or something!"

The woman stared blankly at Tim while feeling his forehead. She shoved a thermometer in his mouth. "You will survive because you are a healthy young man."

A man in a white medical jacket and a pair of dress pants entered the room. He wore a strange pair of glasses that were slightly askew at the bridge of his nose, the lenses an off-peach color.

"My name is Dr. Sluggert. Now we come to the main event."

Tim's heart sank. "At least tell me what you are trying to accomplish."

"Follow me," the doctor said. He led them to an adjoining room that was completely dark.

"Why don't you turn on the lights?" Tim asked.

The doctor flipped the wall switch.

Corpses were all over the room, on tables and in big tanks filled with liquid. The two medical assistants were as surprised as Tim at the scene.

"You appear to be uncomfortable at the sight of death," the doctor said.

"I'm not uncomfortable at the sight of death," Tim said. "I'm uncomfortable with what you are doing."

"These poor souls met such a tragic ending but at least we can say that they are doing some good now," the doctor said. He walked between the tanks, stopped at one and slapped his hands on it like he was banging on bongo drums. "About half of them are assisted suicide," the doctor said. "The other half are victims of car accidents, domestic disputes, full blown suicides, a couple of murders, and several 'unknowns.'"

"I don't believe in assisted suicide. You have no right to take someone's life," Tim said. "How did you collect so many bodies?"

"It's called marketing. We advertised that we were searching for people who would like to participate in experimental research in fighting cancer. We asked for terminal cases."

"You mean to tell me that you misled these helpless, desperate people into believing you could cure them?"

"No. We never promised that we could cure them."

"What did you do when they got here? Make them guinea pigs like you did to me?"

"We're doing valid experiments and they participated before they were relieved of their misery," the doctor said.

"You're telling me that all of these people agreed to be euthanized?"

"They were all put out of their misery."

Tim looked at the bodies. "They didn't come here to die. You people are all cold-blooded killers!"

"We are engaged in a program that is doing everything possible to preserve life… to prolong life, ultimately eliminating death completely."

"So you're involved in the anti-aging program they told me about earlier?"

"Yes, and we are getting closer to reaching our goals."

"You people have reached the height of arrogance," Tim shouted. "Only God controls death and aging! What are you trying to prove by keeping corpses floating around?"

"Their greatest value was the experimentation on their bodies when these people were living, but we are still studying the post-mortem effects of some of our experiments."

As Tim walked around the tanks, he noticed that the bodies were all nude, stripped of their worldly belongings. Many of them had no hair, presumably because of their cancer treatment. In the corner of the room, a rope separated six corpses on tables. "What's the story with these bodies?"

"They are homeless people so we will probably keep them in cold storage until we need to use them. They're basically healthy bodies, as healthy as a dead body can be!"

The two medical assistants broke out in laughter.

"To eliminate death, we must conquer cancer, and that is why my friends in this room have been so valuable." The doctor looked over the room of dead bodies with pride. "They did not die in vain."

"You are a reprehensible person, so don't give me that noble routine," Tim said.

"I expect to go down in history for my cancer research."

"What are you planning to do with me?"

"You can see that all of our friends around the room are deceased and we need some living bodies."

"When you finish with me... then what?"

"I can't tell you," the doctor said.

"At least do me the favor of letting me know if my life ends today or tomorrow or whenever!"

"I do not know what your future looks like," the doctor said. "I have my orders to experiment with you for a few days. That's all I know."

Tim threw his arms up in disgust. "I want to talk with Jon Actund!"

"Oh, you will have plenty of time to talk," the doctor said.

The two assistants led Tim into an adjoining room where he was ordered to stretch out on a table. Dr. Sluggert applied tiny pins all over his body.

"What is this, acupuncture?" Tim asked. "You gotta be more original than that."

"We are simply testing the pressure points in your body," the doctor said. "I need to chronicle which ones are painful and which ones are numb."

The doctor asked Tim about the sensation in various parts of his body after placement of the pins,, using a chart to register Tim's reaction.

After removal of the pins, Dr. Sluggert produced a set of syringes. "We need to test your reaction to these dosages of medicine." He took Tim's left arm, found a vein and sank the syringe slowly into his skin.

"What's this gonna do to me?" Tim asked.

"We'll know soon," the doctor said.

The doctor pulled a peach from his medical bag and began to eat it, gnawing on it like a rabbit. Juice dripped down his chin and on to his white overcoat.

"Delicious," he said as he winked at Tim.

"When do I start feeling something?"

"Any minute now," the doctor said as he pulled out a bag of grapes. He tossed a grape up in the air and caught it in his mouth.

Convulsions started, followed by muscle spasms; limbs, arms, and legs all shaking. "What's happening to me?" he screamed.

The doctor stood over Tim and grinned. "Ahaaaaa!!!"

As Tim looked up, the ceiling above him seemed to spin as he blacked out.

A few minutes later, Tim awoke, but barely, in a strange state of mind. He felt as if he was semi-conscious with one-half of his brain alert, the other half totally disoriented, and his vision blurry.

Still in the examining room, Tim watched as the door opened and a woman peered in. Young and beautiful, the woman made eye contact with Tim.

"Nancy, come here!" Tim cried as he opened and closed his eyes frantically to clear his vision. He could see well enough to distinguish her basic beauty. The woman looked like Nancy. "Come here. I love you." As he reached out his arms, he watched the woman close the door and she was gone. "Nancy!!!" Tim lost consciousness again.

An hour later, Tim awoke again, stumbled out of bed, and found the door of his room locked. He pounded the door with his fist. "Nancy!" he moaned.

Soon the door was unlocked and opened. Jon Actund walked in, accompanied by Lugar.

"Where's Nancy?" Tim demanded.

"I see that our experiments have not sidetracked you. Still blabbering about this woman!" Actund laughed.

"I saw her with my own two eyes. Where is she?"

"You don't look too well, my friend," Actund said.

"Why are you killing me with these crazy experiments? Answer me that."

"Your contribution to science," Actund said as he laughed under his breath.

"I've come all this way," Tim said. "To find her."

"The woman is not here," Actund scoffed as Tim showed him her photo. A strange, unique expression came over Actund's face. "You don't know this woman."

"What do you mean?"

"You're wasting my time," Actund said. "We'll be traveling soon and you're going with us." He motioned for Lugar to follow him out of the room.

Chapter Thirty-Two—St. Augustine

Saturday, August 10, 7:44 a.m.

"Where are we going?" Tim asked.

"St. Augustine, Florida," the security guard said as he led Tim out of the building. "The oldest city in America!"

"I've seen St. Augustine, thank you." Tim laughed. "Why are we going there?"

"Cause that's where the boss is going and that's where he wants you!" the man said. "He's participating in a national conference on aging. There will be all sorts of doctors, scientists, and professors that are attending this shindig."

"Yes! In the city of the Fountain of Youth," Tim said. "Very convenient."

"We've got a plane ready to take us there," the security guard said.

Within minutes, Tim was in a van with three security guards. It pulled onto a gravel driveway and traveled a moderate distance until it pulled to a stop next to a metal pre-fabricated building. Behind it, a sleek airplane idled on a dirt airstrip. Thirty minutes later, the plane was airborne with two pilots, three security guards, and Tim on board.

Tim looked out the window of the airplane as it approached St. Augustine. The lighthouse at the beach came into view first as the plane turned inland and made a path directly over the famous Bridge of Lions. To the right, they saw the Castillo de San Marcos, an old Spanish fort that stood in remarkably good condition. The entire Historic District of the city looked quaint yet regal as the plane flew over.

"What's that?" a security guard asked. He pointed at a huge building situated near the town square.

"That's Flagler College," Tim said. He had spent several summer vacations in St. Augustine with his parents back in his high school years. "It used to be the grand Ponce de Leon Hotel. It was built by Henry Flagler." The men in the plane looked at him with blank expressions. "You know, the railroad magnate. It was turned into Flagler College in 1968."

Shops, churches, museums, and marvelously crafted historic homes dotted the city landscape. "We'll be staying at the Bay Breeze Inn, back near the marina," the lead security guard said.

"Will you take us through town?" Tim asked the driver as they climbed into a van after the plane's landing. The driver looked at the lead security guard in the front passenger seat who grunted his approval.

Sandwiched in between the two other security guards, Tim felt some sense of relief to be back on American soil as the van turned right onto Orange Street. Tim looked back at the location of the old city gates. Many years ago, a huge wall enclosed the entire city of St. Augustine. All that remained of the wall were the posts, two ten foot pillars made of stone, previously attached to the gate at the city entrance.

Tim had read and heard many remarkable stories about old St. Augustine, tales of love, war, wealth, and squalor. The city was founded in 1565 and some of the old buildings had stood the test of time. It was almost as if the van was transported back in time several centuries.

Inside the city gates, the oldest wooden schoolhouse in the country still stood. The cypress and cedar frame building had been a private day school.

The van turned onto Cordova Street and soon they approached Flagler College, awe-inspiring to behold. The college, formerly the Ponce de Leon Hotel, was a beauty in its day, a cathedral of aristocracy and power. Built in 1888, the main building had many wings and two towers. Recognized as the ultimate example of Spanish Renaissance architecture, the structure was listed on the National Register of Historic Places.

"The conference is being held here at the college," the lead security guard said.

"Tell us more about it," Tim said.

"It's the old timer's conference," the lead security guard said.

The van driver laughed. "Not quite. It's the National Conference on Aging and Life Expectancy."

Eagerly, he pointed out the Lightner Museum across the street that housed many items from America's Gilded Age. Originally, the building was another resort hotel built by Henry Flagler, called the Hotel Alcazar.

"Mr. Flagler wanted to make St. Augustine the American Riviera!" the van driver said after he explained the history of the Lightner Museum.

The van turned left onto King Street then passed the Government House Museum and the Plaza de la Constitution, considered the symbolic center of town. At the end of King Street, the van turned left and drove parallel with the bay for three blocks.

Soon the van turned into the parking lot of the Bay Breeze Inn. As the crew climbed out of the van, Tim looked out at the bay. It was a beautiful vista with rolling, blue water and the thick, green landscape of the nearby shore.

Chapter Thirty-Three—Nancy!?

"Nancy!" Tim witnessed a woman getting in a sports utility vehicle with three men. As he opened the door of his motel room, one of Actund's security guards immediately confronted him.

"What do you want?" the man shouted.

Tim pointed at the car as it sped away. "Did you see that? Where are they taking her?"

"Who?"

Tim tried to push the man aside, but the bald, muscular brute was too strong as he grabbed him by the wrist and wrenched his arm. With the upper part of his body immobilized, Tim kicked the man in his right shin.

A struggle ensued as they pushed and shoved each other until they were leaning against the flimsy metal railing of the second story walkway. Tim thrust his shoulder against the man's chin.

Their collective weight forced one section of the railing to come loose, creating an opening that caused Tim and the man to fall over the edge. Tim hit a car in the parking lot with a glancing blow then dropped to the pavement as the man landed face first onto the pavement.

Out of breath and wobbly at the knees, Tim ran after the SUV. The vehicle passed the Statue of Ponce de Leon with the famous Bridge of Lions immediately to the right. It stretched out over Matanzas Bay, leading travelers onto St. Augustine Beach.

A steady stream of vehicles was coming on and off the Bridge of Lions, creating a traffic jam that forced the SUV to come to a sudden halt. The unexpected stop allowed Tim to make up the distance. As he reached the vehicle, he rapped on the rear window. All four of the occupants turned around as Tim failed in his attempt to open the locked rear door.

The front seat passenger rolled his window down and threw a cup of hot coffee in Tim's face, forcing him to fall back and stumble against the curb. By the time he got to his feet, the vehicle was moving again slowly along the street, making a left turn after the statue and heading west on Cathedral Place.

As Tim ran through the road, traffic converged from four different directions. Nearly sideswiped by a vehicle coming from the opposite direction, he dashed through a grassy park called the Plaza de la Constitution to try to overtake the SUV.

A large group of tourists blocked the path in the park. A young black woman walked side by side with a small toddler, forcing Tim to hurdle the child.

Meanwhile, the SUV inched along in the traffic a block and a half up Cathedral Place. As soon as the driver saw Tim approaching, he rolled his window down and aimed a pistol at him. Instinctively, Tim jumped on the back of the vehicle, landing on the top of the trunk.

In an unexpected move, the driver stopped the vehicle in the parking lot of a bank as one of the men scrambled out of it. Tim slid down the side of the vehicle, thrust his arm through the open door and unlocked the back door closest to him. In the next motion, he opened that door, grabbing the woman by the arm.

"Let's go Nancy!"

Tim pulled her out of the car and onto the sidewalk as the woman resisted. Tim saw wild-eyed terror in her face.

"Nancy! It's me!" Tim screamed. "Follow me! We'll find somewhere safe!" He pulled her along until they reached a closed street previously transformed into the center of a walking mall. For several blocks on either side of the street, souvenir and gift shops were open.

The men from the vehicle trailed them on foot. The street was full of elbow-to-elbow shoppers.

"Come on," Tim said. "Let's get lost in the crowd!" They forged ahead into the mass of humanity.

As they ran, Tim looked at the woman's face. She had a sullen, ashen appearance with a frown almost molded into her face.

"I see them," one of the pursuers said from the crowd.

Tim dragged the woman along at a faster pace as they turned the corner beyond a jewelry store and onto a narrow alley where they dodged cardboard boxes and a stray black and white cat. When they reached the far side of the building, Tim stopped long enough to catch his breath. He peered beyond the corner of the building to see the two men running through the crowd.

"I think we tricked 'em," Tim said. He felt a tidal wave of emotion engulf him as he turned to the woman and said, "I love you!" He tried to hug her but she turned away.

Hurt and fear overcame Tim in a way that he had never before experienced. He felt numb, almost cold and chilled in the middle of the summer day. As he looked at the woman, she turned her back to him, her body posture foreign to him.

"Nancy! I love you! Don't you know that?" Tim said.

She did not turn around to face him.

"Why don't you say something to me?"

She took a few steps away from him.

"Speak to me!" Tim shouted. "What have they done to you?" He put his hands on her shoulders and caressed them, but the woman reacted with an immediate cringe.

"What's wrong with you?" Tim moaned. "If you only knew what I've been going through! I've risked my life and I've killed! I've hurt other people in my search for you!" He grabbed her by the left arm and pulled her up to his body.

"No." The distraught woman turned the corner and ran through the narrow alley like a wild animal.

Tim took off after her. As he rounded the corner, he tripped over an uneven patch in the pavement, allowing her to put additional distance between them. As he ran onto Cordova Street, Tim frantically looked in every direction, but he had lost her. Throwing up his arms in disgust, Tim looked at the south end of the street and Flagler College.

A walk along Sevilla Street put Tim in the path of the old Zorayda Castle, a nearby museum. He was on the outskirts of the tourist section. A low-income housing project was located one block away, its units in a sad state of disrepair.

On a hunch, Tim figured that she walked back towards the center of town.

He found his way to King Street, leading directly into the town square. The Government House Museum was on the left side of the road, the seat of local government many years ago.

Tim ran to the grounds of the museum and spotted a young couple leaving the building. He stopped to speak to them.

"Tell me, have you seen an attractive brunette woman running through this area?"

"I saw a young woman a couple of minutes ago. Running? Yes. She was running! Very unusual!" the woman said.

"What direction was she headed?"

The man pointed across the street. "The girl ran into that wax museum. You know, Potter's Wax Museum."

Tim hustled to the museum, housed in an old storefront setting, located near an old-fashioned drug store. A pimply-faced, redheaded teen-age boy stared out from the ticket window.

After he purchased the ticket, Tim reached the first display inside the air-conditioned building. It depicted George Washington crossing the Potomac River. The next display featured Betsy Ross sewing the U.S. flag.

In the adjoining room, he found himself surrounded by a display of wax figures in the likeness of former First Ladies.

Out of the corner of his eye, Tim thought he saw one of the figures move then crouch down in the far corner.

It was a living, breathing person. "Nancy!" Tim cried. "I love you. Let me help."

She responded by cowering in a fetal position.

Tim hurdled a railing that separated the public from the display.

"It's me! Tim! I love you," he said. "I'll help you forget this nightmare." As he bent to one knee, the three pursuing men burst into the room, their weapons drawn.

"Get your hands up now!" one of them shouted.

Tim stood slowly to his feet, boiling with anger. "Look at what you've done to her!"

The second man pointed his pistol at Tim. "Shut your trap. We don't have time for your sad stories. Come out of the corner."

A quick scan of the room revealed no escape route, so an improvisation was needed. Tim reached for the fire alarm and pulled it, creating a shrill sound that cascaded throughout the building.

The men were caught off guard so Tim took advantage of the distraction and burst free, grabbing the woman as he fled. Running like a wild beast with its captured prey, Tim barreled ahead at breakneck speed through the halls of the building.

The woman kicked and scratched at Tim as she tried to pull away. "No!" she said. "Let me go. Please."

Tim was taken aback by her voice, distinctively different from what he remembered about Nancy's voice. It was not soft as he remembered it but a dark tone.

"What've they done to you?"

She broke away and ran out the front door. When Tim reached the outside, a burly St. Augustine policeman approached him.

"How many people are still in the building?" the policeman asked.

"Don't worry. Nothing happened," Tim said. "It was a false alarm."

"How do you know?"

"Some kid came running through the place laughing and telling some other kid about pulling the fire alarm."

Tim ran across the street, looking in every direction. Suddenly, the men who had been pursuing Tim emerged from behind him. They grabbed him by the arms, dragged him to their vehicle, and threw him into the back seat.

Chapter Thirty-Four— A Surprising Encounter

The vehicle turned left off the main highway and took a side road across the street from an alligator farm attraction. Old abandoned homes with broken windows and peeling paint lined the road.

Tim was ushered into the closest abandoned house, void of furniture and fixtures. The cracked wooden floors were uneven; the wallpaper covered with ugly mildew stains.

"What are we doing here?" Tim shouted.

"You'll know soon enough," one of the men said.

The minutes passed slowly.

"Do you really know what you've gotten yourselves into? How well do you know this man Actund who orders you around like puppets?"

"We know that he's a great man and a leader," the driver said. "He has been very successful in Europe with his scientific research."

"You really don't know him, do you? When you were hired, did you know that kidnapping would be one of your responsibilities?"

The driver looked at his associates. "This ain't kidnapping."

"I don't want to be here right now. I'm being forcibly detained against my will," Tim said. "If that's not kidnapping, I don't know what it could be."

"I got a job to do. Don't complicate things for me and my buddies," the driver said.

"That's the spirit!" a voice from behind them shouted.

Tim turned around to see Dr. Vog standing at the doorway.

"What are you doing here?" Tim asked.

"I'm here to celebrate a new era!"

Tim approached the old man. "I'm here to ram my fist down your throat! You've ruined her."

"Such tension. I see that you haven't toned down your attitude since that spree of mayhem in Germany."

"What did you do to my girlfriend?"

"I have no idea what you are talking about," Dr. Vog said. "I would not know your girlfriend from Lana Turner, but you are a fascinating case study, my friend," Dr. Vog said. "Such venom, yet such humor."

Tim sat down on the floor, his hands over his face.

A vehicle approached and stopped, its headlights beaming brightly through the front window, illuminating the men.

Jon Actund entered the house.

"How was your visit at the conference?" Dr. Vog asked.

"It was routine, completely routine. I don't think I've ever been so bored."

"We must deal with a disturbing problem. Young Mr. Jennings continues to be a pest," Dr. Vog said.

"I understand that he caused problems today but he will no longer be our problem after tonight," Actund said.

"What did you do to her?" Tim shouted.

"The woman is back at the motel, safe and sound," Actund said.

"That's not what I meant," Tim said.

"That woman will go down in history as one of the great female icons," Actund said.

"I'm getting tired of your charades," Tim said.

"And I assure you that I am more than weary of you," Actund said.

A man opened the front door and walked into the room—Nelson Porter, the CIA agent. Confused, Tim watched as Porter nodded his head at Actund and shook hands with Dr. Vog.

"I am so glad to meet you," the doctor said. "I believe you work for the Federal Drug Administration."

"Yes, I do." Porter glanced quickly at Tim.

"Mr. Travers has the pull to get our formula accepted by the FDA," Actund said. "When it happens, we'll have instant credibility."

"Outstanding!" the doctor proclaimed. "But do you also believe in our mission? You've been fully briefed?"

"He doesn't need to know our mission," Actund said. "He is being adequately compensated but I was surprised when you requested that we bring Jennings to the States—alive."

"We must be as discreet as possible," Porter said. "We don't want any messy situations." He nodded in Tim's direction. "A dead American means we have too many cops sniffing around and I don't need that. I'm a respected public servant."

"Of course, I understand your concern," Actund said as he cracked his knuckles. "But he has been a loose cannon and troublemaker. In fact, he jeopardized the entire program today."

"Leave him with me," Porter said. "I'll deal with him, otherwise you get no more cooperation from me."

Actund signaled for everyone to leave the house. "I agreed to your terms. I'll be in touch soon."

When the two men were alone, Tim asked forcefully, "What are you doing? Are you some kind of traitor?"

"Of course not," Porter said quietly.

"Explain to me what's going on here. Are you really CIA?"

"Yes. I'm working covertly. I'm gathering information and evidence against this crowd. In fact, we are getting very close to bringing charges against them."

"Hey dude! I have all the evidence you'd ever want. I'm up to my eyeballs in evidence."

"We know that they are a serious threat. I've been given an order to monitor and document their actions in this country. We're limited in what we can observe in other countries."

"You gotta help me get Nancy to safety then get her some professional help."

"We will if it's needed," Porter leaned against the door. "Something big is going to happen at a press conference."

"Tell me more!"

"You don't need to know anything else."

"How have you managed to dupe these people into believing that you're somebody else?" Tim asked. "What's the point of all that?"

"Actund's trying to get this anti-aging formula accepted by the Federal Drug Administration. I'm his contact and I've promised quick and easy approval." Porter looked out the window as he spoke. "The way Actund's got it figured, he will have taken a big step towards credibility and earned the respect and admiration of people everywhere. Who doesn't want to look and feel younger?"

"He really believes you are this FDA man?"

"Yes and when I found out that he had you captive, I convinced him to bring you to the U.S. for the reasons I stated earlier, otherwise you'd be dead now!"

Tim tugged at his collar. "It's hot in here." He walked in a circular motion around the room a couple of times. "You gotta help me, not only get Nancy back, but also to figure out what they did to her head!"

"I promise that we will do that. In fact, I can assure you that the Agency will provide her with the best medical doctors, psychologists, and psychiatrists available… if it's her."

"I know that it's her because I saw her in person, but I'm afraid it may be too late," Tim said. "She's changed. There was a distance in her eyes that I can't even describe. She may be lost!"

Porter started the ignition of his SUV as Tim climbed in and turned on the radio. A local news report was in progress:

"The Aging Conference continued today in St. Augustine. A wide variety of speakers shared their knowledge of many issues. Attendees appeared to come from all walks of life. Many are scholars from out of state. There are employees of government from every level… local, state, and federal. Representatives of several advocacy organizations for the aged are present as well."

"Think how your outlook on life would be different if everyone lived to be two-hundred years old," Tim said. "We'd all be a little more relaxed and probably less selfish."

"You need to be more relaxed and less selfish," Porter said. "Once I check you into the motel, get some rest and get your mind on the big picture. I don't need you to interfere again! By the way, you're welcome."

"What do you mean?"

"For saving your life, getting you out of Europe."

"Thanks. I appreciate it."

Porter paid for an additional room for Tim in the motel that he was staying in near the Historic District.

"Remember, stay out of it. You're gonna ruin our case against this group if you keep interfering. If that's your gal, we'll get her. Get some sleep." Porter shut the motel door as he left.

Worn out and weary, Tim staggered to the bed and collapsed on it. He was asleep within two minutes.

Chapter Thirty-Five—
The Aging Conference

Sunday, August 11, 12:38 p.m.

Springing up out of bed, Tim could not believe that he had slept so long. He staggered to the door and turned the knob. "Locked!"

He looked out the window. Porter had posted two uniformed police officers outside his door.

Famished, Tim opened a bag of cheese crackers that he had bought from the vending machine the night before. As he munched, Tim remembered Porter's comments about a press conference. He looked for a telephone but there was not one in the room. "Porter can't do this to me!" He slumped down in the nearest chair. "He doesn't believe I saw Nancy and she's obviously not a priority to him. I'm not sitting this one out."

The big window in front of the room could be broken with a forceful swing or two from a chair, but Tim thought better of it because of the noise and commotion it would create. The only alternative was a small window in the bathroom. The width of the opening would be very tight but Tim decided to give it a try. The window was a solid pane of tinted glass. He grabbed a small, manual can opener and used it to pry loose the pane and remove it.

Tucking in his shirttail and sucking in his gut made Tim's frame as narrow as possible. He thrust his body upward and through the window opening, slithering like a cold-blooded snake through it. He got stuck around the hips but only momentarily, then he passed through and plummeted to the ground.

Stopping against the corner of the building to catch his breath, Tim saw a bed and breakfast inn behind the motel. A block down the road, he could see the "Oldest House." It was the oldest home in America, a two-hundred-sixty-year-old Spanish Colonial structure.

It was a crisp, bright afternoon. Tim could see Flagler College at the end of King Street. When he reached the gated main entrance to the college, he looked around cautiously, fearing a possible encounter with one of Actund's henchmen.

Upon entering the gate, Tim stood in a neatly manicured courtyard. He approached the first person he saw, a young man with a goatee and long side-burns.

"Where's the aging conference?"

"Is that the meeting with the old codgers, dude?" he asked.

"Yes. That's it."

"Why would I know that? Ask that lady over there." He pointed to a table at the far corner of the courtyard.

"How do I register for the conference?" Tim asked the woman seated behind the table. She was a pleasant-looking young woman..

"We have a fee of ninety-five dollars for registration that helps to underwrite all the expenses of organizing the conference."

"I only want to go to one event. It's a press conference held by Jon Actund."

"The press conference is today at 4:00 p.m. at the Fountain of Youth attraction down the street. You must be a registered and paid attendee to sit in on the press conference." She stuck her chin up in the air and rolled her eyes indignantly.

"I'm not paying ninety-five bucks," Tim said under his breath.

Tim slipped past the woman as she talked to a late arriving attendee and walked into the grand lobby of the former hotel. He felt as if he were in a time capsule because the walls were covered with expertly crafted wooden images of trees and wild animals. A giant, glistening chandelier hung from the high ceiling. The lobby had an aura, a flavor, a smell almost, of the 1920s. Tim could imagine F. Scott Fitzgerald roaming the hallways.

As he looked around the room, Tim observed an unusual mixture of people. College students languished around the lobby, but he also saw senior citizens of all sizes and races.

One of the men that chased Tim all over St. Augustine the previous day was coming down a long hallway. Tim slid into the nearest room, a vacant classroom.

As soon as he slammed the door shut, Tim stood face to face with a very short, odd-looking man. He was probably in his mid-forties with a receding hairline and a wiry handle bar mustache. His eyes had a wild, faraway look in them. A miniature replica of the Eiffel Tower dangled from one of his ear lobes.

"Linwood Smothers. I teach mathematics at the school. Arrrrrr… Who goes there?" The man did a weak impression of a pirate.

"Don't worry. I'll leave."

"Are you here for the conference?" Smothers asked. "We waste too much time worrying about old people and too much money! When their usefulness is over, we need to get rid of them."

"You mean put 'em away in an institution?" Tim asked.

"No. I mean euthanize them, but do it in a quick, painless way." The man almost gloated over the shock value of his comment.

"You're crazy!" Tim said.

"Not at all. I'm merely being practical."

"So you support legalization of murder?" Tim asked.

"Not murder. Euthanasia, my friend." He pulled out a small pack of saltine crackers from his shirt pocket and put one in his mouth. "Quick and simple and cost efficient."

"We're a civilized society."

"But we're already beginning to accept it on a voluntary basis. Noble men and women are declaring that they should be eliminated when there is no medical solution to their ailments. I can hear doctors pulling the plugs now. Listen!" Smothers sarcastically put his hand to his ear and tilted his head as if listening.

The door opened.

An old, feeble man in a maintenance worker's uniform walked into the room.

"Hello, Mr. Bartlow," Smothers said.

In a weak acknowledgement, the maintenance man grunted something below his breath and crept towards the garbage can.

"Take Mr. Bartlow," Smothers said. "He serves very little purpose, quite expendable."

"But what about his family?" Tim asked.

"He has no family. We would be doing him a favor, ending his loneliness."

"It's murder!" Tim said as he left the room.

As he rounded the corner, Tim ran into a small group of people mingling in the hallway and looking at the floor.

"What's the problem?" Tim asked an elderly man.

"Somebody died!"

"Who was it?" Tim pushed his way through the crowd, looked to the floor and saw an old woman face down. Two paramedics leaned over her body.

"What happened?" Tim asked.

"The lady just fell over," a college student said.

"That happens all the time at these conferences," a senior citizen said. "There will be a couple more that fall out by the end of the business day."

The woman's lifeless body was placed on a stretcher. Tim watched as a distraught old man, apparently the woman's husband, fell to his knees in shock and despair, weeping like a baby.

No one in the crowd reacted. Tim almost walked away too, but as he turned to leave, sympathy and compassion overwhelmed him.

"Sir, I'm so sorry for your loss," Tim said. "Let's get you out of this crowd."

"I have nothing now. She's all I had!" the man cried.

Tim grimaced as he patted the man on the back. "I'm sure that she lived a full, satisfying life."

A police officer arrived to speak to the man.

As Tim walked away, the old man's comment rattled around in his mind. Tim had always considered a life of seventy years to be a blessing. He was only about thirty-five percent of the way there himself but he shuddered at how quickly the years were beginning to pass.

His scrambled thoughts shifting seemly every other second, Tim thought about Actund's schemes and their probable universal appeal. He was trying to take advantage of the hope of everybody by conquering death and thumbing a nose at mortality in favor of eternal life.

Metal double doors stood at the end of a short hallway. As he pushed the doors open, warm, dry air hit Tim squarely in the face. He was in the service and maintenance entrance at the rear of the building.

A church across the street was clearly visible. The building was constructed of red brick, its shutters black. The steeple reached majestically to the sky, a metal cross perched atop it.

As Tim looked at the church, he wondered why God had placed him in his situation. He had been lukewarm to God and at no time had Tim earnestly sought God's will for his life. He simply believed in a God who created things and little else.

Until Tiffany's prodding and encouragement, Tim had never been concerned about his relationship with God and His Son, Jesus Christ. Intellectually, Tim could not accept the fact that the Lord would care even remotely about him. But Tiffany was persistent. She had convinced him to go to church.

As a reluctant visitor to Tiffany's church, Tim heard the plan of salvation that God offered through His Son, Jesus Christ. His exposure to the plan had been repetitive and consistent. Tim wondered if perhaps God wanted him involved in his plight in order to strengthen him or for him to have an impact on other people. And what would Jon Actund's master strategy actually do to the world? Would God want people to stop aging? Could he allow eternal life on earth?

"Why am I mixed up in this mess?" Tim asked aloud.

"That's what I keep asking!"

Tim whirled around to find Nelson Porter standing in front of him.

"You found me!"

"You are seriously compromising what we are trying to accomplish."

"Nancy might be at the conference. It's my chance to grab her."

"Now, I've promised you that we will take care of her."

"That's a promise that you can't be confident in making."

"You have to let our way of doing things play out. No interference!" Porter shouted.

"What are you going to do if I don't cooperate?" Tim asked. "Bundle me up and throw away the key?"

"You can't interfere."

As he shook his head in disgust, Tim watched Porter wave at a black SUV as it pulled over to the curb. Three well-dressed men got out of the vehicle and walked towards Tim. He ran behind a restaurant on the other side of the street and turned east onto Cuna Street, noticing a used bookstore down the street.

A second black SUV pulled up and came to a stop down the street when Tim came into clear view. Two men jumped out of the vehicle as Tim shimmied up the side of a chain link fence.

As his pursuers broke into full stride, Tim cleared the fence and found himself in a damp, dirty alley. He ran until he reached the next building, a toy store called The St. Augustine Toy Chest. He ran around to the front of the building and ducked into the store.

The place was a treasure trove of toys and games. A huge pile of stuffed animals and dolls immediately caught Tim's attention. Military figurines lined one shelf, model cars filled up another one, and sporting equipment was crammed into a third. One side of the room was full of classics, including Chutes and Ladders, Risk, Twister, Hula-Hoops, and the Easy Bake Oven. Across the room, the modern favorites, including video games and other electronic gizmos, were available.

A heavyset, small woman, wearing glasses, greeted Tim. "May I help you?" she asked.

"Huh? Yes." Tim looked out the window. "Where's the restroom?"

"It's in the back, but it is not for the public."

Through the window in the front door, Tim could see two of the men approach. Sweat formed on his brow. "Please."

"All right. Follow me."

As the woman walked away, Tim dove headlong into the pile of stuffed toys, burying himself underneath a plush variety of teddy bears, piglets, baby dolls, and dinosaurs.

"Madam, did you see a desperate-looking young man in here?" one of the men asked as he entered the store.

"Why, yes! Where did he go?"

"He's hiding. Let's search the place," the man said.

Underneath the stuffed animals, Tim sat pensively. He could hear boxes moved and toys kicked aside. He sensed one of the men standing directly over him.

"Now that is just about enough!" the woman said. "You have no right to ruin our merchandise."

"She's right. Lay off it. He obviously got away," the second man said.

The front door opened and closed but Tim sensed a trap, uneasy about the entire situation. He listened intently as the seconds dripped by. Dead silence. He did not even hear the woman moving about, a legitimate concern.

After five minutes, he heard movement on the part of the woman as the telephone rang.

"Hello," the woman said.

Tim sprung from underneath the stuffed animals and sprinted towards the door as two of the men emerged from behind a shelf.

One of the men grabbed Tim's shoulder as he swung back wildly, pushing him aside. He reached the other side of the street, ran into a parking lot, scaled a rickety, termite infested, wooden fence, and landed on his knees in a dirty gully. It was overgrown with kudzu and sprinkled with smelly garbage, aluminum cans, empty bags, and assorted paper.

Chapter Thirty-Six—
Refuge in the House of the Lord

A church steeple rose majestically into the sky, white at its base and red near the top. A steel cross was affixed to its apex. Feeling drawn to the church, Tim had a sudden desire to seek refuge in God's House.

He stopped in front of the main entrance to the church, admiring the beautiful stained glass windows that decorated the outside of the building. The front of the church featured four Doric columns, huge oak double doors, and an inviting staircase with brass hand railings.

A middle-aged man came out of a side door.

"May I help you?" the man asked.

As Tim stared at the building, he asked, "Would it be OK to go into the church? Into the sanctuary?"

"Do you need some help?"

"No!" Tim said. "I want some peace and quiet."

"Well… well… I suppose you could go into the sanctuary for a short time. The pastor and the choir director should be here for a while and the janitor, too. We had a great Sunday morning service."

Tim walked up the front staircase, entered the church through the big double doors, and walked into the sanctuary. Struck almost immediately by the beauty and serenity of the sanctuary, he saw twenty pews on either side of the center aisle. Red velvet carpet lined the floor.

The pulpit was a finely carved mahogany structure. A gold cross hung from the ceiling, bathed in streams of light that emanated from bulbs in the ceiling. The shadow of the cross fell neatly against the rear wall behind the choir loft.

"Beautiful, isn't it?"

Tim whirled around to see a wrinkled man with short gray hair.

"It's great!" Tim said.

"I'm Pastor Carlton Wheeler." He extended his hand.

Tim accepted the greeting reluctantly as they shook hands directly in front of the pulpit.

"So this is where you practice your trade." Tim nodded towards the pulpit.

"It's a calling."

"I admire people like you. Always living right and helping people," Tim said.

The pastor sat down on the front pew and motioned for Tim to do the same.

Hesitantly, Tim sat down.

"What can we do for you?"

"All I need is some time alone with God. I need… uh… God to be here with me."

Pastor Wheeler smiled. "God's everywhere, but it does sometimes help to find the serenity of a house of worship. However, let's back up for a moment. Are you homeless?"

"No, I'm not homeless. I have a happy home in Atlanta."

"By the way, I don't think I caught your name."

Tim tilted his head slightly. "I don't think I tossed it."

"If you need help, there's no need for secrecy. We'll protect your confidentiality," the pastor said firmly.

Tim shook his head. "You're better off not knowing the dirty details of my life or how I ended up on your doorstep." Tim stood to his feet. "Why does life have to be such a wild, weird ride?"

"Everybody experiences trials in life." The pastor looked at his watch. "Let me brew us up some coffee in my study and we'll sit down and talk."

"Nah, you don't need to do that. I've been too much trouble already."

"Nonsense. Follow me." The pastor led Tim through a doorway to the left of the choir loft. They walked down a wood paneled hallway, then into a modestly decorated office.

As the pastor prepared a pot of coffee, Tim looked at a well-stocked bookcase. "I wish I had all the knowledge that you have about religion," he said.

"Those books are for show. I'm not very bright but I've got a childlike faith. That's all I need."

Tim picked up one of the pastor's business cards. "I see where you've got all these college degrees attached to your name, so that should count for something."

"It impresses people, but it doesn't impress God." The pastor leaned against his desk. "What brought you here?"

"Actually, I just wanted a quiet place to pray. I have so much going on in my mind." Tim looked out the window. "I wonder about our lives here on this planet. What are our lives worth? We're finite beings that live such a short time and on a grand universal scale, we're completely irrelevant."

"I would argue against that point all day."

"Of course, I'm right," Tim said. "Unless, we can do the unbelievable, defeat death, and live eternally, we are insignificant on this earth."

Carlton Wheeler sat down at a chair behind his desk. "You're headed in the right direction."

"I'm headed in the right direction if what I've heard and seen is true." Tim lowered his head to the floor. "If I told you that it is possible to get a grip on death and overcome it, what would you say?"

The pastor rubbed his chin. "I would say that you are in serious error if you are speaking about life here on earth. That's impossible."

Tim shook his head. "I believe that death has been overcome or at least the means to eliminate death is at hand. But an evil force has control of the situation."

"You will have to explain what you are talking about."

"You will find out soon enough, but don't you agree that we have unlimited potential to change the world once we know that death is not going to stop us?"

"But it can't happen," the pastor said. "God brought order to the universe. The Lord has appointed man to die and shed his earthly existence and then he will face the Judgment Seat of God."

"I believe the Bible, but I also know what I have seen. If we overcome death, then what happens? What about our souls?"

"Are you a Christian?"

Tim laughed. "Of course, I am. My girlfriend gets me to church every so often."

"That's not what I asked you. John 3:16 says, 'For God so loved the world that He gave His one and only Son, that whoever believes in Him shall not perish but have eternal life.' Have you accepted Jesus Christ as your Lord and Savior?"

Tim looked to the floor again. He knew the answer was a big *no* but he did not want to admit it. "Listen, I told you that I am a Christian. Now back off."

The pastor put his hands up as if to surrender. "Fine."

"Do you want to live forever? You might have the opportunity," Tim said.

"In Heaven, my friend. In Heaven."

"God should be supportive of allowing his creation to forego the pain and suffering of death," Tim said.

"He has a plan that makes physical death insignificant. Our eternal life can be assured."

"Then you believe that this development that eliminates death could not be in God's will?" Tim asked.

"It could not be."

"I've got work to do. Is it OK if I spend some quiet time with God in your sanctuary?"

"Certainly. I'll be here awhile so I'll lock up when you leave."

Quietly, Tim walked into the sanctuary, sat down on the first pew, lowered his head, and silently prayed. He sought God's guidance and will for his troubling situation.

A peace came over Tim unlike anything he had ever experienced. He felt confident that everything would work out.

Chapter Thirty-Seven— Renewing Acquaintances

As Tim walked away from the church, he saw a figure behind a tree on the far side of a cemetery.

"Stop!" the person said as he came into clear view. He was a tall, young man, very slender in build with sandy brown hair. His face was angular and distinctive with a high forehead and a small scar that ran across his chin.

"Who are you?" Tim demanded. "Wait a minute! I know you!"

"I'm a friend," he said.

"I don't need a new friend, especially you! You're one of those CIA agents that locked me up in Denmark."

"My name is Matt Stowe. You're right. I'm with the CIA."

"Where's Nelson Porter?"

"Nelson Porter is not aware that I am here."

"What are you doing?"

"I sympathize with your situation because I know about your girlfriend. I had a sister who was a victim of Jon Actund. She was little more than a tool in his games after she became fascinated with his charm."

"Where is she now?"

"She's dead," Matt Stowe said quietly.

"I'm sorry. What happen?"

They put some psycho drugs into her and burned her inside organs."

"That's bad. I'm sorry. What's the plan? Is the CIA gonna apprehend him?"

"No. They want to continue to monitor him with surveillance." Stowe grimaced. "That's unacceptable."

"But Nelson Porter talked like something could develop after the press conference."

"He's only talking. Besides, I have my own way of doling out justice."

Tim looked warily at the man. "Are you working with Nelson Porter?"

"I work with him. That's how I know so much about you and this whole situation," Stowe said. "But I'm talking to you independent of the Agency. This is personal for me."

"Won't you lose your job?"

"I'm not worried about that stuff. I'm just glad that I was able to leverage my access to information within the Agency to follow Actund."

"Don't you think Actund's insane?"

"No, he's not insane. The Agency has done a profile of the man and he's not insane, criminally, or in any other way. He's got a diluted, perverted thirst for power."

"In other words, he's insane!" Tim said.

"I'm trying to give you a serious analysis of the man."

"But that's double-talk." Tim's face turned a crimson red. "I know this Jon Actund better than you do. He's insane and he's evil."

"The man is evil. No question about that."

"I've looked into his eyes," Tim said. "I've seen the face of evil and I know that he kills. I've seen him plotting and planning, drooling about his evil ideas."

"You don't have to convince me because he ended the life of someone I love dearly," Stowe said. "I've got important business to take care of at the press conference. I'll take you with me but stay out of the way."

On the way to the press conference, Tim wrestled with his emotions. Relieved to have met someone that sympathized with him, Tim, however, was not sure he could trust Stowe.

"Do you have arrest powers?" Tim asked.

"No. Actund is really a public relations hog," Stowe said. "He wants to play this event up in a dramatic way by having it at the Fountain of Youth when he should have had it over at the college."

"Look at the media," Tim said as the vehicle turned into the parking lot. There were television vans lined up along the street, all representing local stations. Local radio station and newspaper reporters had assembled as well.

The Fountain of Youth attraction was a popular tourist stop. There was a small sign at the entrance, surrounded by tall trees, shrubbery, and bushes.

Stowe and Tim walked past the ticket window and met an attendant standing at a turnstile.

"We're here for the press conference," Stowe said.

The attendant motioned them around the turnstile and through a private gate. They walked through a garden filled with dandelions and roses as the sweet smell of the flowers floated all around them.

A mannequin, Juan Ponce de Leon himself, dressed in full regalia of Spanish armament stood guard in front of the main building. They walked to an open patio dotted with folding chairs lined up in rows. The chairs faced a platform with a podium and microphone. Several television cameras were lined up in front of the podium.

As Stowe walked away, he said, "Stay clear of me."

Confused, Tim sat down at the end of the third row of chairs as he noticed a spring that was reputed to be the actual Fountain of Youth, gushing forth fresh, clean water, behind the platform.

A steady mix of people descended on the place. Several uniformed policemen milled around the area.

With noticeable enthusiasm, a swarm of elderly people marched down the path and into the press conference area, a mixture of men and women. Some of them were spry and alert; others slow and anemic. Most of them were smartly dressed in summer wear and at least half of them wore big straw hats with broad, rounded bills, obviously to block out the stifling Florida sun.

"Mr. Actund is very impressive because he truly cares for senior citizens. He should run for public office," a woman seated behind Tim said to a friend.

"How do you know about him?" Tim asked.

"We were sent a biography and a DVD about him at the senior citizens center."

A buzz came over the crowd as a group of well-tailored men descended the hill and entered the patio area. Uniformed and civilian security personnel surrounded the group of men. Jon Actund stood front and center in the crowd of leaders as he acknowledged the audience, flashing a broad smile and waving energetically.

Rage and indignation nearly overwhelmed Tim as the senior citizens seated near him applauded and waved their hands at Actund. From the original group, ten men stepped onto the platform, including Actund. One of the men approached the podium as the others sat down in folding chairs.

"That guy looks familiar," Tim said to the elderly man sitting next to him.

The man leaned over and said, "That's William Marks, the famous network weatherman." Marks was well known for publicly recognizing citizens who had reached one-hundred years of age.

A couple of lame jokes told by Marks lightened the mood. As he spoke, Stowe lurked to the right of the platform.

Next, Marks introduced the men who sat on the platform. The first person acknowledged was the senior U.S. senator from Florida. Seated next to him was an attaché for the United Nations, followed by the Director of Public Health for Florida, the executive director of the public policy think tank that had organized the conference, and a high-level assistant to the U.S. Surgeon General. Several other dignitaries were recognized and finally, Jon Actund was introduced, sitting smugly at the end of the platform as he took in the whole scene.

The senator highlighted legislation that he had sponsored in support of the elderly, and his fight for increased funding in the federal budget for senior citizen programs.

The jovial William Marks returned to the podium. "Now I would like to introduce a man with a sincere interest in our senior citizens. He is a philanthropist at heart and a successful businessman and entrepreneur—Jon Actund."

Confidently, Actund stood up from his chair and walked to the podium as the senior citizens in the audience responded with enthusiastic applause.

"I am deeply touched by your warm welcome," Actund said as he winked at two elderly women in the front row. "I feel the energy and love that you shower on me."

The crowd cheered enthusiastically.

"I recognize the fantastic contribution that all of our senior statesmen and women are contributing to society," Actund said. "Therefore, it is with great pleasure that I announce my contribution of $10,000 towards the establishment of The Institute of Senior Citizen Studies. It will be a public policy, issue-oriented organization that will serve to raise public education and concern for issues related to seniors as well as research medical issues directly impacting this vitally important segment of our population."

The crowd broke out into thunderous applause.

"The institute will be located here in St. Augustine and will be on the cutting edge of medical research. In fact, I am proud to announce to you today information that will literally change the world as we know it." Actund paused with a gleam in his eye.

"I plan to end the aging process. I will literally stop Father Time in his tracks." Actund thrust his arm straight out with his palm open in a dramatic pose. "In our world, there is no reason for us to succumb to death. If we have the desire and the heart, we can accomplish anything. In our modern society, we are prepared to accept any challenge head on, especially when it impacts our very health and lives."

Actund continued, "I love life and I treasure every day. I get a kick out of watching children play in the park. I enjoy the fellowship of family and friends." He walked in front of the podium. "Why can't it go on forever?"

One of the older men arose from his chair and shouted, "Preach it, brother!"

"The brightest minds in the world have come together to work on our project. Let me introduce to you one of the most brilliant men I have ever met—Dr. Bernard Vog."

Dr. Vog emerged from the front row and climbed the stairs to the podium. Tim could tell by the expressions on the faces of the VIPs on the platform that they were surprised. Actund was invited to announce his financial contribution but he was taking advantage of his time in the spotlight.

Grinning widely, Dr. Vog stood in front of the podium. He cocked his head slightly to the right and put his hand to his ear. "Do you hear anything? Listen closely." Dr. Vog slapped his hand on the podium. "Yes. I hear it."

"I don't hear a thing," a woman in the audience shouted.

"Listen closely," the doctor urged. "We should all be able to hear our molecular clocks ticking. From the moment you are born, that clock is ticking steadily towards the inevitable, our demise. Our cells cannot replicate. As time moves forward, we begin to break down and without a replenishment of our weary, broken cells, we become inflicted with a weakened immune system causing heart disease and other maladies to overtake us."

"As a gerontologist, I have spent many years researching the fascinating subject of the aging process. The underlining goal has been to produce the most effective weapon to ward off the impact of aging on our bodies." The doctor paused to clear his throat. "There have been anti-aging creams introduced into the market composed mainly of alpha-hydroxy acids. This topical solution can create smoother skin, reduced sallowness, and make better color, but it's purely cosmetic."

William Marks and Actund exchanged heated words in low tones at the back of the platform.

"Dehydroepiandrosterone. Say that one five times blindfolded," the doctor laughed. "DHEA, for short, is one of many endocrine hormones in our body. There has been extensive laboratory research done on the subject. This hormone is a potent anti-carcinogen. It appears to retard diabetes and reduce cardiovascular disease." The doctor pointed at his head. "It even enhances our memories but alas, it's volume in our body declines as we grow older." He put his hand to his brow and shook his head demonstrably. "Estrogen, ladies… Estrogen contributes to a longer, healthier life, So keep taking those pills."

Actund returned to the podium. "Doc, aren't we all tired of getting old? Arthritis, bursitis! It's discouraging."

"I agree but through exercise and healthy eating habits, we can live longer. But nobody is immune. Alas, death is inevitable," Dr. Vog said.

"Until now!" Actund said loudly.

A low murmur reverberated in the crowd.

"Years of research and development have been dedicated to the lofty goal of conquering the aging process, but we have discovered that a group of modest pioneer doctors has already vanquished the dragon of aging," Dr. Vog said.

"Death has been defeated so I plan to be an eternal man! We have uncovered the most significant scientific discovery in human history!" Actund's voice brimmed with enthusiasm. "We will soon make available a drug that will stop aging… period. Doctor, give us the background."

William Marks tried to interrupt. "We have to continue with the rest of the program."

There was an immediate hostile reaction from the crowd. "Let 'em finish," someone shouted.

A flustered Marks looked back at the other men on the platform. The senator motioned for Marks to sit down.

"Through the years, rumors have circulated in Europe about a wonder anti-aging drug," Dr. Vog said. "We discovered that a group of doctors and scientists worked secretly at an abandoned factory in the 1940s. The result of their work was a drug that stops aging in its tracks. The drug combines the best aspects of ten previously created pills to supplement diminishing hormones. Its strongest component is a scientifically enhanced version of the DHEA hormone. But there were several other elements to the drug that have been unknown because the formula to create it was lost. However, through sheer determination, we have discovered the formula. Our lives will never be the same!"

The crowd erupted in loud applause.

A young man shouted, "How do we know the formula works?"

"Oh, it works!" Actund said.

"Where's the proof?" the young man demanded.

Actund snapped his fingers in the direction of the doctor who in turn walked to the back of the podium and down the small staircase. Dr. Vog stepped behind a blue curtain that had been set up as a backdrop and returned with a woman.

Tim stood to his feet. "Nancy!"

Chapter Thirty-Eight— Woman in the Spotlight

The woman was dressed in a neatly pressed gray business suit, a white blouse and her hair was coiffed in an old-fashion style.

"Here's your proof," Actund proclaimed. "This woman is eighty-five years old."

Half the crowd broke into applause while several people scoffed with hisses and a scattering of boos.

"The woman voluntarily, and bravely I might add, took the drug," Actund said. "As you can see, it completely halted her aging."

Dumbstruck by the comments, Tim stood to his feet, nearly shouting out, yet holding back.

"Let's have the woman speak!" a young male newspaper reporter in the crowd said.

Actund smiled broadly as photographers and video camera operators walked toward the podium. "Be patient friends," Actund said. "I realize that some of you are skeptical, but I am staking my reputation on this announcement, and the good doctor likewise."

"You don't have a reputation, at least not in the United States," the young reporter said. "We don't know anything about you. You're asking us to take a great leap of faith, to throw common sense out the window."

"You underestimate the ingenuity and the inventiveness of the human spirit. If a goal is set, and the motive is pure, then the sky's the limit," Actund said.

From the second row, an elderly man sprang to his feet. "Cut out the sassafras and let the girl talk."

Actund smiled. "I'm happy to oblige, so let me introduce Miss Hilda Carr to you. She was born in Salina, Kansas in 1920 and worked for the American Red Cross after finishing school. In her work, she was asked to relocate to Austria in the early stages of World War II."

"That's Nancy's grandmother's name," Tim muttered furiously.

"A woman of profound courage," the doctor said, picking up the introduction. "She understood the historic significance of the work of the small group of researchers. This woman stepped forward and bravely volunteered to be a test case. We are very close to developing an updated version of the drug that will allow us to replicate what you see before you for the public at large."

Actund put his arm around the woman. "I present to you Miss Hilda Carr!"

"What are they doing?" Tim said with gritted teeth.

"Thank you for being here," the woman said. She spoke in the same sullen tones that Tim had heard earlier. "I am not a good speaker, so I only want… I have never been in front of this big a group, but it is important that you are here. I admire the older people. It is something…" she hesitated. "I have never been near this many older people."

"Honey, you're older than any of us!" a black woman said from the second row. The crowd howled in laughter.

"Uh," the woman hesitated. "I feel like I did when I was twenty-two."

"And what kind of lifestyle do you live?" Actund asked.

"I exercise every day and I read three books a week. I tend to a garden and quilt sweaters."

"Have you had any health problems in recent years?" Actund asked.

"None at all," the woman said in a low tone.

"Let's get some objective analysis from Dr. Vog," Actund said. "Recently, he gave her a complete physical exam and certainly has most of the answers about the woman's health."

All eyes turned to the doctor. "Her vital organs are in fine condition. Her blood work was smooth as silk. She has the dexterity and motor skills to handle any task and all at eighty-five years young," Dr. Vog said.

"I don't believe it. I just don't believe!" an elderly woman blurted out.

Tim seethed.

"I assume that you have documented proof that the woman is who you said and the age is accurate," a reporter shouted.

Actund hesitated shortly then responded. "Yes. We have all that information documented."

A tall, distinguished man stood up and asked, "Where has this woman been all these years?"

"In seclusion in Europe," Actund said. "A woman of privacy and modesty. That's why she should be commended for stepping forward with her story."

The senator broke in. "Mr. Jon Actund is a pioneer, a man of vision. He has presented the most important medical breakthrough since the discovery of penicillin. Let's show our appreciation!"

The crowd stood to their feet and applauded thunderously. Tim sat slumped in his chair, stewing over the turn of events.

"Thank you, Mr. Senator. Thank you friends, one and all," Actund said proudly. "I appreciate your support. When we are prepared to move forward with the final formula, please work with me as we secure Federal Drug Administration approval. With everyone working together," he pointed at the people on the platform. "We can change the course of history."

"I admit that I may be slow sometimes," William Marks said as he stepped forward. "But you're saying that literally no one will die in the future?"

"Yes. That is the ultimate goal," Actund said.

"Now I'll never get Green Bay Packer season tickets!" Marks said.

"Seriously, there are numerous questions that come to mind as we consider such a drastic change in society," the Florida Director of Public Health said. "The world will be overpopulated and government services will be stretched to the limit."

"Many issues must be resolved. Population control will be paramount," Actund said.

"I have a question," Marks said. "If we give the formula to our babies, then is Willie Nelson gonna have to stop worrying about babies being cowboys? Cause they aren't ever growing up!!! Terminal babies!"

The crowd laughed nervously.

"There will be many questions to resolve," the senator said. "I will call for a summit of international leaders to convene, in two months, in Miami to consider important issues surrounding the formula, ethical, medical, regulatory."

"Ah yes," Marks said. "We will call it 'The Formula Summit' or 'Miami's Fabulous Formula Summit' or 'Miami's Anti-Death Summit' or something like that."

"In all seriousness," a man said as he stood to speak. "Theological and ethical considerations are going to come into play here." It was the pastor that Tim had met at the local church, Carlton Wheeler.

"Hey, we got a party pooper!" Marks laughed. "Let's move on."

"We should address these issues immediately," the pastor asserted.

Actund was visibly uncomfortable with the direction of the discussion, but under the circumstances, he could hardly be uncooperative.

"I'm not sure that the majority of you have stopped long enough to consider what this proposal would really do," the pastor said. "To remind you, we are already eternal beings."

"Already competition," Marks said.

"The question is where will we all spend eternity, Heaven or Hell?" Wheeler continued. "The Bible says, 'It is appointed unto men once to die, but after this the judgment.' We are mortal to this earth and we can't bring about eternal life in Heaven by ourselves. There's only one route to take to eternal salvation and that is by accepting Jesus Christ as your Lord and Savior."

Tim listened intently as Actund became visibly agitated.

"Are you doubting the claims of Mr. Actund?" Dr. Vog asked.

"I don't doubt his sincerity, but it's an agenda based on a false foundation," Wheeler said.

"You're forgetting one thing," Marks said. "That good looking woman over there is eighty-five years old."

"I haven't seen any proof, but even if she is that old, eighty-five years is not eternity. This world has many pleasures and much good is all around us," Wheeler said. "But our place is with God in Heaven. You are re-writing the Bible! It's absurdity!"

Infuriated, Actund stood to his feet and glared at Marks. The master of ceremonies got the message and quickly thanked the pastor. "Comments must be brief."

"Differences of opinion," Actund said. "I must respond that my team of scientists and physicians has concluded quite convincingly that the formula will completely eliminate the aging process. People will still get diseases not related to aging and die in car accidents and get murdered so the population will not swing out of control." He walked to the left side of the platform. "But my friends, to ensure that overpopulation does not overwhelm us, there must be a great degree of cooperation among the brotherhood and sisterhood of nations. Amen?"

"Amen!" several people in the crowd shouted.

"An important point must be stressed. Please help me promote a greater cooperative spirit between the nations of the world, and the big nations must take the lead." Actund said as he turned to the United Nations representative. "Will you help us work together on this grand opportunity?"

"Uh… Uh… We certainly want to promote cooperation among member nations," the U.N. man said.

"Then you will help? Let's hear it for our man!!" Actund urged the crowd.

"I made no commitments. It will probably be referred to our health care subcommittee for consideration," the U.N. representative said.

"We know you have to go through the proper channels and all that," Actund said.

Dr. Vog returned to the podium. "We envision the serum taking two forms, liquid and capsule." He put on his reading glasses and pulled out some notes from inside his coat. "Man has studied aging for ages. Experiments, both privately and publicly funded, have researched and scrutinized every facet of the issue. From the famous 'Methuselah' fruit fly gene to the more recent Harvard University study of centenarians, we have done our best to thwart the efforts of Father Time. Now we are succeeding. Any additional questions from the media?"

A reporter rose to his feet. "If I take this pill today…"

"There is no pill yet," the doctor interrupted. "But we nearly have everything in place to begin production soon."

"When the pill is ready, if I take it, will I be young like I am now for the rest of my life?" the reporter asked.

"When the formula is perfected, aging will stop with consistent usage of it. But before we get to that point, I suspect that there may be some slow incremental aging associated with it until a person's appearance levels out."

"So you're gonna have to take them like vitamin supplements?" the reporter followed up.

"That is a true statement," the doctor said.

"How's this supposed to impact social security?" a gray-headed, wiry middle-aged male reporter asked.

"That issue, and other policy matters, will be addressed quite enthusiastically by our elected officials," Dr. Vog said.

"We need more proof about the woman," the reporter said. "How do we know that she's not some good-looking Florida babe?"

"She is a good-looking babe… at eighty-five years old," Dr. Vog said.

The audience laughed heartily.

"Do you have proof or not?" the reporter asked.

"We've already given you her name. Dig my friend. You're a good reporter… Dig! Find that information," Actund said.

"Don't worry. We will," the reporter said.

"To get you off to a good start, I thought I would help." Actund reached underneath the podium and pulled out a manila folder. Actund produced a copy of a birth certificate. "It reads 'Hilda Estelle Carr, born January 31, 1920, Salina, Kansas Memorial Hospital.' Solid documentation."

"I'll verify it," the reporter said. "When did she have that physical exam?" "She looks great on the outside, but she could be dying inside."

"She had a complete physical examination only two months ago," Dr. Vog said. "She's in excellent condition."

Tim could barely withstand the anger that he felt as he listened to the comments. He did not believe a word of it.

"I appreciate everyone attending today," Actund said. "We will announce the dates for the summit soon. I encourage everyone to come together and make the most of this historic opportunity. We need the support of government leaders, the business community, academia, and citizens from all walks of life. Now get out and spread the good news!" Actund let out a howl of enthusiasm that sounded like a coyote in heat.

The crowd laughed and applauded as Actund took an exaggerated bow. He turned to the men on the platform and shook everyone's hands.

A loud explosive sound rang out. Most members of the crowd crouched down to the ground.

"Look! He's been shot!" someone shouted.

On the stage, Actund had crumpled to his knees as blood spewed from his back.

Tim scrambled to the front row to get a better view. He could see that Actund was turning a pale color, his eyes rolling to the back of his head as people attempted to help him. Suddenly, a commotion developed to Tim's right. A group of men, including uniformed police officers, had converged on Matt Stowe.

"He still has the gun!" one of the police officers shouted as he produced handcuffs.

A second police officer tackled Stowe as a man in civilian clothes joined the fracas. Chairs were knocked all over the patio area. As paramedics came to the aid of Actund, Tim noticed Nelson Porter approach the law enforcement personnel who had custody of Stowe.

"What are you doing?" Porter asked. He flashed a card with his CIA credentials. "He's with the Agency."

"I don't care who he is, I saw him shoot the guy!" a police officer said.

"That's preposterous!" Porter said.

"I saw him do it! I saw him do it!" a thin young man said. He wore denim coveralls and had a big, toothless smile.

"Let me talk to him," Nelson Porter demanded.

"The man had it coming to him," Stowe said in a casual way.

"But you just ruined your own career… and life!" Porter shouted.

"I did it for my sister and her memory."

Dr. Vog led the effort to save Actund as several women in the audience cried. Within a few minutes, Actund was delicately placed on a stretcher.

"Is he dead?" Tim asked a paramedic.

"It's close. We have to get him to the hospital."

Within the crowd of onlookers, a rumbling of angry discourse started.

"We should lynch the person that did it," someone shouted.

"There he is over there!" another man said. A small part of the crowd, in mass, approached the law enforcement personnel who had surrounded Stowe.

An odd sight, Tim had never seen an unruly mob comprised of senior citizens.

"He killed our savior!" an old man shouted as he pointed at Stowe with his cane.

"Let's get him!" another man grumbled.

As the crowd moved toward Stowe, they were met head-on by the police, security guards, and plain-clothed security personnel. Pushing and shouting started. Then someone threw a chair. A second wave of uniformed police officers came rushing onto the scene. They had billy clubs in hand.

The elderly group was no match for the police so they backed away.

Shortly, an animated discussion began between Nelson Porter and the police officers who had handcuffed Stowe. The officers hustled Stowe away, running down a short paved walkway that led to a police van. Porter trailed right behind them.

Tim stood alone and confused. "Where's Nancy?"

The woman was nowhere in sight. Frantically, Tim climbed up onto the platform. From the higher vantage point, he still could not see her so he ran behind the curtain and down a slippery, grassy hill into a soggy marsh with shoulder-high weeds and deep black mud.

As he trudged along, he noticed to his right that there was a long, rickety, wooden dock, nearly hidden by the growth of weeds.

Standing on the narrow and very unsound structure, Tim saw that the deck was at least three hundred feet long, made of splintering wood and reached to the mouth of Matanzas Bay. In the distance, The Bridge of Lions was clearly visible.

A roaring noise pierced the sky, the sound of an outboard boat motor starting. From within the marsh, a boat emerged with three people aboard, two men and a woman.

The boat passed directly in front of the dock.

"Nancy!" Tim shouted. "Where are you going?" Lugar was seated in the boat as well as a man that Tim did not recognize. He dove onto the boat as it passed the dock, landing on Lugar, who fell flat on his back.

The two men wrestled with each other, Tim thrusting his knee into Lugar's stomach and his elbow into his throat. Lugar grappled desperately with his free hands to get a grip on Tim's shirt.

The man operating the motor slowed the speed of the boat to a crawl while Lugar grabbed a wooden oar and swung it. Tim ducked under it. Immediately, Lugar unleashed a forearm thrust, catching Tim squarely in the jaw, the force pushing him backwards and over the side with a thunderous splash into the water. Tim was submerged for about ten seconds, his head coming to the surface in time to see the boat speeding away.

A few seconds later, a personal watercraft appeared on the scene with a teenager driving. He stopped as he approached Tim's bobbing head.

"Help me!" Tim screamed. "I need your help!"

"What 'chu doin' in the water?"

"I need to hitch a ride with you," Tim said. "See that boat way down there? I gotta catch up with it."

"I don't know. I'm not supposed to mess with strangers."

"Let me ride on the back. You drive."

"I don't even know you."

"We'll get acquainted later," Tim said. "I'll give you five, no make that ten dollars!"

"OK, I'll do it." The boy stopped his craft long enough for Tim to climb aboard.

The personal watercraft accelerated so quickly that Tim nearly fell off, but he grabbed the side and hung on. Soon they were bouncing over the waves with energy and force as the boy let out a rip-roaring shout, a huge crested wave the source of enthusiasm.

They could see the boat ahead of them as it approached the Bridge of Lions. "I've never been this far down the river," the boy shouted.

The boat went under the bridge, abruptly turned right and slowed down as it entered the Municipal Marina. There were two docks at the marina.

Suddenly, a teenage girl on a personal watercraft flew across the water, nearly colliding with the boy and Tim. The sudden diversion sent Tim flying off the watercraft and into the bay.

It took twenty seconds for the boy to circle back and pick up Tim. When they reached the marina, the boat and its occupants were gone.

As Tim climbed up on the nearest dock, he came face to face with the barrel of a gun.

Chapter Thirty-Nine— Porter's Patience

"I should blow you away here and now," Nelson Porter said as he stared at a wet, shivering Tim.

"Did you see Nancy?" Tim asked. "She got off a boat at this marina."

"Are you talking about the woman on the platform?"

"The woman? You mean Nancy?"

"We believe that there's a chance that what Actund said was legit."

"You're as crazy as he is! The name that they used is her grandmother's name."

"It doesn't take a great leap of faith to conclude that his theories could become reality. You've seen the kind of experiments that they've done in Europe."

"That was Nancy on the stage, not her grandmother," Tim said. "Obviously, they manipulated Nancy into claiming that she is her grandmother, a bogus scheme that will amaze and shock everybody."

"Do you know for a fact that her grandmother is dead?"

"Well… No. She got lost in Europe or something and they never found her."

"Then the possibility exists. Have you seen a photo of the grandmother?"

Tim thought about the photo at Aunt Linda's home but he did not want to admit that there was a striking resemblance. "I don't quite remember."

"Nancy drowned."

"They never found her body. I'm telling you that was her standing on that stage."

"There's only one way to find out who that woman was and that's to track her down," Porter said. "You will be able to tell if you spend time with her."

"That's what I've been trying to do!"

"Listen carefully. I don't want you to get out of my sight. Stay with me at all times. Do you understand?"

"Yes. Absolutely," Tim said. He climbed into Porter's vehicle in his soggy clothes.

Porter drove up and down the road several times but they saw no sign of the woman.

"There's always a possibility that the woman could be someone else completely. Not Nancy or her grandmother, simply a look-a-like," Porter said.

"I don't believe it."

"It sure would be a miracle if it's your girl."

"I believe miracles can happen, don't you?" Tim asked.

"Sure. I've read about them."

"I've read about miracles too, in the Bible," Tim said quietly.

"There were some pretty good ones back then. You might call it the heyday of miracles," Porter said.

"I'd like to see miracles happening again. It might give us some hope in this world."

"Are you a religious man?" Porter asked.

"A few weeks ago, I would have said no, but I would have to reconsider that issue. I have sure had a lot of opportunity to reflect on my values, my life in general," Tim said. "It's been a wild ride lately."

"And it may get even wilder," Porter said.

"Sometimes I don't think I'm worth much of anything. I'm taking up space and wasting my life away."

"You don't really believe that," Porter said. "Be more positive."

"I might have found my purpose, my reason for existing right here. I am helping to break up the plans of a madman."

"If either one of us was the dishonest type, we could try to get our hands on that anti-aging formula and profit from it," Porter said.

"I would never try to profit from it. In fact, I'm not sure what I would do if I had that formula in my hands right now," Tim said.

Chapter Forty—Back in the Game

Monday, August 12, 11:18 a.m

"Jon Actund is dead," Porter said.

The news was difficult for Tim to grasp. Jon Actund, the invincible and charismatic leader, was dead. As Tim sat down in a chair in his motel room, he felt a strange mix of emotions and uneasiness because Actund's death could affect his pursuit of information. He also felt deprived of any satisfaction that he could have had from extracting revenge against the man. "The pain that the man has caused…," Tim muttered.

"The other news is that Dr. Vog won't tell anyone where the woman is staying," Porter said. "They want to shield her from the media. They believe that her elusiveness will help create an aura of mystery about her."

"Unbelievable," Tim said. "Did you know that Matt Stowe had that connection to Actund?"

"No, of course not. In hindsight, though, now I know why Matt wanted the assignment so badly."

"Don't you think that it's about time that we went to the local police?"

"We're working with them in an appropriate way, but they could not help to answer your questions. Actund's death has created a major complication, but your answers are gonna come if you trust me."

"I keep hearing that...."

Tuesday, August 13 9:03 a.m.

"Tiffany, I'm in St. Augustine," Tim said. "It's a long story but I'll explain everything when I get home, hopefully in a few days." He hung up the motel room phone without giving her time to ask questions.

Anxiously, he turned on the television in his motel room. Dr. Vog stood in front of a podium to begin a press conference.

"My good friends," the doctor said. "I stand before you in mourning. My colleague, Jon Actund, is no longer with us, but his legacy will continue. I assure you that our memories of him will never fade away. I consider it my obligation and my burden to begin a new program in his memory. Introducing the Jon Actund Academy!"

The doctor unveiled a full color diagram of a building, modern in appearance, but practical in layout.

"Within the walls of this building, brave young men and women, stout of heart, will emerge to promote through legislation, public dialogue and everyday living, the concept of unified governments, working hand in hand. The first common goal that our organization will promote among young people, and eventually to the governments of the world at all levels, will be proper diet, exercise, and preventive health care. We ask for the acceptance and support of the public. The finances are in place but we need moral support. JAA will be located here in St. Augustine."

Tim watched the announcement with incredulity. "Talk about pulling something out of your hat," he muttered. "They're going after the young and the old."

"I will not comment on the circumstances surrounding Mr. Actund's death. The authorities are conducting their investigation so we must allow them to do their work," Dr. Vog said. "Now I will open the floor for questions."

"What is this going to be? Some kind of brainwashing camp?" a young newspaper reporter asked.

"My good man, the people are tired of skeptics and negative attitudes."

"But you're talking about one world government, aren't you?" another reporter asked.

"I am talking about a unified, peace loving population in this world that we inhabit."

"Where are these young people going to come from?" another reporter asked.

"They will come from far and wide, hopefully from the four corners of the earth."

"How realistic do you think this concept is?" the young newspaper reporter asked.

"It's as realistic as it is revolutionary."

"Even if it is realistic," a young female reporter interjected. "It will take years and years to make it happen."

Dr. Vog laughed. "I am very optimistic because, with a little luck, I believe that the next generation could usher in a new era. This young generation of leaders will be called The Empowerment Brigade."

Tim cringed when he heard the name because it was the first time he had heard it said in a public setting.

"When will you get us some information about the curriculum? This is some kind of high school, right?" the young woman asked.

"No. It is more encompassing than that. A child will begin first grade at the academy and finish sixteen years later with a bachelor's degree."

"When do you expect the first class to enter the program?" a radio reporter asked.

"In eighteen months."

Tim watched in fiery anger.

"Where in town do you plan on having a headquarters?" the radio reporter continued.

"St. Augustine Beach would be a lovely location," the doctor said. "Plenty of open space and a peaceful setting."

"Why not the Historic District?" the radio reporter asked.

"I am a great aficionado of history and tradition," the doctor said. "I could not upset the landscape of the Historic District."

"Let's get to the question that everybody's asking. Where's the wonder woman, the ageless wonder?" a grizzled, gray-headed male newspaper reporter asked from the back of the room.

"You will see her again soon because another public appearance is planned," the doctor said. "There will be an announcement soon."

"Will you allow the media to interview her? A Q&A type scenario?" the same veteran reporter asked.

"Yes. We would anticipate a question and answer session."

"Will it be in the next week?" the reporter asked.

"I'm sure it will be." Dr. Vog looked in the direction of one of his assistants and pointed at him. "Mr. Drake is handling all the arrangements."

Tim was familiar with Mr. Drake because he had seen him frequently in Europe. The man had struck Tim as being a wicked-looking scoundrel with bad manners and even worse breath.

Thirty minutes after the press conference ended, Nelson Porter returned to the motel. "We need to have a serious discussion."

"I'm ready."

"You will be pleased to learn that we have collected quite a bit of additional vital information, beyond what you gave us, on this organization, the Empowerment Brigade, and its European operations."

"I hope that you have everything now!"

"Your verbal opinions and observations alone won't cut it in a court of law."

"I beg to differ."

"We needed physical evidence of wrongdoing."

"It's about time," Tim said, shaking his head. "What did you get?"

"We found evidence of terrorist planning, including plotting to bomb certain buildings and kidnap certain people."

"Finally!"

"But we need more. We want you to wear a wire."

"I'm listening."

"Set up a meeting with the doctor and wear a wire on your body. We need you to get him to acknowledge on tape that the organization is planning the kidnapping and possible murder of federal officials of the United States as well as United Nations personnel."

"Why would he say it to me and not you?"

"Because he knows that I'm with the federal government, even though he thinks it's the FDA, so he won't confide that type of information to me. But he knows that you already know their plans. On U.S. turf, though, you may have to coerce him to get him to talk about it."

"I think you know my decision already. When do we go to work?"

"Tonight."

"Let's do it!"

"I go back and forth about that woman's identity. It could be some actress they found that happens to look like your gal. Everybody's supposed to have a double in the world."

"Right!" Tim said sarcastically. "But she says she's Hilda Carr, her grandmother's name. I think that they tricked her into claiming that she is her grandma because it will benefit their plans. Nancy could pull it off because she knows all about her grandmother. I want this strange situation to end, so here's the deal. I'll do whatever you want as long as you get me medical proof of the woman's identity."

"It's a deal."

"Give me some details."

"You will need to set up a meeting for tomorrow night at 6:30 at the big fort, Castillo De San Marcos. You will meet with the doctor at the far northeastern corner of the fort at the top."

"Why such a public place?"

"Because we need to draw the doctor and his lieutenants out in the open, backed into a corner," Porter said with zeal in his eyes. "If we get the incriminating comments on tape, we will rush in there at the fort and grab him and his friends."

"Let's talk about a minor point, my safety! Those characters want me dead and I'm gonna walk right into their lap. They might shoot me on the spot."

"Not in a public place."

"I don't trust 'em so you gotta let me have a weapon."

"I think that we can arrange it. We plan on having you covered with some of our agents who will be dressed like tourists."

"I want help, medical or whatever, for Nancy," Tim said.

Nelson Porter shook his head. "You have to keep in mind that… whoever she is… she's a free woman."

"I understand but all I can do is ask you to help me piece together some information about the experiments that they performed on her, to give us some basis for helping her."

"I think we can help there," Porter said. "If they did perform experiments, as you say, on her. Alternatively, we could find out that she is willingly working with them."

"Impossible," Tim said.

Wednesday, August 14, 6:17 p.m.

Tim approached the fort, known as Castillo De San Marcos, with caution and fear. An imposing landmark, he remembered visiting it when he was a child.

Construction on the fortress began in 1672 and was completed many years later. The native coquina stone quarried on nearby Anastasia Island was the main ingredient in its completion.

As Tim walked across the wooden drawbridge at the entrance of the fort, he saw the large number of tourists in attendance on the relatively mild Florida summer evening. As Tim approached the creaky, wooden staircase that would take him to the top level of the fort, he felt on the inside of his jacket for the reassuring presence of a small caliber firearm and to ensure that the wire that he wore was snug and hidden.

When he reached the top rung of the staircase, Tim saw the doctor and six of his cronies standing against the outer wall of an open-air walkway. A handful of tourists milled about on the far end.

"I bet you were surprised to get that call from me," Tim said. "I've been doing a lot of thinking and I want to join your group."

"When you told me your intentions over the telephone, I was perplexed," the doctor said. "Obviously, I'm skeptical so you must convince me that you are sincere."

"I understand completely. If I were in your shoes, I would be just as skeptical. If there is one thing that you need to realize about me, it is that I am very practical." Tim walked to the wall and looked out over Matanzas Bay.

The doctor gave an appreciative nod of his head. "Elaborate."

"I don't want to be on the run. I know that at some point one of your friends here was going to hunt me down like a stray dog and put me out of my misery because I know too much about your organization. The other night you were only trying to appease temporarily the FDA man. I don't want to fight. Instead, I'll join."

"Do you really want to abandon everything else in life and take up our cause?"

"Yes, because I understand the incredible possibilities of your organization."

"Frankly, I do not trust you." The doctor walked slowly around Tim, looking him over with a skeptical glare. "Why should we welcome you after all of the havoc that you have created?"

"Several reasons. I don't like to brag but I have a lot of talent. But even still, if you don't trust me, it's better to have me near, at an arm's length, rather than roaming all over the place like a loose cannon."

"There are easy ways to deal with problems," the doctor said coldly as he motioned for the nearest crony to approach.

The man gave his weapon to Dr. Vog. The doctor rammed it against Tim's face.

"Let me do it, boss," the crony said.

"I don't believe that you will kill me because there are tourists all over the place," Tim said.

"We would not do it here," Dr. Vog said.

"Don't you think that there has been enough bloodshed already?" Tim asked as the doctor gave the weapon back to his assistant. "Let's save it for when we infiltrate the State Department and the Defense Department. After all, assassinations of important government officials are being planned, right?"

"How did you know that?" the doctor asked through gritted teeth.

"I've been with you folks long enough that I know what the game plan is," Tim said as he gave the 'thumbs up' sign and cracked a wry smile.

"We would anticipate having to do that at some time in the future," Dr. Vog said.

Tim was pleased that he had coaxed the comment out of the doctor. "Would it involve bombing government buildings?"

"Yes. It would," the doctor said. "It's time to move forward with our goals. For a while, we were like a rudderless boat out in the waters." He walked to the side of the fort and stared out at the bay.

"You like the water?" Tim asked.

"I respect the sea that's over the horizon, that vast world, a world with more mystery underneath its surface than anyone imagines, a characteristic not unlike the Empowerment Brigade. We are visible but so much has yet to come to the surface and when it does…"

"And I want to be a part of it," Tim said feebly.

"Then you will do as I say and answer directly to me."

A woman in a red dress appeared from behind a wall.

"Nancy!" Tim shouted.

"Finally, I know what you are doing and I don't like what I just heard," the woman said to Dr. Vog. "It's insanity and I don't want anything to do with it. You misled me."

The doctor appeared to be more annoyed than surprised. "There's no turning back for any of us because I have the missing piece of the puzzle." He pulled a sheet of paper from his coat pocket. "The missing element of the formula."

The woman grabbed the paper from the doctor's hand and ran down the staircase.

"Get it back!" the doctor shouted. "That's the only copy!"

One of the assistants produced a weapon and aimed it at the woman as she fled.

Instinctively, Tim pulled out his pistol and fired at the man who fell, wounded, to the ground. In a rapid whirlwind of motion and confusion, several of the people who had appeared to be tourists produced weapons. In response, the cronies brandished their own weapons.

The real tourists ran for cover.

Tim counted four agents. Three additional agents ran up the staircase while two others repelled up the side of the fort.

"Drop your weapons!" the lead agent said. "You're outnumbered.

"Yes. We are in a pickle," Dr. Vog said.

"My name is Agent Stewart with the Federal Bureau of Investigation. You are under arrest. Drop your weapons!"

"On what charges?" Dr. Vog asked, feigning innocence.

"Threats against federal officials, terrorist conspiracy, and more."

"There is a misunderstanding," Dr. Vog said.

"No! Afraid not! Now tell your men to drop their weapons."

The loud, rumbling sound of a convoy descended on the fort. It included marked FBI vehicles, S.W.A.T. vans, St. Johns County Sheriff's vehicles, and City of St. Augustine police patrol cars.

"We're in trouble," one of the cronies said.

"They aren't taking us alive," one of his associates shouted.

"You're outnumbered," Agent Stewart said. "Time to surrender."

Dr. Vog rubbed his chin and arched a bushy eyebrow. He lowered his head thoughtfully. "It cannot end this way."

"You're on our home turf now!" Tim shouted. "We're not gonna tolerate your games."

"We can take hostages!" one of the cronies said as he pointed at a distraught group of tourists huddled in a nearby corner.

"That would appear to be our best option," Dr. Vog said.

Tim recognized Nelson Porter's voice as it blared out from the lead agent's two-way radio. "Agent Stewart, what's the status?"

Stewart described the scene. "And sir, we've got civilians up here."

"How many?"

"Eight. Two adult males and three adult females and three children."

"Is there any way that they can safely get to the lower level?"

"I wouldn't want to risk it. They'd have to run directly by the subjects, and they're talking about hostages."

"We have already cleared out all the civilians from the lower level and we are currently removing them from the grounds," Porter said.

Without warning, one of Vog's assistants fired his weapon in the direction of the agents. Everyone scattered for cover as best they could behind walls and garbage cans.

"What's happening?" Porter screamed over the radio.

"One of these nuts fired off a round," Agent Stewart said.

"Dr. Vog, listen to reason," Tim said. "You don't want to get in a fire fight with these guys."

"Nobody else will fire their weapon unless I order it," Dr. Vog said. "We will negotiate with you."

"You're not in a position to make demands," Agent Stewart said.

"I suggest that you listen," Dr. Vog said. He pointed at the tourists. "We have leverage."

Agent Stewart shouted into his radio. "They want to negotiate with us but I'm worried about the civilians."

Thirty seconds later, Porter's voice came over the radio. "We have cleared all the other civilians off the grounds. We are going to attempt to communicate with the subjects. We've set up a microphone and a loudspeaker."

"Go for it," Agent Stewart said.

Nelson Porter's voice boomed out loudly over the microphone system as he stood on the grass sixty feet below. "This is Agent Nelson Porter with the federal government. We strongly urge you to lay down your arms and come out peacefully."

"We have been forced to defend ourselves," Dr. Vog shouted. "We are innocent visitors to this national landmark and we find ourselves under siege."

"Let's end this encounter before anyone else gets hurt," Porter said.

"If we turn ourselves over to you, we have no assurances that we will live to see another day," Dr. Vog said.

"We don't harm individuals in our custody," Porter said.

"I am sorry but we cannot surrender to your forces of oppression. Our cause is a great one. As the leader of our movement, I cannot allow you to imprison us. We recognize that we may pay the ultimate price, but our followers will carry on."

"We know about the Empowerment Brigade and your European compound," Porter said. "It would be to everyone's benefit if you called for the closing of that facility."

The doctor laughed. "You do not realize the enormity of our operation and the commitment to our cause. We won't close our doors like a traveling circus."

"That may be true," Porter said. "It would have been better for everyone if you had not been so secretive. In an open forum, we could have exchanged ideas."

"Your culture has compromised itself to the point that there is no possible way to live peaceably."

"Obviously there will be disagreements, but you need to be present to argue your point of view," Porter said. "If you get yourself hurt here today, then you are completely out of the picture."

"There is something to be said for martyrdom," the doctor said.

"I don't believe that you're serious," Porter said. "Jon Actund is your martyr."

"These men that surround me are my family," Dr. Vog said as he exchanged quick glances with his cronies.

"I think our biggest priority now is to get these civilians out of the way," one of the agents said as he stood next to Porter.

"As a show of good faith, would you please allow the innocent tourists up there to go free?" Porter asked.

"We will allow the children to go free, but the adults must stay," Dr. Vog said.

"The children need their parents," Porter said.

"Yes, but we may need a bargaining chip or two!"

One of the cronies ran over to the tourists and rounded up the children, leading them to the staircase. They were frantic, turning back to the parents, crying uncontrollably as they were nudged along.

"We want this situation to end in peace," Porter said. "We would like for you to put down your arms and come out. We won't harm you or your men."

"Do you think I was born yesterday?" the doctor laughed. "We've been backed into a corner. We will not be incarcerated by your shameful judicial system."

"You can afford a good lawyer," Porter said.

"Porter needs to stop wasting his breath," Tim said as he wiped sweat off his forehead.

"We will give them a reasonable amount of time to come to their senses," Agent Stewart said.

"How long is that?" Tim asked.

"Hard to say."

"Are we gonna sit here and let them dictate our actions?"

"They aren't dictating our actions," Agent Stewart snapped.

Thirty minutes later, there was a stirring among Dr. Vog's men.

"I would like to announce our demands," Dr. Vog shouted down at the law enforcement personnel outside the fort.

"Go ahead. We're listening," Porter said.

"In one hour, we want a helicopter to land here on the top floor of the fort. We want to be safely transported to a private plane that will then fly us to Cuba."

"That's a tall order," Porter said. "You don't want to go to Cuba anyway."

"I am serious. We must seek refuge."

"How do we know that our pilot will be safe?"

"He will be," Dr. Vog said.

"I'm not sure that we can pull it off," Porter said. "I'll get back to you."

Two minutes later, Porter radioed Agent Stewart. "We will surprise them with tear gas canisters. As soon as the gas spreads, you better come out and apprehend them."

"Everybody put your gas masks on," Agent Stewart said as he handed Tim a spare mask.

A high-pitched noise could be heard from the outside of the fort as three silver, metal canisters sailed through the air and landed very close to the doctor and his men. The tear gas seeped from the canisters, filling the air rapidly. Everyone without a mask started coughing and wheezing.

"You bloody…" The doctor could not finish his comment before he choked up.

Agent Stewart led the charge towards the opposition. "Drop your weapons and put your hands up!"

The members of the Empowerment Brigade reacted in different ways. Two of them dropped their weapons, holding their hands up to the sky. One of them pointed his weapon but was overcome with tear gas, sending him to his knees. Meanwhile, Dr. Vog ran towards one of the fort's walls.

Two of the FBI agents corralled the civilians and ushered them down the staircase as one of the cronies cross body-blocked Stewart.

"Your time is about to run out," Tim said through his gas mask as he approached Dr. Vog.

Seconds later, three of the agents approached Agent Stewart and helped him to his feet.

"Under international law, I demand clear passage!" the doctor shouted.

"What are you talking about?" Agent Stewart barked. "I'm only going to tell you this one time. Give up!"

"I demand clear passage!" the doctor said as he climbed on top of the wall.

Delicately, Tim approached the doctor. "Don't jump."

"Stay out of this situation!" Agent Stewart screamed.

"The Empowerment Brigade has arrived. The movement and the way of life will continue regardless of what happens to me! I am willing to be a martyr!" Dr. Vog shouted.

Out of the corner of his eye, Tim noticed that television station trucks and radio vans had descended upon the fort and video cameras and microphones were already trained on Dr. Vog as he spoke.

"He has a television audience at his call," Tim said. "He knows what he's doing."

"Join the Empowerment Brigade! You will live forever!" Dr. Vog said. "You will live in luxury and wealth! We will eliminate the oppressive U.S. government!"

"I've heard enough," Agent Stewart said as he motioned for his colleagues to move in. Two of the agents jumped on top of the wall and pulled the doctor to safety.

Chapter Forty-One—Tiffany's Plea

Confused and exhausted, Tim sat in the back of an ambulance outside the fort on the grass lawn, waiting to be checked by a medic. The local police ordered an evaluation of everyone for possible problems related to the tear gas.

Tim looked up to see Tiffany standing outside the back of the ambulance, looking as lovely as he had ever seen her as her blond hair glistened in the sunlight.

"Tiffany, you're an angel!" Tim said as exhaustion overwhelmed him. "Why do you keep wasting your time with me?"

"Let me climb up there and show you." She stepped up into the back of the ambulance and kissed him. "I love you."

"But I'm very unlovable and I have been completely unfair to you. I've played with your emotions in a downright sorry way." Tim turned her head so that they would be looking at each other, their faces only inches away. "This nightmare is not over because Nancy is out there somewhere. I gotta find her and you're the person that has the kindest heart, the warmest disposition, of anyone I've ever met. You need to find someone that deserves you."

Sadly, Tiffany's face turned red and tears formed in the corner of her eyes. "But I love you," she said.

"How did you find me?"

"After you called, I decided that I just had to come down," she said. "I caught a quick shot of you on TV in my motel room, then it only took me ten minutes to get here."

"This situation has been nasty," Tim said. "But I have to see it to its end. The bond that I shared with that woman can't be broken. You will never understand."

"But I do understand. The emotions that you are feeling are very personal and complicated. When you saw that woman, all the old memories came rushing back to you. But listen to me. Everything that I saw and read in the media about this woman can only lead to the conclusion that it's not Nancy. For your sake and happiness, I wish it were her, but it's not! They're saying that it is actually an older woman, as wild as that idea sounds."

"Yeah but it's a big sham."

"I've been praying for you night and day because I want you to find happiness. I believe in my heart that this situation will be resolved and that you will accept Christ as your Savior. That's my prayer for you."

Tim lowered his head. "You're truly amazing. Your dedication and persistence are incredible, while I've been rotten to you."

"God loves you so much that He sent his only Son to earth in the form of a man to die for your sins. I've been praying for you so long and I believe that you've gotten something out of the visits to church with me."

"I haven't gotten anything except a good feeling that I get when you're happy."

"I don't believe you. You need to stop long enough to pray and reflect on what you've heard."

"I will admit that I've heard a few good messages from your preacher, but I'm not much on studying the Bible."

"That will come later," Tiffany said sympathetically. "When you accept Christ, you will be a baby, spiritually I mean. You have to take it one step at a time."

"I'm so tired," Tim said. "Can't we talk about it later?"

"This is the most important thing in the world. We shouldn't put it off. You need to accept Christ as your Savior now."

"It's a miracle that I'm even alive," Tim said. "You don't know the half of what I went through!"

"I'd like to hear about it. I really would."

Tim put his head in his hands. "I don't want to talk about it now."

"After you rest, we need to have a long talk," Tiffany said. "God has spared you this long, but who knows what the future holds. You need to have assurance of your salvation."

"Listen," Tim said. "I believe in God and all, but I don't feel comfortable with what you're asking me to do. You want Jesus to be my leader and my Savior."

"Yes!"

"I'm not worthy, for starters," Tim said.

"No one is worthy so that's why God sent his Son Jesus to die for our sins, including yours, mine, and everyone!"

"In a way, I'd like to commit to this program, but I'm too much of a maverick and I can't follow rules very long."

"It's not about following rules," Tiffany said. "It's about admitting that you are a sinner, believing in your heart that Jesus died for your sins, honestly repenting of your sins, and turning away from those sins. Then you accept Jesus Christ as your Lord and Savior and start following him. You can do it."

"I want to believe that I can do it, but it can't be that simple."

"It is that simple. I've been praying fervently for you!"

Tim patted Tiffany on the cheek with his hand. "Let's hope it pays off."

A medic appeared at the back of the ambulance. "Mr. Jennings, we think you should go to the hospital for observations."

"No. Like I told you before, I'm fine, a little weary, a little fried, but I've got stuff to do!"

"No, Tim," Tiffany said. "You need to be on the safe side."

"I'm fine. I didn't take a bullet or anything like that."

"Mr. Jennings, you've been through a traumatic experience. Please go to the hospital," the medic said.

"Traumatic is my middle name," Tim said. "I'm fine."

Tim noticed Nelson Porter standing behind a van.

"Tiffany," Tim said as he hugged her. "I need to talk to someone. Will you go back to your motel? I'll meet up with you later."

"OK. I'm staying at the Winter Haven Inn," Tiffany said. "I'll come looking for you if you don't come soon."

"We got what we wanted on tape for evidence," Porter said as Tim approached.

"That's great, but what about dealing with the operation in Europe?"

"It gets sticky because it's an international problem, but I can tell you that the developments of today will give us the momentum and justification we need to stop this Empowerment Brigade."

"When will you order your men to start looking for Nancy? You know, she grabbed the missing piece of that anti-aging formula and ran with it after she overheard what they were really doing."

"I know. I know. My men are looking for her. That information is evidence."

"I feel twenty years older than when I got into this situation," Tim said. "The concept of stopping the aging process is very appealing to me right now."

"This topic will not go away, the goal of putting a stop to aging," Porter said. "No matter how this plays out with the Empowerment Brigade, people are craving youth. This woman, whoever she is, holds many answers. I want to find her, too."

"I'll hang around a little while," Tim said.

Chapter Forty-Two—The Truth

"We located her," a St. Augustine police officer shouted. "She was seen on a construction site at 348 Plainstafford Boulevard. There is a high-rise building under construction there."

"You have to let me go and help her!" Tim said.

"I'll let you go, but I'll talk to her first," Porter said.

"I understand," Tim said. "But we can settle this identity issue once and for all."

When they reached the construction site, Porter and Tim were briefed by a local uniformed police officer. The construction crew was evacuated from the building but some of them continued to mingle around a big, raging bonfire where garbage and debris were being burned.

"The lady is way up there near the top of the building," the policeman said. "I think she's gonna kill herself."

Tim craned his neck upwards. On the seventh of the eight floors, through the open sides of the uncompleted walls of the building, Tim caught a glimpse of a woman walking as she dodged wiring, concrete, and plywood. Sections of the walls were complete in some places. However, in other areas, the opening was large enough to see deeply into the structure of the building.

"We better get up there fast!" Porter said. He motioned for Tim, the policeman, and one other City of St. Augustine cop to follow. Their only route was a staircase in the far corner of the building.

As the first man to reach the seventh floor, Tim leaned over to catch his breath. Seconds later, he spotted the woman. She stood fifteen feet away.

"Nancy!"

"I don't know you and I've never known you. You are wasting your time and emotions," she said as she walked to the far side of the seventh floor.

Slowly, Tim approached. "You've been through a difficult situation. If you will only give me time, then we can sort all this out."

"You don't understand! I'm not Nancy! I had a granddaughter named Nancy, but my name is Hilda!"

"You're Nancy Proctor."

"My granddaughter was Nancy Proctor."

"What?"

"You must be looking for Nancy, my granddaughter. She's dead."

"Nancy Proctor of Atlanta, Georgia?" Tim asked.

"Yes. She drowned at a lake."

"Talk!" Tim shouted.

"I'm eighty-five years old. Nancy was my grandchild."

"You look exactly like her. It's too bizarre to believe. There's a generation between both of you. I don't believe you."

"You better believe me because I'm telling you the truth! I wish Nancy were alive more than you do! I understand that we look alike, but I never met her. I've seen photos from the newspaper websites."

"I saw a photo of you from years ago. It was wild how much you two look the same," Tim exclaimed as reality began to set in.

"I was part of a secret experiment."

"I've never seen a girl look that much like her grandmother," Tim said. "So you're telling me that the anti-aging stuff works?"

"Yes. It works and I'm the living proof."

"But how did you get involved in the organization?"

"I needed the money that Mr. Actund offered me after they tracked me down. I agreed to tell them my story and what happened in 1942. The information explained at the press conference was true. I told them what I knew about the anti-aging formula and I agreed to make one appearance here in the U.S., then go back into seclusion in Europe."

Tim was stunned. Slowly, he sat down on the dirty floor. "I don't know what to say. I loved her so much! You don't know how much I loved her!"

"I wish she were alive, too. You understand that I never had the opportunity to meet Nancy so you are more fortunate than me, but I loved her, too."

"I'm not sure that I can believe you," Tim said. "Nancy had a birthmark on her lower back. Would you please let me look so I'll have peace of mind?"

"If you wish." The woman turned around and pulled up the back of her blouse. She had no birthmark.

"She's dead," Tim muttered as his face turned ashen and his eyes glossed over with tears. "You don't know what I've been through in search of her." Tim felt faint as his head began to spin and a general weakness overcame his entire body.

"She was my flesh and blood," Hilda Carr said. "At least she didn't have to endure what I experienced."

"What do you mean?"

"The side-effects of the anti-aging formula! I've had to put up with constant headaches, pain in my joints, and I vomit a lot! But the worst part is that I have a weak heart."

"You've been going through all that for decades?"

"Yes! Of course, I look young but on the inside I am in poor condition." She pulled a piece of paper from one of her pockets. "This wonder drug may not be worth the paper it's printed on, and you know what? I have the only copy with the missing element."

"How did you get it?"

"I took part of it at the end of the war when all the confusion and chaos was taking place," Hilda Carr said. "Recently, Dr. Vog searched me out from old laboratory records. When I returned to Europe, I found him on my doorstep. They had parts of the formula that I did not have, and likewise for them, I had what they were missing. I shared my information only recently. But they deceived me into believing that it would be used for good. What a dupe I've been!"

"But what were you doing at Petrie's business? I caught you there on video."

"That was before I encountered Dr. Vog. I was attempting to buy the rest of the formula from Mr. Petrie, but he turned out to be a scam artist," she said. "I was still in the area when I saw the tragic accident involving the young man."

"What good will it do you now?"

"I hope that if I can get it in the hands of the right doctors, then they can study it and determine the best way to reverse or eliminate the side effects for me or anybody else."

"All this struggle, fighting, and death for something that's only going to hurt people," Tim said.

"Young man, I'm so sorry for your loss! I truly am."

"Thank you."

Tim turned around to see Porter and the two police officers standing behind him.

"We heard the discussion," Porter said.

The sun began to set on the skeleton of a building as Tim walked to its edge. "This is a lot to take." He looked down to see the construction workers throwing debris into the big fire.

"Why did you come up here?" Tim asked. "It's not safe."

"I was very upset when I found out what Actund and Dr. Vog were really planning," Hilda Carr said. "I wanted to be alone after everything I have experienced."

Tim felt a bond, a connection with the woman. She was related to Nancy, but he also sympathized with her enigmatic existence.

"Let's go," Tim said.

As Hilda turned to leave, she caught her shoe on a loose piece of wood, losing her balance, and falling backwards out of the open frame of a building. Tim grabbed her by the leg and struggled desperately to pull her up but his grip was not firm, his fingers quivering and aching. His palms turned red in his awkward physical position and he could not hold on. Tim looked down in horror as Hilda Carr fell into the burning heap of fire.

A moment before Hilda went into the fire, the piece of paper that she held in her hand came free, and like a leaf, fluttered harmlessly to the ground.

The fire raged fifty feet in the air, the heat overwhelming. Above the flames, high in the sky, Tim stretched out on a hard steel girder in a numbed state of shock.

As darkness fell on St. Augustine, Tim walked slowly down the staircase with a burdening sensation of loss because Nancy was gone. He would have to face that reality once and for all. And he felt a strange, different kind of loss over Hilda. Her mysterious ways and sketchy background reverberated in his head and he realized that she would always maintain a strange, dark corner in the recesses of his memories.

Chapter Forty-Three—A Dilemma

When Tim reached the first floor, he looked for the piece of paper that came out of Hilda's hand and floated to the dusty ground, but he was quickly hustled away by a policeman to the construction company's trailer. He looked back at the bonfire. Through the towering red flames, he could see the media reporters descending on the site with their cameras, microphones, notepads, and lights. Their buzz of chattering voices cut through the humid air.

Inside the trailer, Tim encountered the scornful glare of several plain-clothed law enforcement leaders as Nelson Porter stood in the corner.

"Promise me that you will not leave town. Get yourself a lawyer and we'll talk," Porter said.

Tim walked out of the trailer and headed in the opposite direction of the media crowd. He stopped in his tracks as his mind raced back to the piece of paper he saw fall to the ground. His desire to tie up the loose, convoluted issues in his mind forced him to go back to the bonfire and search for the paper.

Two crime scene investigators were scouring the area as Tim walked quietly up to the edge of the fire. He saw a white paper, crumpled and torn, on the ground, so close to the fire that one edge of it was singed. He snatched up the paper and walked away.

As he reached the other end of the high-rise building, Tim looked at the paper and saw that there were two versions of the text, English and German. He read of a drug formula to eradicate the aging process in human beings. It was complicated and certainly not easily understood by a layman, but Tim knew that the paper in his hand was the source of much bloodshed and death.

His quick, impulsive decision was to turn the information over to the police. In his physically exhausted and mentally bereaved condition, Tim considered the ramifications of that choice as his disgust and anger with everything that he had witnessed and experienced weighed heavily on him.

A stark reality hit Tim Jennings in the face. He knew that there would be no end to the madcap quest for the Fountain of Youth. However, the information that he learned from Hilda about the side effects of the formula caused him great concern. The woman appeared young outwardly, but Tim was sure that if the tragic accident causing her death had not happened then, she would eventually die from the side effects. The Empowerment Brigade's claim of conquering death would be revealed as a sham in the end.

A feeling deep within his being pressed on Tim's heart and mind. The entire premise and foundation of the quest for eternal youth was wrong. A growing lack of respect for senior citizens by society had some bearing on the trend. The human desire to stay young forever was present everywhere in society, much of the desire driven by vanity. Physical appearance was too important to scores of people in modern society.

Tim understood and appreciated the need for good health and physical fitness. In fact, he exercised regularly and was very concerned that obesity was becoming a serious problem. However, the primary motivation behind the movement and attitude was to do the impossible… eliminate death.

The steeple of a church several blocks away caught Tim's attention. He looked at the cross at the top of the steeple and his thoughts about Tiffany and her deep, sincere faith captured his emotions. In his heart, Tim knew that her way of life made sense. Through her own walk and witness, Tiffany was an inspiration.

Tim realized that the search for eternal life apart from God was a losing battle. The supposed miracle formula that everyone had desperately sought would only lead to heartbreak and death, and the Bible did stress that everyone experiences physical death. The effort of the Empowerment Brigade was ultimately wasted because God would provide eternal life in Heaven.

As the flames from the bonfire shot up into the darkening sky, Tim crumpled the paper containing the formula in his hands and threw it into the fire.

Over the next twenty-four hours, Tim constantly thought about Nancy and Tiffany as he holed himself up in his motel room. His grief over Nancy's death was repeated as he went through the mourning process a second time. He cried several times over the morning, afternoon, and evening, becoming numb in his body, emotions, mind, and motivation.

Tim spent a great deal of time in bed, tossing and turning. He had set himself up to believe that Nancy was alive. He retraced the steps that he had taken in his search for her, scolding himself for not using some measure of common sense and level-headed thinking that would have led him to conclude that Nancy was gone forever.

Embarrassed, he felt like a village idiot, actually a cross between Don Quixote and the village idiot. He wallowed in self-pity but the young man also felt guilt because of the people he had hurt along the way. He had been inconsiderate and cold to Tiffany. Even after the nightmare ended, Tiffany had understood Tim's desire to be alone for a few days. Her patience, dedication, and loyalty were incredible.

Chapter Forty-Four—The Most Important Decision of Tim's Life

Monday, August 19, 11:02 a.m.

Tim opened his motel room door to find Tiffany standing before him, wearing a dress made of a pink chiffon fabric and a cream-colored ribbon in her hair.

"You are the most beautiful woman I have ever known!"

Tiffany blushed. "Don't say that."

"But it's true. You're the most wonderful girl in the world and I'm the biggest stooge in the world for the way I treated you."

"I understand what you were going through."

Tim motioned for her to sit down in a chair in front of the window. As he sat across from her, he admired her smile. A tear formed in the corner of Tim's eye. "I don't deserve you." He shook his head and stared out the window. "Why are you so kind and devoted to me?"

Tiffany's smile widened. "Because you are a man of character and you have love in your heart. You've demonstrated those traits that are so important in a man the last few months."

"What do you mean?"

"Hoping to recapture the first real love of your life with Nancy," Tiffany said. "That was very noble and romantic. You went to the ends of the earth for love and any woman would admire that in a man."

"Sure but you loved me, too. I had no right to do you that way."

"But Nancy came first. You knew her first and loved her first so I can respect that, but the bottom line is I wanted you to be happy."

"But my happiness meant that you would not be happy, because if I found Nancy alive, then it would have been over between us."

"I could have accepted it." Tiffany looked out the window. "Honestly, in my heart, I never believed that she was alive, but I am being sincere with what I am about to say. I was hoping and praying for your sake that she was alive. I didn't feel that way at first, but later I did because I wanted you to be happy. I hope you believe me."

Tim pulled his chair closer to Nancy and softly put his hand on her cheek. "I believe you and I will always be grateful."

"And I would have been thankful to God for allowing me to have the short time that I did experience with you if it had worked out that way," Tiffany said.

"You're amazing!" Tim said.

"No! You are one of the most amazing men I have ever met. Your testimony of the last few months has been inspirational because perseverance, loyalty, and determination are the mark of a great man."

"You got the wrong man, that's for sure."

"I don't think so," Tiffany said as she kissed him. "You have many admirable traits and good, traditional qualities. We need more of those qualities in people."

"You're embarrassing me," Tim said. "Let's talk about you. Get me caught up on everything that you've been doing since I was in Atlanta."

"I started a new job. I'm working as an administrative assistant at my church where I spend part of my time helping with the church's day care program," Tiffany said. "I've been reading some interesting books on history and traveling. I want us to visit cities out west, possibly San Diego and San Francisco."

"We have a great country," Tim said. "I appreciate it even more after hearing the ranting rhetoric of Jon Actund. We're blessed to be living here."

"I'm so happy because you've returned and now everything is complete. It hasn't been easy to wait, but I've been able to spend my days with two of my favorite things, my church and children. You know, the ones in the day care program," she said, beaming with joy.

"You have some good folks at that church."

"They are fine people and many of them have been praying for you. In fact, your name was on our prayer list on Wednesday nights, plus some of the ladies and I formed a prayer chain for you."

"It must have worked, because I made it through in one piece."

"And you had faith in God, didn't you?"

Tim was thoughtful. "I did have faith in God, but I didn't think about it all the time. I did have faith, for sure. In fact, I prayed to Him in some tight spots." Tim lowered his head.

"That's great." Tiffany smiled sympathetically.

"But I'm such a loser when it comes to God," Tim said. "I'm being honest when I say that I was only falling back on praying to God when I was desperate, and that's not good."

"But it's natural," Tiffany said. "Don't feel bad because you are beginning to develop a relationship with the Lord. But you do know what the most important step is, don't you?"

"Yes. We've talked about it so many times."

"You need to accept Jesus Christ as your Lord and Savior."

Tim's eyes grew moist and his face turned a bright red. "I'm ready. Help me."

"In I John 5:13, the Bible says, 'I write these things to you who believe in the name of the Son of God so that you may know that you have eternal life.' Do you admit that you are a sinner?"

"You better believe it," Tim said with a nervous laugh.

"Then you must repent, or turn away from your sins."

"I do! I do!"

"Then you're ready to except Christ and have eternal life."

"Yes I am!"

Tiffany moved up on the edge of her chair as she pulled out an evangelical tract from her purse. They prayed the following prayer together: "Dear God. I know that I am a sinner and unable to save myself, but I do believe that You love me, and that You sent Your Son, Jesus, to die on the cross for my sins. Right here and now, I repent of my sins and I ask You to forgive my every sin and give me the gift of eternal life as I accept Your Son as my Lord and Savior. Thank You, dear God, for hearing and answering my prayer, and for giving me eternal life as You promised You would. Moving forward, please lead, guide, and direct me. Amen".

Tim stood up from his chair. "I don't feel that different but I do have a sense of relief and peace inside."

In excitement, Tiffany hugged Tim repeatedly. "That's the beginning. We're both babes in Christ, growing together. We'll have such happiness while we study Scripture together, developing our relationship with God."

"I'm excited," Tim said as he pulled Tiffany close and kissed her. "You're actually going to give me another chance?"

"Of course, because I love you!"

"And I love you!"

Chapter Forty-Five—Resolution

Monday, August 26, 9:17 a.m.

In the aftermath of Tim's experiences, it became increasingly clear that his knowledge of the internal secrets of the Empowerment Brigade were very valuable because Nelson Porter was adamant to other government officials that he would settle for nothing less than the complete collapse and elimination of the organization. Additionally, the CIA agent assured Tim that he would not face any criminal charges in the United States for anything that happened over the course of the summer.

"I know that I interfered with an official investigation, so thanks for cutting me some slack," Tim said to Porter in a telephone conversation. "But here's the deal. I did help bring those cowards down."

In the ensuing days, Tim met with Nelson Porter, personnel from the FBI, the CIA, the State Department, and the Defense Department to describe in detail everything that he knew about the Empowerment Brigade. He described the key personalities that he had encountered and rehashed the rhetoric that the leaders spewed in front of him. Additionally, Tim actually had a map of the Empowerment Brigade's compound in his possession that would prove to be valuable. But the most important intelligence that Tim provided was a good estimate of the weaponry of the group, both active and stockpiled.

Eventually, federal law enforcement officials were comfortable with the information that they had gathered about the Empowerment Brigade's headquarters. Through masterful planning, solid communication, and adequate support from the government of Germany, a surprise assault was carried out on the compound. The U.S. military served in a supporting role.

The Empowerment Brigade's most ardent members in the compound offered stiff resistance, but when the shooting stopped, the compound collapsed and the true believers and sympathizers that remained standing were taken into custody. Most of them were European, but there were several Americans on the long list of people indicted and charged with varying offenses.

Both the American and the European media had a field day with their coverage of the legal process and how it dealt with the offenders. The major television networks broadcast special reports on the leaders of the Empowerment Brigade and their backgrounds. In death, John Actund took on almost mythical status.

Ultimately, all of the major surviving offenders received punishment in the European courts. The top lieutenants of Actund received life sentences, including Dr. Vog. Most of the supporting cast received eight to ten years of jail time. Matt Stowe received thirty years in prison for killing Actund, with the possibility of parole after fifteen years.

The long-range agenda of the Empowerment Brigade was uncovered in a document that was found in a safe at the compound. It was entitled, 'The Empowerment Brigade Manifesto', a hardbound volume that chronicled in detail the subversive agenda of the organization.

The document made for a chilling read. Tim had gleaned their basic goals during his ordeal, but the hate-filled details were indeed frightening. Jon Actund and the Empowerment

Brigade were arrogantly bold in their vision because they believed that they could infiltrate the United Nations. Initially, at least five U.N. Ambassadors would be recruited, brainwashed, bribed, cajoled, or blackmailed into aligning themselves with the organization. Two of the nations represented would be Eastern European, two nations would be Western European, and one would be from the Middle East.

Of course, the indoctrination of ambassadors and the prospect of winning over the populace of an entire country were two entirely different issues, but incrementalism was a key term that the leadership of the Empowerment Brigade stressed and nurtured. In other words, patience and a single-minded determination were essential to success. However, there was no mention in the document of the plan to clone human beings.

Additionally, the baby that Dr. Vog claimed was cloned could not be located and he disavowed any knowledge of the topic.

As the media focused on the story, Tim Jennings emerged as a celebrity and a folk hero in the eyes of many people. Deluged with requests for interviews, he was not comfortable with the attention. He simply wanted to return to private life, but he did reluctantly grant several interviews and provided information for a magazine profile as he predicted that his fame would be fleeting and people would soon forget about him.

After the ordeal, especially in the United States, the senior citizen community was completely deflated by the conclusion of the story. Their hopes for a modern day Fountain of Youth were dashed when they learned about the side effects that Hilda Carr experienced. Despondency overtook scores of elderly citizens who lived in nursing homes and assisted-living centers.

The American Academy of Retirees demanded a congressional investigation into the situation. When pressed to name who should be investigated and exactly the reasoning behind such action, the leadership of the organization could not say, but sit-ins were staged in Washington, D.C. at government buildings by senior citizens. Isolated outbursts of violence were carried out by a few elderly people. When an old man threw a cane through a window, the media and the public reacted, not with indignation but with laughter. Recognizing the vacuum that had developed over the longing and desire for eternal youth, numerous entrepreneurs of questionable virtue and scruples appeared on the scene in the United States to take advantage of gullible people with products and schemes to meet their desires.

Saturday, September 30 4:09 p.m.

As Tiffany took two sodas out of the refrigerator, Tim waited at his kitchen table, reading newspaper stories about the ordeal and the anger of the elderly. "Hopefully, this stuff will die down soon," he said. "I've heard nothing about the cloned baby. That outfit claimed that they cloned a human being, but the authorities have not been able to find evidence. A baby's a pretty significant loose end. I saw it with own eyes, so it's out there somewhere."

"I believe you."

"Thanks."

"Are you sure that you don't want to start up your old business again?" Tiffany asked. "I'll help you!"

"The business is in complete shambles because of Bud's indifference while I was gone, and besides, I need to go in a different direction. That office will always be a reminder of Lance's death. I expect Marino to be charged soon so that will come as a relief. Hey, I might write my memoirs on this thing, a TV mini-series in the making!"

"Seriously, you have quite a story to tell and your testimony could be an inspiration to many people. It would be great if you spoke in churches and to young people. God has a purpose for your life and He makes everything work out for the best. You can be a witness to many lost folks who need Jesus in their lives."

"Some good might come of this stuff in the end."

"I know it will!"

"You've got it all figured out," Tim said. "You can be my manager and girlfriend, all rolled into one!"

"I accept!"

The doorbell rang.

The pizza deliveryman stood at the front door. "Sir, you ordered a large sausage pizza. Wait a minute, you're Mr. Jennings. I've seen you on TV," the young man said. "I followed all the news and I wanted to say that I admire you. You're an American patriot and a hero!"

"I'm not a hero."

"Yes, you are! All my friends think so, too. You fought for what you believed in, protected our country and hung in there!"

Later, Tim told Tiffany about the exchange. "I'm not a hero. If I'm a hero, we need to redefine exactly what that word means."

"You're too modest," Tiffany said. "I was right. You can get out there and be a role model for people."

"The foreign cops haven't had their say yet. I left a lot of messy loose ends over there and they may want to hang me in the streets. If I am extradited, then my goose is cooked. You'll probably never see me again. Maybe I am a criminal. I'm certainly a killer."

"It was all in self-defense in a very dangerous situation," Tiffany said.

"It used to be that I couldn't even kill a bug, but I ended the life of two human beings. That's a lot to live with and what do I have to show for it? I don't even know what happened to Eric."

Tiffany hugged Tim. "Would you stop it? You're a wonderful man, a strong person. That's the great thing about you."

"Now I'm more of a realist and I'm going to enjoy and appreciate the blessings from God that I've taken for granted in the past. If you're constantly worried about prolonging your future, then you can't enjoy your blessings now," Tim said.

"That's why being a Christian is so great because you know that your eternal salvation is secure. When we pass from this life, we will be in the presence of God. His love will overwhelm us and we will be with loved ones and friends who have gone on before us."

"I want to go to Lake Lanier."

"But why? I thought you said that you would never go there again after the accident."

"I need to go up there one last time to settle things in my heart and head," Tim said.

"Do you really want to do that? There are so many bad memories up there."

"Yes. I need to go up there one more time, then I can let go of the past."

Within twenty minutes, they were driving up Highway 400 with Tiffany at the wheel. Tim was very quiet on the entire trip, praying silently a great deal of the time and reflecting on the love of God.

"This is a great place," Tim said when they arrived at the area of the lake where the accident happened. It was one of the most secluded and least utilized of any of the parks bordering the lake. To get to the shore, they had to park the vehicle in a gravel area and trek up a slightly elevated hill that jutted out over the surface of the water. From the apex of the hill, they could see watercraft of various sizes and designs moving across the surface of the water.

"It's beautiful," Tiffany said. The water glistened under the late afternoon sun as a cool breeze swirled all over the tree-lined shore.

"Will you give me a few minutes?" Tim asked. "This is the last place I saw Nancy. She waved to me as she walked across that dock down there.

Tiffany returned to the vehicle and waited patiently as Tim stood quietly at the top of the hill, gazing out upon the waters. He knelt on one knee and prayed.

"Are you OK?" Tiffany asked when Tim returned to the vehicle.

"Yes. Let's go home."

Sunday, October 1, 8:02 a.m.

As soon as the alarm clock sounded, Tim sprung up out of bed, ate a granola bar, quickly showered and dressed. He wore a dark blue pinstriped suit that was a bit musty as he had not worn it in three years.

As the morning sun rose in the Atlanta sky, Tim drove to Tiffany's house. When he arrived, a huge smile swept across her face as she saw him.

"I'm ready for Sunday school," Tim said emphatically as he looked at the Bible that he held in his hand. "I've been so stubborn that I shut out the one true source of peace and strength available to us. I'm ready to make up for lost time."

"My prayers have been answered," Tiffany said. "I knew you would follow God's direction. I guess we won't need to put out those chocolate donuts in the fellowship hall anymore to get you in the door!"

The Sunday school class that Tiffany attended was growing in membership. The parking lot was nearly full when they arrived and as they walked toward the church, the couple was greeted by the very friendly smiles and comments of members.

As Tim walked hand in hand with Tiffany, he looked up at the church steeple as it rose in the direction of Heaven, its cross visible in all directions. He felt the awesome power of God as he turned to Tiffany, smiled, and entered the building with her. Tim Jennings had faith in God, and he was at peace.

CPSIA information can be obtained at www.ICGtesting.com
Printed in the USA
LVOW11s1058121113

360984LV00004B/4/P